LILITH

THE KING FAMILY VAMPIRES BOOK ONE

by Jason D. Mepham

Copyright @ Jason D. Mepham

Jason D. Mepham has asserted his right under the Copywright, Designs and Patents Act 1988 to be identified as the author of this work.

The characters featured in this book are fictional. Any resemblance to persons living is purely coincidental.

ISBN 978-1-4716-7468-6

This book is sold subject to the condition that it shall not, by way of trade or otherwise, be lent, resold, hired out, or otherwise circulated without the publisher's prior consent in any form of binding or cover other than that in which it is published and without a similar condition including this condition being imposed on the subsequent publisher.

First published in Great Britain in 2012 by the author.

www.publishnation.co.uk

Lilith is dedicated to my parents Alan & Christine. I thank them for their continued guidance and support and love them both dearly.

I would also like to thank Sue Millward for the lovely front cover art. She brought Lilith to life in the way I could not! Thanks also to my technical consultant, Julie Haughton.

I would have been lost if not for my editor's skill and ideas, so a BIG thank you to Lisa Jones. You have taught me a lot and I really hope we can work together again.

I would also like to take this opportunity to thank my fellow British writer, Karen Mahoney for her advice and encouragement. Go discover her now!

I also dedicate this book to all the dreamers out there.

Finally, I would like to mention the fabulous Anne Rice, without whom this book would never have been written. It was her incredible Vampire Chronicles that introduced and seduced me to the genre, so thank you Anne!

"Without passion we are truly dead."
(Angelus, the vampire)

"The vampire's blood is all powerful. It's magic blood."
(Lilith, the vampire)

Author's Note

What merely began as an idea back in October of 2006 stayed that way. Just an idea. I had wrote the introduction but quickly lost interest in the story of Lilith. That was my trouble. I would have these seemingly good ideas but would then quickly forget about them. Lose the thread as it were.

But while at my work in the September of 2008, almost 2 years after I had started this novel, my bosses son spoke words of encouragement to me that I have not forgotten.

"If you enjoy writing then you should write."

I went home that afternoon and thought about what he had said. Oh believe me when I say I didn't really have any intention of picking up a pen or typing on a keyboard. However, I found my introduction to Lilith amongst a discarded pile of magazines. I began to read it and it was as if my mind was suddenly opening up to the possibilities. I loved what I had written and found myself hooked. I wanted to carry on reading the story but of course couldn't because it hadn't been written yet!

I have had a fascination with vampires for as long as I can remember. I love all there is to know about them. I like some parts of the mythology about them but not others. So this was why I took some elements and carried them into my story, but wanted to add a few of my own into the mix.

So this being the case, if I really was going to write a book. And I mean a really serious attempt at a novel, the chances were it was going to be about vampires. So in the space of approximately four months I continued the story of Lilith and completed it on 2nd January 2009. After editing, and extensive rewrites, the novel was finally finished 3rd April 2012.

Since I have created Lilith, friends and family have asked me how much of me is in the character of Alex. I answer them by saying not much actually. However, the whole concept of Lilith started out as a fantasy. My fantasy. I have had dreams of meeting a mysterious woman such as Lilith and having her take me into her world. But there my resemblance to Alex ends.

As to Lilith herself, it is true I have often dreamt of a long, black haired woman with amazing green eyes. I do not know who she is and nor do I know if she is a vampire or not. However, this woman feels very real to me so it is on this mysterious and ultimately nameless creature, that I base the character of Lilith on.

Jason D Mepham, April 2012

Lilith and Alex will return in "Eponine"

Lilith: The King family vampires book one

Prologue

She came in the dead of night; in the early hours of a Friday morning. Outside rain was falling steadily and the glow of the full moon faded in and out with the passing clouds.

How do I know this? I don't sleep. Well, not on a regular basis. For years now, I have got by on 3 or 4 hours sleep a night and on this night nothing changed. Except that everything changed.

I turned over in bed for what must have been the tenth time. I was desperately trying to get some sleep. I made the mistake of glancing at the red numbers on my radio alarm clock. 3.23. I had to be up in less than 4 hours and so far all I had been doing was dozing on and off.

I had just pulled the covers up and fluffed my pillow once again when I clearly heard my name being called. I sat up and listened, but all I could now hear was the continuing rain.

I figured it must have been my imagination or something, because I wasn't going to admit to myself that my insomnia was affecting my mind. I was about to lie back down again when I heard my name being called again. This time it was louder and was most definitely a woman's voice.

I got out of bed and stumbled across the room to my window. I pulled the curtain back slightly, as I was naked, and peeped out. I live in a high apartment building so I looked down into our car park below. At first I couldn't see anyone, for half the car park lies in darkness, but then the moon came out from behind the clouds again and I saw her.

This mysterious woman, for I didn't know her, was standing there in the pouring rain, just staring up at me. Her hair was long and dark, probably black, and she wore a white flowing dress that billowed out around her as the wind began to pick up. Then for the third third time she called my name and held out her open arms. I stared at her, completely lost for words. Then as I continued to watch, the woman stretched out her arms and suddenly began to rise off the ground. She was floating inches and then metres off of the rain soaked tarmac. She kept her arms outstretched and continued to rise upwards until she was level with my window on the seventh floor.

I was stunned to say the least and stumbled backwards, falling over my chair and crashed with a bump onto my bedroom floor. I sat up, and through the gap in the curtains I could still see her floating outside. Now that I could see her more easily I saw how beautiful she really was. Breathtaking in fact. Yes, her long dark hair was indeed black; the way it was being swept about in the wind and rain, it looked like a raven's wing. What I thought originally was a dress was actually a white nightdress. The top two buttons were undone and I could clearly see the woman's slender neck. The nightdress also had a rather severe split down one side so that I got a generous view of the woman's right leg. Judging by the edges of the split I would have said the dress had been torn by branches or something similar rather than by a pair of hands or blade. Her lips were full and red but her face seemed a little pale. As to her eyes, I couldn't tell, for at that moment a gust of wind blew her hair into them, although she remained completely at ease and in seemingly perfect balance.

As she continued to float there, again she held out her arms in a pleading gesture. And this time she spoke more than my name:
'Let me in. Please.'
Her voice was so soft and light, almost a whisper, yet I clearly heard the words as if she'd spoken them into my ear.
I grabbed the edge of the quilt and covered myself up before stepping nearer to the window. Who was this woman? I was totally entranced and transfixed by this wonderful vision before me. Slowly but surely I could feel the fear evaporating from within me. And yet, I did not open the window.
'Who are you?' I managed to ask her. It vaguely occurred to me that my neighbours might well hear us and wondered, if they happened to look out and see her floating there, would they believe it any more than I?

The woman slowly shook her head and the saddest expression came over her features, almost as if she was about to burst into tears.
'You know who I am.'

At this I was truly confused, because as far as I was concerned I had never set eyes on her in my entire life. Not even someone who vaguely looked like her.

'I'm sorry,' I said, 'but I don't know you. I don't even know what you are or how you're managing to just float there.'

'Let me in,' she said again, 'I will explain everything.'

Looking back on this now I still can't believe how calm I remained. And despite the bizarre and fantastic nature of this visitation, I reached out and opened the window. Without the slightest hesitation, the mysterious woman floated closer and pulled herself into the room.

'You're not a spirit then,' I said, 'because how else would you have been able to grip the window frame like that?'

Elegantly she stepped down from the sill and looked at me.

'No, I'm not a spirit.'

Without another word she suddenly came at me and kissed me full on the mouth. The kiss, both powerful and intoxicating, was like no other I had received before. I was about to put my arms around this gorgeous creature when she suddenly stepped back and turned away.

'You have no idea how long I've waited to do that.'

Still aware that I was naked behind the quilt, I went to the bed and sat down with it wrapped around me.

'Who are you?' I asked again, 'What are you?'

'Where am I from? What is the secret of the universe? Is there a God?' she said in a mocking voice, 'so many questions and such a limitless amount of time.'

I didn't know what she meant by that but said nothing. I just sat and stared at her in silence. Then she slowly turned to face me and said:

'My name is Lilith and I am a vampire.'

I was about to burst into laughter but I suddenly remembered the way she had floated in mid air. As I recalled this I instinctively moved back, but she simply shook her head.

'I will not harm you Alex.' Lilith then stepped up to the bed and sat down on the edge of it, looking at me. I don't know why, but my mind chose that moment to recoil in horror that she was sitting on my bed in a soaking wet dress. But then, for the first time I saw how green her eyes were. They seemed to shine with amazing radiance. There was something clearly inhuman about them, something supernatural for sure.

I watched as a single drop of rain ran down the length of her bare left arm, seeing that her skin took on a slight sheen that I didn't see in my own.

'How do you know my name?'

As I said this, Lilith actually laughed, which wasn't an unpleasant sound in the slightest.

'How could I not? I've been searching for you.'

'But why? I don't even know you.' I said, becoming flustered.

'You may think that now, but soon you will remember.'

'Remember what?'

'Everything!' she actually winked as she said this.

Lilith turned her gaze from me to my bedroom walls. Her eyes went from one poster of a famous female celebrity to another.

'You always did have a taste for the ladies.' She laughed, and looked at me again.

I didn't know what to say to that, so just stared at her silently.

'Well?' she asked. 'Don't you have any more questions for me?'

I hugged the quilt cover more tightly and knew what to ask first.

'How old are you?'

Lilith sighed and looked at her alarmingly long fingernails. They were painted blood red.

'I was born in the year 1556. I'm sure you can work it out from there.'

I was astonished. The woman before me was 450 years old.

'Next question.'

I was finding it very difficult to concentrate. I found no matter how hard I tried I couldn't take my eyes off her. And when her gaze fixed onto mine, I could quite literally feel my spine tingling.

'How do I know you won't harm me?' I spluttered out.

'I've already fed this evening.'

And suddenly she was lying beside me holding my chin in her hand. I hadn't seen her move and yet here she was, her cool hand cupping my chin so that we locked eyes. I vaguely remember her hand upon my chest pushing me down onto the bed but my mind was still coming to terms with the speed she had moved.

'Besides,' she smiled, 'why would I wish to harm you when I've been searching for you all these years?'

I didn't have an answer, so instead I pulled my head back. She let go but continued to lie there, a small smile playing across her lips.

'How did you do that? Move so fast I mean?'

'Because I can.' she grinned and for the first time I saw her teeth. They gleamed white and appeared normal except for the two fangs that extended down further than the rest.

'You really are a vampire!' I said rather stupidly.

Again Lilith laughed, then alarmingly raked one of her nails across her wrist, drawing blood.

'Here, a taste.' she held up her wrist to my face. I instinctively drew back but there was nowhere to go.

'Taste.' she said again, more insistently.

This time she more or less forced her wrist to my mouth. I kissed the snow white skin, smearing the blood that was still dripping from the self- inflicted wound.

'Go on.' she urged.

I tentatively ran my tongue over the cut and allowed the blood to settle in my mouth. I didn't really taste it, swallowing it straight away. Why was she making me do this? Drinking her blood would make me a vampire too wouldn't it? But Lilith shook her head and forced me to take some more.

'Drink it and know me.' She said firmly.

I wasn't in a position to argue so this time I licked at her wrist, then sucked at it. Now a greater flow entered me and I finally savoured the taste.

Suddenly the whole room seem to turn slowly around and I realised I was becoming dizzy. Not only this but also drowsy too. I found it difficult to keep my eyes open.

'Don't fight it,' Lilith whispered. 'Let the power of the blood take you and know me all over again.'

In my head, a torrent of images began to come to me. I saw a castle from centuries ago, its walls high and intact. I saw a woman slaying a knight with a sword that cut off his helmeted head. The woman was Lilith. I saw her drink the blood of the fallen man and then beckon to someone lurking in the shadows of the wall. A man stepped forward, a dark hood on his head hid most of his features but as he came toward her, he pushed the hood back and I was looking at myself. He didn't have my face or features; yet somehow, I knew this powerful man was me. The man held a sword as if ready to strike out at Lilith, but instead he dropped it on the ground and held out his arms. I saw her smile and step into his embrace and I saw these two were lovers. She kissed him and I clearly heard her say the words, 'It is time.'

Then suddenly she bit deep into the man's neck. He made no sound and did not struggle at all, just standing there as Lilith continued to drink from the wound she had made. Slowly he sank to his knees and the woman went with him. I could see this as clearly as if it was happening right there in my own room. Lilith took one final mouthful of blood before pulling her head back. The man was mortally wounded; I could see the light beginning to fade in his eyes, but still he did not cry out.

Now, Lilith scratched her wrist, holding the man's face to it, and as she had done with me seconds before, encouraged him to drink.

'Take it and know life eternal.' she was saying. The man did not reply, but instead continued to drink her blood.

'That's it. Good.' She encouraged him.

I realised that with each passing second, the man was becoming stronger. It was as if her blood was keeping him from death. Not only that but revitalising him, re-building him, until Lilith pushed him gently but firmly away. She staggered back a couple of steps, clearly weakened. The man was sitting up looking at her, licking a last drop of blood from his lips.

'Lilith, am I?..'

'Yes,' she answered. 'You are now like me, a creature of the night. Immortal'

The man stared at her as I gazed at the scene unfolding before my eyes. The room seemed to sway again as three more knights suddenly appeared on the castle battlements, swords at the ready. They marched forward with purpose in a line, while Lilith gave a loud hiss and flashed her teeth at them. They suddenly began to charge the weakened vampire but before they reached her, something flew through the air and intercepted the attack. The newly formed vampire smashed his arms into the lead attacker's armour clad chest. Even from where I was witnessing the scene, I clearly heard the sound of breaking ribs as the knight hurtled backwards with the force of the blow. The second knight swung his sword in an arc at the vampire but he easily avoided it and sent a savage kick to the man's face, breaking his jaw and several of his teeth. The last knight was still brave despite the loss of his comrades. He faced the vampire, keeping his sword up and distance between them. However, he had forgotten Lilith. She was now stronger but far from fully recovered, and I saw her circle around behind the knight, calling:

'Severin, this one's mine.'

The male vampire shrugged and answered 'as you wish.'

He stepped away and before the knight could turn his attention on Lilith, she was upon him. The sword went flying, as did his arm, for with one powerful strike of her hand she dismembered him.

The knight went down onto one knee and tried to fend her off with his one remaining arm, but Lilith knocked it to one side and ripped off the man's helmet. Then with astonishing speed she gripped the knight by his hair and threw him with ease high over the castle wall.

I don't know how, but I knew the battle was over. I also somehow knew that the castle belonged to Lilith and that she had just defended it from enemies unknown. Now I saw her approach the vampire she had created. The one called Severin.

'Kiss me my love.' She smiled at him.

Severin smiled too but then saw that the second knight he had kicked was still alive and trying to crawl away, blood dripping from his shattered mouth.

'Going somewhere?' Severin walked over and deliberately stepped on the knight's hand.

The knight screamed and cursed but this was quickly ended when the vampire gripped the man's head and easily snapped his neck with a simple twist of his now supernaturally powerful hands.

As the dizziness began to fade, the last images I saw were of the two vampires embracing once again and sharing a lasting kiss.

Chapter 1

Lilith pushed herself away from me and rose from the bed. Without saying a word she threw the curtains back and gazed out into the night.
Her silence un-nerved me so I decided to speak.
'I saw myself, in the vision.'
Slowly, Lilith turned her steady gaze upon me.
'As you once were.' she said softly.
'How do you mean? As I once was. I don't understand'
Lilith sighed and closed the curtains again.
'You believe every living thing has a soul?' she asked.
I shrugged and replied, 'I guess so.'
'Well, it's true. And if an animal dies, their soul is free to move on. But humans were made differently.'
'How do you mean?' I asked.
'When a man or woman dies,' she explained. 'Our soul is released but the only place it can go is back into another body. Don't ask me why, but for some reason our souls need flesh and bones as a host.'
I found this concept bizarre, to tell the truth.
'How do you know this?' I asked. 'Who told you?'
'My sire, Christiano told me. He is a great and wise man.'
'So you are saying that human souls are timeless? That they never die or fade?'
'That's exactly what I'm saying.'
'And the soul also takes memories from one host body to the next?'
Lilith looked at me and just for a moment a look of sadness came to her expression.
'Always but for a reason I do not know, the next body doesn't always recall its previous existence.'
'So I was this Severin in a previous life?'
Lilith simply nodded.
'But I had no knowledge of this until I drank some of your blood.'
'The vampire's blood is all powerful. It is magic blood.'
'But I saw you turn this Severin into a vampire. Where is he?'
As soon as I said this, Lilith looked at me sharply.
'Don't you get it?' she snapped. 'If you're here, Severin must be dead mustn't he?'
I looked at her, unable to do or say anything other than nod my head.

'How did he die? How did I die?' I stuttered.
Lilith sighed and shook her head.
'It doesn't matter. Ancient history.'
The passion in her voice revealed her true accent to me for the first time. It was definitely Southern Ireland in origin.
I was still very much in awe of her but this didn't stop me from reaching out a hand and placing it on her shoulder.
'Please tell me. I'd like to know.'
Lilith took my hand gently into hers and brought it up to her lips. She kissed my finger-tips and ran my palm over her cheek. She really was cool to the touch but not overly so. Then she slowly sat down beside me again.
'I won't tell you what happened to Severin. I will show you the beginning of the end.'
And without any further words, she again sliced her wrist open and offered it to me. This time I did not hesitate and dipped my head towards her wrist, my mouth already open.
Once again the room began to spin and my vision became blurred. When it had cleared, I saw a different setting.
Lilith was there, sitting on a chair. As the scene came into focus, I realised this was a ballroom. There were many tables and chairs and people all seated around. I'm not a history buff by any means, but judging by their dress, I would have said this was the late 1800s.
Sitting across from Lilith, was Severin. Neither had changed in appearance from the castle scene I had witnessed earlier, all that was different was their clothes. Lilith was dressed in a magnificent lilac ball gown, her breasts tightly concealed beneath a lace bodice, raven hair set in a mass of curls. As for Severin, he was immaculately dressed in a dark dress suit, rich with ruffles and frills. For a moment my sight of them was obscured by other couples dancing to the music that the small orchestra in the corner had begun playing. But suddenly I was again looking at Lilith, this time through Severin's eyes.
'May I have this dance my lady?' I heard him say. His voice was deeper than mine, yet seemed so familiar.
'But of course my darling.' Lilith smiled without showing her fangs and allowed herself to be gently pulled to her feet by a powerful hand. And then they began to glide across the floor. Slowly at first, carefully avoiding the other couples. Lilith only had eyes for Severin. She kept her gaze locked onto his/mine as they continued to glide and twirl around the floor. As the dance and music continued I saw Lilith's blissful expression change and a frown appeared.

'Damn it!' she cursed.
'What is it my love?'
'Archer has found us.'

Slowly Severin turned his head, never stepping out of the dance's rhythm. Through his eyes I saw a thick-set man standing across the room. He too wore a dark dress suit, but not made from the same fine materials. Two even bigger men stood either side of him. All three of them were staring at Lilith with what can only be described as hatred.

'What do you wish to do?' Severin asked, still swaying with the music.

Lilith turned in his hands and leaned her head towards his ear.

'We can't afford to cause a scene. Not here. We should leave.'

'Agreed.'

With that one word, Severin bowed towards Lilith, still holding her hand, and they began to slowly make their way towards the garden exit, putting couples between themselves and the newcomers.

Without looking back, Severin and Lilith made their way into the garden and with no apparent effort at all, leaped high into the air and landed gently upon the roof of the grand house.

From his position I could still see through Severin's eyes. We were looking at the ground where Archer and his companions had just emerged from the ballroom. They cursed and glanced about but had not spotted the two vampires.

'Shall we take them?' Severin whispered.

'Not here. There are too many people about.'

'Then where?'

'Patience my darling.'

And with those words Lilith kissed Severin full on the lips and I actually felt her fangs bite into his flesh. Blood quickly flowed into each other's mouths as they kissed deeply.

Slowly my vision came back to me and once again I found myself sitting on my bed with this remarkable woman beside me.

'Who's Archer?' I asked.

Lilith sighed and stood up. With her head bowed she took a couple of steps away from me. It looked to me like she was lost in thought or remembering a bad memory.

When she turned to me, there were tears running down her face.

'Archer was the man who killed my beloved Severin.' she sobbed.

I didn't know what to say but felt I had to do something, so I beckoned her to me. Without hesitation Lilith came into my open arms and I held her until the tears had stopped.

She dabbed at her eyes with her sleeve and gave a short laugh.

'That's the first time I have cried in fifty years.'

'I'm trying to understand this,' I said. 'I thought vampires couldn't die.'

Again Lilith sighed, then looked at me, her stunning green eyes now clear of tears.

'I take it you have read stories about vampires? Seen movies?'

'Of course.'

'Well, some facts are true. We are, as you have already seen in the visions very strong. We move very fast and we can levitate. We don't grow old and disease cannot harm us. I look exactly the same as I did when I was sired by my master Christiano. I have outlived all of my friends and family by many centuries. The more years that pass, the greater our powers become.'

'There are others?'

'Of course. Perhaps more than you would think.'

This news shouldn't have surprised me but for some reason it did.

'And you drink blood to survive?'

Lilith bowed her head in answer.

'Although, the older we become the less we need the blood. When you are first sired the blood lust is overwhelming at times. Not so much now.'

'Okay,' I said. 'I've read all the vampire chronicles by Anne Rice. A lot of what you're saying is mentioned in her books.'

Lilith laughed at that and her eyes shone even brighter.

'Well, perhaps Ms Rice has, shall we say, inside information?' Then with a sly smile, Lilith was suddenly over the other side of the room, where she picked up a photograph.

'Who is this?' She asked, holding it up for me.

'That's my friend Stephanie.'

'Your girlfriend?'

I shook my head.

'No, just a friend, but she means a lot to me.'

'As true friends should.' Lilith put the photo back down and was once again at my side.

'So how exactly do vampires die?' I asked.

'Direct sunlight is our worst enemy and biggest fear. Even the oldest among us fear the power of the sun. We can move around in daylight but few of us choose to do so.'

'Okay. What else?'

'Any sharp objects directly into our hearts or brain will destroy us. We are not too dissimilar to humans in this respect. The only other thing that can harm us is fire.'

'So it's true? That you have the ability to heal yourself?'

Lilith nodded.

'Not only ourselves but others too.'

'How do you mean?'

Lilith was suddenly holding my wrist, although once again I hadn't seen her move.

'Watch.' she said and to my horror she drew one of her nails across my skin. I instinctively tried to pull my arm away but Lilith held firm. Blood instantly began to run out.

'Watch.' Lilith said again and as the wound continued to bleed, she dipped her head towards it and just before she made contact with her mouth, she must have bit her own tongue because drops of blood dripped from her open lips. I watched as the drops landed onto my open wound. Then Lilith gently smeared the two bloods together and in amazement I saw the cut close before my very eyes.

'But how?' was all I could say.

Lilith smiled and winked at me for the second time that evening.

'I told you. Magic.' Then she kissed me and again stood up.

I massaged my wrist but why, I had no idea. There was no pain and not the slightest indication it had ever been injured.

'You should sleep. You have work.' Lilith said, glancing at the clock.

The same old red numbers now showed 4.12.

'Yes I do, but how can I possibly sleep after this?'

Lilith smiled. 'Good question.' she said.

'How about you? Do you sleep?'

Again Lilith laughed.

'Of course, silly. And no, not in a coffin but a nice comfortable bed. A bit like this one.'

And with that she was suddenly lying stretched out looking at me.

'You want to sleep here? With me?'

'That was the idea, yes.'

She beckoned me to lie down beside her but I hesitated.

'Look, I have already told you. I will not harm you. You are perfectly safe.'

I was still a bit nervous but nonetheless I lay down beside her. With a casual flick of her wrist she had pulled the duvet over the two of us and suddenly I was naked in her arms, my head resting on her shoulder.

Suddenly the rain soaked night gown didn't bother me at all, and being this close to her I was aware of the lavender fragrance that emanated from her skin.

'Go to sleep Alex. I'll still be here when you wake up.'

'But…'

'Go to sleep. Trust me.' She whispered in the darkness. It wasn't exactly a command but the words had an immediate effect and I felt my eyelids grow heavy and soon I fell into a soundless sleep.

Chapter 2

Sure enough, when the alarm woke me at 6.45 I turned to find Lilith sound asleep beside me, her left arm draped over my chest.
   I gently removed it and got up. After completing my toilet and shower I returned to the bedroom to dress for work.
   My work is in I.T. for a small company, which I found to be tedious but it pays the bills.
   I had just chosen my tie when I heard Lilith stir.
   I glanced over at the bed; she was looking up at me with those same beautiful eyes I had dreamed about.
   'Uh, morning.' I said.
   She smiled and glanced at the clock.
   'Good morning.' She stretched out an arm and sat up, her raven hair spilling down over her shoulders.
   'When you return, I shall still be here.'
   'How do you know what time I'll be back?'
   Lilith smiled and flashed her fangs at me.
   'Oh, my dear Alex. I know everything about you. Where you were born, who your parents are, where you went to school, your first girlfriend, first job...'
   This un-nerved me and made me angry.
   'Oh, really?' I snapped. 'Then how come you didn't know Stephanie is just a friend of mine, huh?'
   'I do know. I was testing you to see if you were being truthful or not.'
   I opened my mouth to shout something rude at her but thought better of it. Instead I finished tying the knot in my tie.
   'Why would I test you?' Lilith said. 'Because I don't like being lied to. Severin did it just once in all the years we were together.'
   I looked at her sitting in my bed. I couldn't help but glimpse a shapely breast through the split in her nightdress.
   I turned away and asked: 'How long were you together?'
   I heard Lilith sigh and slump back onto the bed.
   'Severin and I were together for over 200 years.'
   I was so astonished I didn't know what to say. After a few seconds of silence I mumbled: 'A long time'
   'Yes,' Lilith answered, 'and yet not long enough.'
   Suddenly she was in front of me, gently gripping my arms.

'But there were mistakes made with Severin. I know that now. After all these years I know where I went wrong, know where and when I got careless and failed to look after the one I loved so much. That won't happen with you. I promise you that Alex, I promise'

With those words she kissed me, and grabbing my hand, placed it upon her left breast. I have no idea how long the kiss lasted but I was aware of the fact she had slipped my hand inside her open nightdress. And of course I was very aware of the fact I was stroking and caressing her naked breast and all the while we were still kissing. I felt a little prick as my tongue grazed her fang, and her tongue licked the blood that came and went within a matter of seconds.

As if on cue, Lilith broke the kiss and slowly withdrew my hand from her dress.

'Go to work. We will talk later. We have much to discuss, you and I.'

'What do I tell them? I mean, can I mention you?'

Lilith laughed and playfully tapped my shoulder, saying: 'Of course, but who would believe you?'

Chapter 3

Who would believe me? She had a point of course, so, after a quick slice of toast I left her alone and drove to work.

My office isn't too far from my apartment, but even so it's a wonder I ever made it there. My mind was so full of Lilith it was a miracle I didn't crash.

But I got there safely and pulled into my parking space. My colleague Paul had just arrived and was getting out of his BMW. It was quite an old one but still looked good, especially compared to my poor old Nova.

'Hey Alex,' he greeted me. 'You look like shit!'

We both laughed and I locked the Nova's door.

'Yeah,' I agreed. 'Didn't get much sleep last night.'

We started walking towards the building.

'Had a woman over did you?'

'Something like that.'

Paul stopped me by grabbing my arm.

'Hey come on, tell me! Who was it?'

It annoyed me that my colleagues always wanted to know all about my sex life. In our department it was a well-known fact that I was the only single guy. The fact of the matter was, now that the other five guys and four girls were either married or engaged my sex life was the only one they were interested in.

'I only met her last night.'

Paul laughed his dirty laugh.

'Sex on the first date? You sly old dog Alex.'

'No, we didn't sleep together. Well, I mean we did but didn't… Look, can we talk about something else please?' I said, becoming exasperated.

Paul shook his head and carried on walking towards our office.

'Wait until the others hear about this. Never knew you had it in you to fuck on a first date.'

I groaned inwardly and trudged after him, knowing what I was in for once the others heard Paul's untruthful version of events.

Once inside the building I made my way to my desk, only stopping to pick up my mail and a coffee from the machine.

Our department consists of the ten of us all on the one floor, each person with their own desk and computer.

Luckily for me, Paul worked on the far side of the room behind a small partition. Opposite my desk worked Karen, who I liked. She had long straight blonde hair and a lovely figure. I had always had fantasies about the two of us getting together but knew she was hopelessly in love with her husband Simon.

I had just sat down when she approached me and sat on the edge of my desk.

'Don't worry about Paul. You know how he is.'

'Yeah.' I said looking up at her, pleased that she had come over.

'Don't let him get to you. If you're happy then I'm pleased for you. About time you found someone.'

And with that Karen went back to her own desk. Normally I would have watched her every move, almost like a stalker but today my mind kept wandering back to the woman waiting at home. What was she doing? I remembered the things Lilith had said. About me being the reincarnation of her long lost lover and the fact vampires clearly existed after all. Would she go out? Could she? I mean, it wasn't a sunny day by any means. If she went out, would she attack someone? I had left her my spare key in case she wanted to go and Lilith had tilted her head to one side and said: 'Maybe."

It had been the slightest gesture but as I thought of it now, I felt a warmth within my chest of the kind I hadn't felt in a long while. I tried concentrating on my work but was finding it difficult. All the letters and numbers on my computer monitor kept merging and didn't seem to make sense as I continued to think of Lilith. How many vampires were there? Where did they all live and go? How had they remained a secret all these years? Just how many deaths of innocent people had been caused by a vampire attack? What had Lilith been doing all this time since Severin had been killed? I still didn't know how or why he was killed. I had so many questions that I knew I needed answering but would have to wait until the end of the day.

I was glad the teasing about my love life wasn't too bad in the end. Even at lunch where we all shared the same small canteen, not much was said. Just the odd light hearted remark here and a bad joke there. Still, I wished now I hadn't mentioned a woman at all and vowed to myself that I wouldn't talk of Lilith again.

I got back to the apartment about my usual time of five thirty. As soon as I opened my front door I smelt cooking.

I shut the door behind me and called out Lilith's name.

She emerged from the kitchen wearing one of my t-shirts and very little else judging by the long slender and extremely bare legs I got a good view of.

'Welcome home, Alex.' She kissed me briefly and went back into the kitchen.

I followed her and was amazed to see two decent bits of gammon under the grill and eggs frying in the pan.

'Even after four centuries I don't know how to cook very well.' Lilith smiled over her shoulder at me as she turned the gammon over.

'No, no. This will be fine,' I said. 'I'm just surprised that's all.'

'In what way?'

'Well, firstly you've obviously been out to get the gammon and secondly I didn't think vampires ate or drank anything apart from blood.'

Lilith laughed and turned to me.

'Where's the fun in that?' she said. 'We live year after year after year. Why would we just drink blood? How boring!'

'So you can digest food the same way we can?'

'Of course.'

'I've never given it much thought.' I admitted.

'Supernatural beings or not, we still have to use the lavatory Alex.' Again Lilith laughed and I felt a bit silly.

'Now, why don't you go change out of that shirt and tie. This will be ready when you come back.'

I didn't argue so set off for my bedroom. When I got there the bed was all freshly made. Clothes that I had left out had been put neatly away. The thought of a domesticated vampire made me laugh out loud.

I changed into jeans and a t-shirt and joined her at the table in the lounge. Lilith had even opened a bottle of red wine.

Before we started eating she chinked her glass against mine.

'To you my darling Alex. My search is over.'

To say I was speechless would be an understatement. This extraordinary woman had called me her darling. I simply nodded and drank when she did.

We made small talk while we ate the meal. She asked me how my day had been and I told her it had been difficult to concentrate. I left out the bit about the teasing though. I asked what she had been doing with her day. Lilith was vague to say the least.

'This and that.' Was all she told me.

I didn't press her for details so we finished the meal and tidied up.

After, she came and sat beside me on the couch.

'Tell me more about Severin.' I said.

Lilith stopped stroking my hair and shrugged.

'Wouldn't you rather make love?'

Naturally, that got my attention. I looked at her and Lilith was gazing at me with those wondrous eyes of hers, while her hand was stroking my leg.

'Come.' With that single word, she grabbed my hand and led me towards the bedroom.

As soon as we got there, Lilith slipped the t-shirt off and stood completely nude. I had been with a few women in my time but none compared to the slender beauty before me at that moment. She was simply magnificent in every detail. I drank in her body from the top of her head down to her toes and knew this was absolutely right, that this was supposed to happen.

'Know my body as you knew it before Alex,' she said as she began to undress me.

The love making was fast and frantic at first, almost as if the wait for her had truly been so very long. But the second time was a lot slower, more passionate and gentle.

Afterwards we kissed and lay there together in each other's embrace.

'Oh Alex,' she whispered. 'Why did it take so long to find you?'

I didn't say anything because I didn't have an answer for her. Instead, I just held her tighter.

'You are so beautiful.' I said as I kissed her neck.

'Thank you. As are you.'

No one had ever called me beautiful before and I was still thinking about that when Lilith sat up in my embrace.

'I want you to come away with me.'

'What?' I said. 'Where?'

'To my home. What was our home and will be again.'

'But Lilith, I can't just leave. What about my job?'

'What about it? You don't need it any more. You will never need anything now that you have me Alex.'

Chapter 4

I didn't understand what she meant. And I was too distracted by her gently stroking my face and hair to question her. I was quietly amazed that she hadn't scratched me, with her nails being so sharp.

We continued to lie there, naked in one another's arms.

'You must have so many questions,' Lilith said softly. 'You can ask me anything.'

The first question that came to mind was one I had intended on asking the previous night but had somehow slipped my mind.

'How old were you when you were created?'

'Sired,' Lilith corrected me. 'Created sounds too godlike, and I was thirty one.'

'You don't believe in God?'

'In all my 450 years I haven't seen any evidence of his existence Alex.'

To be honest I wasn't convinced I believed in God either but to hear the notion of divinity dismissed so easily was a bit of a shock. But I let it pass.

'So you don't think vampires are one of God's creatures?'

Lilith sighed in that now familiar way of hers.

'I don't know. I just know I was sired against my will at the age of thirty one. And that I have hated the last 120 years and more than once thought about walking into the sunlight.'

It never occurred to me that Lilith might not like being who she was. But to hear her talking of suicide certainly surprised me.

'You've been tempted to destroy yourself?'

'Yes. I've been alone for a very long time.'

'What about other vampires?'

'We tend to keep our distance. I know some vampires but don't really call them friends as such.'

'Can you sense other vampires?'

'Yes, but only the younger ones. The elders can shield their minds. Their presence is far harder to detect. Fledglings are easiest because they haven't the knowledge to properly protect themselves. For instance there is a young one not two miles from here, wandering the street in search of an easy kill.'

I looked at her and copied her action by running my hand through her hair.

'How many of you are there?'

Lilith shook her head.

'I have no idea but we are more common than you think. As part of the vampire code, all young ones are taught to hide their kills. A high percentage of bodies deemed 'unknown cause of death' are actually vampire kills.'

'How?' I asked, intrigued.

'After we feed, we do the blood trick I showed you last night. We seal the wounds.'

I nodded and tried to imagine Lilith killing someone. I was finding it difficult until I remembered the vision she had shown me of her killing that knight at the castle. Despite this, it hadn't horrified me at all that she had killed her foe so easily.

'Do you know how many people you've killed? How often?'

I was truly beginning to realise what it might mean to be a vampire for the first time.

'I have no idea,' Lilith said. 'We are taught not to keep count; supposedly it helps our conscience. And I don't kill very often these days.'

I stopped stroking her face at that.

'You don't?'

'I haven't killed in a while Alex.'

'But you told me you had fed last night.'

She nodded and gave a small smile.

'I have learnt with time that I no longer need as much blood. Certainly not enough to kill everyone I meet now.'

I can't explain why, but this came as some relief to me. A small grain of comfort that this cold killing machine laying naked beside me might not be such a monster after all.

'Okay,' I said. 'Is it true vampires can read minds?'

'Only the very oldest of us. I, at a mere 450 cannot.'

'So who is the oldest vampire you've met?'

Lilith kissed me and began stroking my chest.

'I haven't met him but I have heard of a vampire called Zang Zing in China. It is reported he is over 4000 years old, if he's real that is.'

I think I gasped out loud at this piece of news. What must it be like to live so long? It was hard enough to imagine living 450 years, let alone 4000.

'But now Alex, I grow hungry.'

'Hungry? But we haven't long eaten.'

Her hand slid onto my groin.

'There are more ways to hunger, my love.'

It was now ten in the evening and Lilith and I were walking hand in hand along an almost deserted street. I had lived in the same town for many years and yet for some reason things didn't seem that familiar to me any more. Perhaps Lilith was correct, maybe it was time to move on.

'So where do you live?'

Lilith was now dressed in a short green dress she had purchased earlier in the day. I was back in jeans and a sweatshirt. I was quite cold to tell the truth, being an October evening but Lilith didn't seem to mind.

'I have a home in Camden Town. A quaint little place you will love; as you did before as Severin. He chose it after we left the castle.'

'The castle? You mean the one from your vision?'

'The very same.'

'What happened to it?'

'I sold it to a Duke. It had served its purpose and I no longer needed such a huge place.'

'Served its purpose?'

Lilith slowed and looked at me.

'I had made a few too many enemies and needed a place where I could protect myself.'

I could see that pain had returned to her eyes so I stopped my line of questioning. Instead I gripped her hand tighter and kissed it.

'Show me with one of your visions,' I said, 'if it's easier than talking about it.'

Lilith nodded and gave me another small smile like the one she had given me not long ago in bed.

'I will, but later. Is there a tavern around here?'

I laughed and pointed across the road.

'Will that one do?'

'I'm sure it's fine.'

Half an hour later we were sitting opposite one another, a bottle of wine between us. Being a Friday evening it was busy, with people of all ages in there. I didn't go out much so I didn't know anyone in the place.

We got one or two looks, but no one bothered us until closing time, when two youths approached us. I could instantly see they were drunk and when one of them spoke this was confirmed.

'What you doing with this loser?' One asked. 'A babe like you needs a real bloke, know what I'm saying?'

His words were slurred, which made his companion laugh even more.

Lilith smiled up at him.

'If you want to show me what a real bloke is capable of, then by all means lead the way.'

And with that, she stood up and pushed her way past the two youths. I was about to follow when Lilith told me to wait there.

The young men were eager to follow this beautiful woman and ignored me completely, muttering to one another about what they'd do to her.

After a few seconds I followed anyway, curious to say the least. And I think after the wine we had drunk I had perhaps forgotten exactly what Lilith was and what she was capable of. To all intents and purposes I wanted to make sure she was alright. Stupid I know.

The two youths were shouting after her;

'Where ya going? We can do it here!'

'Oh come now boys. A lady wants a bit of decorum.'

Lilith was walking at a fast pace towards the park. When the youngsters realised where she was heading they giggled like idiots and ran to catch up. I did the same, knowing they were too drunk to even notice I was following.

Lilith entered the park and walked towards the nearest bench. There was a single light above it, the only one for quite a distance, no other benches being near.

She sat down and waited for the guys to catch up. She saw me then and gave a slight wave of her finger as if in disapproval at me disobeying her.

'Go on then love. Get that dress off,' said the bigger of the two, eagerly stepping towards her, his arm reaching for her shoulder.

She smiled and opened her mouth in a hiss. The youth froze when he saw the teeth exposed, but his mate egged him on.

'It's Halloween soon, she's dressed up. Get her!'

I stopped walking and simply watched as Lilith slowly got to her feet.

'I shall give you one chance,' she said. 'If one of you can lay just one finger upon me, then you can have me without resistance.'

The two youths looked at one another and suddenly one of them rushed at her, only she was no longer there.

Lilith had leapt high onto the park light and stood in perfect balance looking down at them, her arms crossed over her chest.

'What the fuck?' The one who had rushed her looked up and staggered back, probably in amazement, or befuddled with drink. Most likely both.

'How did you do that, bitch?' The other one asked.

I couldn't help but laugh, which made Lilith laugh too.

'What in fuck's name is going on?' Both youths started to head towards me.

I was just thinking of what to do when Lilith again leapt high into the air and this time landed in front of the startled youngsters.

'He is not ready for you yet,' she hissed, and lashed out a hand that sent the biggest youth flying backwards several feet.

The other youth tried grabbing her, but Lilith grabbed him first and held him in the air above her head by his shirt.

'I could kill you so very easily. Don't make me.'

With that, she threw the guy across the wet grass as if he weighed no more than a dinner plate.

Meanwhile, the first youth had staggered to his feet and had pulled out some kind of knife.

'I will slash your face, bitch.' He bellowed and began to run at her.

Lilith crossed her arms again and smiled.

'Take a free shot.'

The youth, fair play to him, didn't hesitate and slashed the knife in a wide arc. I saw blood immediately appear on Lilith's right cheek, as she rolled her head with the blow.

'Fuck you bitch! I got ya, I got ya.' He taunted her.

Lilith glanced at me before turning slowly back to face her attacker. I saw his eyes go wide in astonishment at something I couldn't see from where I stood behind her, and suddenly he was writhing in pain as Lilith grabbed the same arm that carried the knife and twisted it with no effort at all. But even from where I stood, I clearly heard the snapping of bone and the knife dropped harmlessly to the ground.

The young man was crying as Lilith shoved him away from her. He sat on the grass cradling his broken arm and rocking slightly, just like a baby.

Lilith glanced at the other youth who was now running in the opposite direction. Satisfied she turned back to me.

I don't know why, but I was surprised to see that there was no evidence that she had been slashed at all. Her cheek was as perfect as before.

'Come my love,' she said calmly, 'let's leave this boy to his misery.'

And so, hand in hand again, we left the crying youth alone in the park and went back to my apartment. We weren't to know it yet but his companion, who ran away like a coward, would be the catalyst for me becoming the being I am now. But I am getting ahead of myself.

Once inside the door, Lilith led me to the lounge and sat me down at the table. She sat opposite and looked at me.

'Any questions?'

'You could have killed them. Easily. Why didn't you?'

'And what would that have accomplished? I think it is safe to say they have learned their lesson and won't be much trouble to people from now on. Agree?'

I nodded and saw the sense of her words.

'You could have fed on them.' I suggested.

Lilith shrugged and then took my hand in hers, her eyes sparkling.

'Ah but Alex, tonight I intend to feed on you!'

Chapter 5

As soon as Lilith had said that, I looked at her in horror and backed away from the table.

She gazed at me and shook her head.

'What's wrong my love?'

'You,' I pointed my finger at her. 'You want to kill me. You said you wouldn't harm me and now you want to kill me.'

Lilith continued to sit and gaze up at me.

'Kill you? Yes and no.'

'What? What does that mean?' I stuttered, more confused than ever.

I knew it was pointless but I had backed away a bit more.

I was well aware Lilith could catch me without even trying but this change of events was affecting my judgement.

'I want to give you eternal life. How else can we be together forever, darling Alex?'

'But I thought…'

I stopped. The truth was, I didn't know what I thought.

'Thought what? That you'd remain the same weak human you are until your dying day and then I'd come and whisk you away into my world?'

I didn't know what to say and just stared at her.

Lilith got up and turned away from me. She went and stood by the window and looked out at the night.

Was this my opportunity to at least try to escape? I must admit it did enter my mind but something she had said made me uncertain.

'You called me weak.' I muttered, leaning against the wall by the door.

'All humans are weak to me.' She snapped.

'Of course.' I nodded and in that instant had made a decision.

Lilith turned as I walked towards her.

'When you were sired,' I said. 'You said it was against your will?'

Lilith bowed her head in memory.

'Yes,' she replied softly. 'Christiano had almost killed me when he forced me to drink his blood.'

'He attacked you?'

'Yes. I was just another victim to him and was going to be left to die when something changed his mind.'

'What?'

Lilith looked at me then.

'Christiano once told me that he wanted to create something that the passages of time wouldn't change.'

'And that something was you.' I finished.

Lilith nodded.

'Don't you see Alex? I want to sire you as you are now, young and beautiful. Not when you are old and grey.'

'But why me? Why not some other guy?'

Lilith shook her head and had suddenly grabbed my hand.

'You know why. You have Severin's soul. You will become as he once was, only this time I will not fail you.'

'Were you really to blame for his death?'

Lilith glared at me and in a fit of rage smashed her fist deep into the living room wall.

'Yes, it was my fault. I should have been there. Should have protected him, from his own impetuous self.'

'Show me.' I demanded, sounding braver than I felt.

Lilith shook her head but I had taken hold of her bleeding hand and without hesitation tasted her blood.

Once again the room seemed to spin as the visions began to take shape and form until I was looking at Lilith through Severin's eyes.

They had obviously just made love because Lilith was lacing up her bodice.

'What are we going to do about Archer?' Severin asked.

Lilith turned and gave a mocking wave of her finger, similar to the motion she had made to me in the park earlier.

'We make love and you want to talk about Archer?'

Severin shrugged and got off of the bed.

'He is a threat that has to be dealt with, Lilith.'

'I agree,' she murmured. 'And he will be, in time.'

'Why not now? We know where he sleeps tonight, at his brother's farm.'

Lilith appeared to give it some consideration before shaking her head.

'No. I feel it would be more prudent if we killed him with far fewer people around.'

'No!' Severin actually shouted at her. 'What I did to his sister was a natural thing for a vampire to do.'

Lilith glared at Severin.

'Yes, but you got careless. You were caught and only just managed to escape. He has sworn vengeance ever since.'

'I can take him. Easily.'

Lilith placed her hands gently but firmly upon Severin's shoulders. She gazed into his eyes and he tried not to look at her.

'Look at me Severin.'

When he did Lilith kissed him on the mouth.

'Listen to me, my love. You are still so very young for a vampire. You still have so much to learn. There's still so much for me to teach you.'

'I know my Lily. But I am sick and tired of being hunted by this inferior being! He thinks of us as monsters, nothing more.'

'I know but promise me you won't go there. Stay here while I go and see Christiano. Promise me.'

Severin bowed his head and muttered he would stay.

'Good. I shall be back as soon as I can. I am actually intrigued as to what my sire wants.'

'Maybe I can meet him one day?'

'If he wishes it. You know how vampires like their privacy, my love.'

'But you will ask him?'

Lilith smiled and kissed him once again.

'Indeed I will. Be safe lovely Severin. I love you.'

And with a last embrace Lilith was gone from the room.

Suddenly the affects of Lilith's blood wore off and I was once again back in my familiar lounge. I noticed that her hand was now fully healed.

'I'm sorry for losing my temper.' Lilith said quietly.

I looked at the hole in my wall and shook my head.

'A bit of plaster will fix that. No problem.'

Lilith gave me a half smile and again turned to the window.

'You know, it's a wonderful thing. Vampiric vision.'

'I'm sorry?'

'My vision. I can see so clearly. The darkness holds no secrets from me now. Certainly no fear.'

'You see in the dark?'

'Of course!' Lilith laughed. 'Extremely well.'

'Like other nocturnal predators I guess.'

'Yes.'

There followed a silence between us and I started to think about what I had seen in the last vision.

'When you went to see Christiano, was that the last time you saw Severin, Lilith?'

She didn't answer me at first. She just continued to stare out of the window at the night.

'It wasn't the last time I saw him. It was, however, the last time I saw him alive.' She turned back to me and the tears were back in her lovely eyes.

'Tell me what happened. Let it all out.' I said.

'No. I will show you. It's the best way.'

And with that Lilith once again drew her nail across her wrist and told me to drink.

Chapter 6

When the vision first came I thought something had gone wrong. I couldn't see hardly anything but then I realised I was again seeing through Severin's eyes and I was in the clouds.

I could make out the land below. I passed a church steeple and over a couple of fields before dropping down to make a silent landing by a large barn.

Just across the yard was a big farmhouse in need of repair. There were holes in the roof and the paint was peeling from the walls, while lights were on in at least three of the front rooms.

I made my way silently but swiftly over to the house and around the back. There was a maid with her back to me, sweeping the porch with a poorly constructed broom.

Without a word or sound I placed a powerful hand across her mouth, yanked her head back and bit deep into her throat. I could feel the blood rush into my own mouth and throat as the maid struggled uselessly against me. I continued to drink until I felt her life fade dead away. I dropped the dead body to the porch and bit one of my fingers. With my blood I sealed the bite mark on her neck before entering the house. Apparently the notion about vampires needing an invitation to enter a private house was myth.

Still seeing through Severin's eyes, I made my way through a cluttered kitchen. There were pots and pans all piled up by a dirty sink. Presumably it had been the maid's next task.

From the kitchen I walked into a short hallway and heard voices coming from the left.

I stopped and listened to what they were saying.

'That monster and his whore will die very soon.'

'Aye, you can count on us Mr Archer, sir.'

As Severin I hissed in anger and entered the room.

There stood Archer against the fireplace. One of the men I had seen in the ballroom vision was also there but the third man was not to be seen.

'You!' Archer snarled but I could see the fear in his eyes as he took a step to his left.

'The monster, at your service.' Severin said pointedly, taking a firm step towards Archer.

The serving man held an axe as if he'd been chopping wood and I vaguely recalled seeing a pile of logs by the barn's entrance.

'You can't hurt me with that!' I snapped and before the man could do or say anything I was on him, ripping the axe from his hand and smashing his head into the wall.

Archer took his opportunity to run and I let him. I was beginning to realise this had become a game to Severin.

'That's right Mr Archer,' I mocked. 'Run like the coward you really are.'

I entered the hallway slowly and heard the front door slam. I turned to follow but suddenly there was a very loud explosion and I was lying on the floor.

I felt a tremendous pain and sudden wetness in my right leg and looked down to see it was in tatters. I gasped in shock and looked up to see the third man from the ballroom holding a shotgun, smoke curling out of the barrels.

I heard the front door re-open and turned to see Archer come back in, another axe in his hand.

I tried to get to my feet and realised that the man with the shotgun was reloading. I hissed at him, showing my fangs in the angriest snarl I could muster but he knew I was helpless. He finished reloading and fired again. This time the shells shattered my chest. I was blown along the hallway towards Archer, blood and innards flying out of my broken body as I went. By some miracle the blast had missed my heart but I now knew I was at the mercy of the man standing above me.

Archer looked down at me and there was actually a sad expression on his face.

'Are you in pain sir?' He asked, with what sounded like genuine concern.

I coughed up blood and tried to crawl away but my strength was fast failing and my vision was becoming more blurred by the second.

'Oh look Mr Timkins. The monster's leg is almost healed already.'

'It is indeed Mr Archer, sir.'

I looked down at myself and realised it was true. Maybe I would be alright after all and get away, back to the arms of my love.

'This ends now monster. For the death of my sister, Edith!'

I looked up and saw Archer swing the axe back. I just had time to whisper one blood-soaked word.

'Lilith.'

My vision cleared and I became aware of Lilith crying as she lent against me. We held each other up because I am sure that at that moment either one of us would have fallen over.

'I'm sorry Lilith. I'm so sorry.' I held her close to me, harder than I had previously. I felt her respond and I was almost crushed by her strength.

I put up with the constricting embrace until I could bear it no more.

I gasped out loud and Lilith must have realised what was happening because she relaxed her grip a little.

'What happened next?' I asked.

Lilith shook her head.

'No, I can't.'

'Please tell me. End the story and we will never have to mention it again. Ever.'

Lilith sobbed and continued to hold me as she recounted the last of the tale. Her mouth was right by my ear so she whispered it.

'I had not gone very far to meet Christiano. So after a brief conversation we again parted ways and I made my way back to our house in Camden.'

Lilith then removed her arms from around me and went to sit at the table, where I joined her.

'Severin wasn't there waiting for me. I thought it odd for two reasons. One he said he would be and two, I knew he had already fed so he wouldn't have gone out for that reason. So I immediately felt uneasy and that something was wrong.'

She became silent so I held her hand across the table and encouraged her to go on.

'I remembered the conversation we had had before I left and suddenly I knew without doubt that was where I would find my love. And so I took to the skies and made my way directly to the farmhouse.'

I nodded but didn't say anything. Lilith looked at me as she continued her narrative.

'There was a fire burning when I got there. As I landed I saw Archer throw something onto the pyre. I also saw another man with a shotgun standing watching.'

'Timkins.' I muttered.

Lilith nodded.

'Anyway, I perceived that he was the greater threat and so was upon him before he even knew I was there. I happily ripped his throat out with my fingers and threw him through the side of the barn. Archer by this time had hidden. To this very day I still do not know how he eluded me.'

She was silent for a moment as if dwelling on that fact.

'Anyway, I made my way over to the fire and realised a body was burning on it. It was so badly charred that I did not know who it was.'

Again she fell silent and bowed her head. I merely waited for what I thought was coming. She confirmed it.

'Then I saw the head. My lovely Severin's head, lying on the ground defaced, mutilated and barely known to me. They had decapitated him and burned his body. I've no doubt the head was to follow.'

I nodded in silence and felt her loss.

'I screamed my Severin's name. Over and over. I cried a thousand tears there and then and have cried thousands more since. He was gone. Truly gone. Never to return, my love. Oh my Severin…'

Surprisingly Lilith didn't start crying again but just sat there, supernaturally still, her hands still clasped in mine.

'I did the only thing I could do then. I kissed Severin's lips one last time before putting his poor head onto the fire to burn with the rest of him. You see now how I failed him? How it was my fault?'

I shook my head and squeezed her hand.

'No, it was his fault Lilith. He was young and impulsive. He disobeyed you and paid the ultimate price.'

Lilith sighed deeply and got up. She went back to the window and opened it.

'I need to be alone for a while,' she said. 'I will return.'

And with that, she climbed out of the window and was gone. I rushed over to try to see her but she had been swallowed up by the night.

I realised it was late and so made myself ready for bed. I left the window open for her and turned out the light.

I think the visions had somehow drained me physically, as well as emotionally because I actually fell asleep very quickly. I remember dreaming of being chased by something I couldn't see and yet not being frightened of whatever it was. I used to have that dream quite often as a child and would wake every time in a cold sweat. But not this time. I slept on until I felt the bed move slightly.

I opened my eyes to find Lilith laying there looking at me, her cheeks full of colour.

'Shss,' she whispered. 'Go to sleep Alex. Fear me not.'

'You look different.' I said.

'I fed a few minutes ago. Now go to sleep.'

'What? Who was he?'

'She. And I have no idea. But she will live. Kiss me and sleep well, my love.'

I brushed her hair with my hand as I kissed her on the mouth, my tongue again scratching itself on her fangs.
'Thank you for telling me about Severin.'
Lilith slowly nodded and stroked my face.
'You are the only one I've told. Even my master doesn't know the story.'
'Then I am truly honoured you confided in me.'
Lilith laughed.
'You always seem to know just what to say and when. But it grows late now. Sunrise is a mere 4 hours away so it is time for sleep. Goodnight my sweet Alex.'

Chapter 7

I woke up to find the bed empty. I glanced at the alarm clock; it read 9.25. Shit! I was late for work. But the previous night's events and drama had overwhelmed me. I had completely forgotten that it was the weekend.

I got out of bed and wandered naked down the hall. I heard the shower and poked my head around the bathroom door. There stood Lilith in all her nude glory, clearly enjoying the warm water because she was singing softly but loud enough to be heard over the cascading water. I didn't know the song but she seemed happy.

I was about to leave her to it and return to my bedroom when she called out.

'Come and join me my love.'

I had no idea how she knew I was there but I joined her in the shower with a smile.

'Before you ask,' she smiled, splashing me. 'Vampires aren't afraid of water.'

'What about Holy water?'

'I don't know. I guess it helps if you have something to believe in, not that I make a habit of taking a bath in the stuff.'

I put some shower gel onto a flannel and gently soaped Lilith's breasts.

'That feels nice,' she admitted.

'Good, I'm glad,' I continued to apply the soap and water to her naked body. 'So what was that song you were singing?'

'An old Irish folk melody. My father taught it to me when I was a little girl.'

'So I was right.' I said.

'Right?'

'Yes. When you become passionate about something, your accent becomes stronger. Most of the time I would never have guessed where you come from.'

Lilith nodded, water dripping down from her nose and chin.

'Most vampires lose their original accent after a few centuries. I was born and raised in Dublin.'

Lilith was now soaping me down. Long, gentle strokes with her hand and flannel. It was erotic to say the least.

'It's not fair,' I said. 'I hardly know anything about you and yet you claim to know everything about me.'

'You'll get to know me over time. What's the rush?'
I shrugged; I guess she had a point.
'Anyway, no more talk. I think we should take advantage of our nakedness.'
So we began kissing and were soon making love there in the shower as the lovely warm water crashed down upon us.

Lilith declined my offer of coffee so I sat alone at the table in the lounge in fresh jeans and shirt. She was once again in the green dress she had worn the previous day.
'We can get you more clothes if you want.' I suggested.
'No need. I have plenty back in Camden.'
I nodded and took a sip of my coffee while Lilith again stood at my window.
'I wouldn't be standing here if it wasn't so cloudy.' She said.
'Do you miss the sun?'
'I don't miss something I have come to fear, so no.'
'No I mean being able to walk under a cloudless, sunny sky? Or to sunbathe even.'
Lilith shrugged.
'I never did those things really before I was sired. I was never allowed to play with other children much and as soon as I turned 14 I was sent to the fields to pick fruit.'
'You worked at the age of 14?'
Lilith turned to me and smiled.
'You forget Alex. We are talking over 400 years ago. Things were a lot different then.'
She came across the room and held my head to her chest and kissed the top of my head.
'I notice you haven't said anything more about me giving you eternal life.'
I felt a sinking feeling grow in my stomach but at the same time knew it was only a matter of when and not if she would mention it again.
I did the only thing I could think of doing and that was to tell her the truth.
'I'm afraid.'
Lilith lifted my chin up so she could look me in the eyes.
'Why afraid? Of dying or of being reborn into something more incredible than you can possibly imagine?'
'I don't know,' I admitted. 'Dying is something I simply don't want to think about. Not yet. Not at the age of 35, Lilith.'

She stroked my face and continued to look at me.

'Listen my love. You saw the vision of when I made Severin, yes?'

I nodded.

'And you remember how quick and painless it was for him?'

I tried to think back to the first ever vision she had given me. I recalled the scene perfectly as if watching it on video.

'Yes, I remember.' I said softly.

'Do you know how it was so painless for him? But incredibly painful for me?'

That intrigued me because I assumed it was all the same. I shook my head in answer.

'Well then, I will tell you,' Lilith sat down on my lap and stroked my hair as she spoke. 'As you know I was almost dead when Christiano forced me to drink from him. It was a vampire equivalent to rape. Violation. I had no choice in the matter. Even at full strength it would have been useless to fight him. I was literally seconds away from death when he forced me to drink the magic blood. As I drank from him I got similar visions like the ones you have seen. Only it was all about him. As he fed me I saw Christiano kill one person after another. He was spiteful. In the visions I got from him I knew that he had always been a bloodthirsty and sadistic killer. He was evil in the strongest sense of the word. And yet, something made him choose me to be his third creation.'

Lilith altered her position slightly before continuing.

'Of course I have since learned that vampires have the ability to control what they show victims with their vision powers. That's why I can show you certain moments from my life. It also helps that you have a former vampire's soul. This is why you are able to see through Severin's eyes. But anyway, Christiano deliberately sent me those blood soaked visions as I became one of his kind. There is nothing worse that you can do to a new-born vampire, believe me. It fills them with an instant bloodlust and drives them almost insane until they get their first feed. I went through that and remember it as clearly as if it was yesterday.'

The more she spoke of her master, the more I disliked this Christiano. I certainly didn't want to meet him.

Lilith slid off my knee and got to her feet.

'With Severin it was the exact opposite. I was careful to show him visions of sleeping and smiles. Me at peace so he would be peaceful as the change took place. I had read many vampire scriptures and wanted to do the right thing when I finally chose who I would sire.'

Lilith dropped to her knees and stared up at me again.

'And that is what I promise for you my dear Alex. You will hardly feel a thing my darling. You will drift off as I take your blood. You will get sleepy and then the visions will begin once you taste my blood. All the visions I will send to you will be full of tender and peaceful moments. You will only know the change once you've opened your eyes for the first time.'

I didn't know what to say, just stared at that lovely face. There was still a glow to her cheeks from her feed the night before. Or perhaps it was from the shower we had shared. I wasn't sure.

'Please Alex,' she said, 'please let me give you this gift. Become as strong and fast as I am. Never fear sickness again. Let me end this life so you can start a whole new one in a completely different world with me at your side for all times.'

I still couldn't answer her. I was just too confused. My heart was saying yes, let her do this. But my head was telling me no, that this was not right and that I should reject her offer. I needed time and space to think, although I still wasn't sure it would solve anything.

'Lilith,' I said. 'I am going to go out for a while, an hour or two. I want you to remain here and I will come back okay? I will think about all you have told and described to me and you will have my answer when I come back. I promise.'

Chapter 8

I made my way past familiar shops and headed for the park, where Lilith and I had encountered the two youths.

The sun was refusing to come out and it seemed to me the cloud cover would remain just as dense for the rest of the day. Perhaps it would even rain.

I nodded a greeting to a man I saw regularly around town, although I didn't know his name. There were too many instances like this I decided, considering I had lived in the town for twelve years now.

I walked around the park, stopping for a moment to watch the grounds man painting the white lines for the local football team. They evidently had a game this afternoon.

I thought to myself that I had never taken the time to watch them play. I was always busy doing this or going there. It seemed to me that time was always in short supply.

This of course would all change the minute I granted Lilith her wish to make me a vampire. But was it reason enough? Was time really worth literally dying for?

I started walking again, leaving the man to work on his pitch.

I walked past the tennis courts and was surprised to see a guy in there coaching a girl.

He was encouraging her to follow through with her racquet and I recalled when I used to play regularly. I used to love tennis and wondered why I had stopped playing. Again, time was a factor. There was that word again. Time. Funny how often it was suddenly cropping up in the most trivial of things. Perhaps it had always been there but now I was only just noticing.

'Oh Lilith, what have you done to me?' I said out loud and carried on walking past the courts.

I began to walk towards an un-occupied bench when a familiar figure sat down before me. It was an ex girlfriend of mine, Elizabeth.

'Oh, hi Alex,' she said, seeing me approach.

We had parted on good terms and had remained good friends. Her smile was both genuine and warm.

'Hi Liz. How's you?'

'Good thanks. Got a promotion at the bank. I'm now assistant manager.'

'That's great news, congratulations.'

'Thanks. Hey, sit with me a while. John's with the kids in the playground at the moment.'

John was her husband and father to her two boys. I had only met him a couple of times but liked him well enough, and the boys were great little guys.

I sat beside her, keeping a wide enough gap to let any passer by know we weren't a couple. I don't know why I did that. Force of habit I suppose.

'So how are things with you?' she asked.

'Not bad. Job's the same and the Nova is still running.'

Elizabeth laughed and playfully hit me on the shoulder.

'You still have that same old banger? I can't believe it.'

'Yeah.' I laughed too.

She had always teased me about my choice of car. Ironic really, as Liz couldn't even drive.

'So how's your love life Alex?'

'Well... It's actually pretty good.' I admitted.

'Really? That's great. Who is she? Anyone I know?'

'No. She's new to the area.'

'Okay cool.' Elizabeth looked at her watch. 'Damn, is that the time? I really should get going. Nice seeing you again Alex. Take care of yourself.'

We hugged briefly and she walked away, leaving me to sit there.

Elizabeth had spoken that word again. Time. It was almost as if Lilith was tormenting me with it. I was half expecting to see a calendar come walking towards me, just to fray my nerves that extra bit more.

I sat there in the almost silent park. The birds were singing their various songs high in the trees. A lone squirrel was going about his or her business, bouncing along the ground briefly before scurrying up a large oak tree.

'Not a care in the world.' I muttered, watching him until he disappeared behind the branches.

Despite it being October, the leaves were still very much in abundance. They had lost their brilliant shades of green and were now yellow and brown, but they were still there, hanging on to the tree they were born to.

I would be reborn, I realised, if I gave in to Lilith. I still wasn't sure. I had said I would give her my answer in an hour or two but was that enough time?

Damn it! There was that dreaded word again. I remembered a line spoken by Malcolm McDowell in the Star Trek movie Generations: 'Time is like a predator. It's stalking you and in the end it will hunt you down and make the kill.'

Whether I liked it or not, I found those words perfectly true. Did I really want to grow old and weak? Face maybe one illness after another? Did I want to take a chance that I might lose my faculties later in life and have to be cared for?

As I continued to sit there I shook my head. The answer was no. The answer was NO! I had made my mind up. I was going to consent to Lilith's wishes.

I felt something awakening within me, something that made me smile and laugh out loud. It was the relief you get after a huge burden has been lifted from your shoulders. I was going to become a vampire and I now knew I was ready for it.

I had just got up from the bench to start my way back when I felt a sharp pain in my side. I felt it with my hand and realised it was wet.

To my horror I saw it was covered in blood.

Then I saw the same youth who had run from us the night before, a bloodied knife in his hand.

'Thought it was you, bastard!' he snarled and calmly walked away.

I tried to go after him but already I was growing weak and felt my legs growing heavier by the second. I collapsed to the ground in front of the bench and knew I was in serious trouble. I desperately looked around and saw no other people close by.

'Lilith!' I shouted as loud as I could.

Why I shouted her name instead of for help I don't know. Perhaps something was telling me that she was the only one who could save me now.

'Lilith!' I shouted again, hoping that somehow she would hear me with her superior hearing.

Again I tried to get up but my strength was fast failing. It was getting harder to see or think straight.

'Lilith, help me!' I screamed and managed to crawl a couple of feet away from the bench.

Where was everyone? Why wasn't anyone coming to help me?

And then in my blurring vision I saw a familiar pair of boots step up to me.

'Oh, my poor Alex.' Lilith knelt down beside me and cradled my head in her arms.

'Lilith, help me. Please.' I could barely get the words out now.

'Do you want my gift, my darling?'

'Yes. Yes I do.'

Lilith smiled, despite the fact I was dying in her arms and then pulled my shirt away from where the wound was.

'Not here.' She muttered and quickly dragged me behind some bushes.

Lilith then dipped her head towards the wound and I immediately felt her mouth suck at the blood that was flowing out of it. This stung quite a bit but that was all I felt. My vision was so dark now I could barely see. I could just about make out her hair as she continued to suck and lick my blood.

'Alex.' Lilith shook me slightly and I realised I must have passed out for a few seconds, perhaps longer.

'It is time.' With those words she bit deep into her wrist and placed the open wound over my mouth. I almost gagged on the blood, there was so much of it. Lilith had obviously bitten into a main vein.

'Yes Alex. Yes. Drink it all and be strong again.'

I did as she told me and sucked at her wounded wrist. But already the fountain was running dry. Her healing powers were so great that the wound had almost healed. She bit into it a second time, urging me; 'Faster my love. Drink faster and feel the change.'

Visions were coming to me thick and fast. I saw the two of us earlier that morning, making love in the shower. I got a vision of Lilith sound asleep, a contented look upon her face. Another vision showed her laughing and dancing in moonlight. And still I drank on until Lilith gently but firmly pushed me away from her.

I collapsed on the earth behind the bushes and trees. I was vaguely aware of two people walking past nearby, lost in their own private conversation. But I was exhausted and just wanted to curl up into a ball and sleep. But even as I felt and thought this I became aware of a power building within me, slowly at first but building in force and substance. Power and strength rushed through my entire body. I felt it flow through my fingers, my hands and arms, down my legs and into my feet. It was like a wave of pure and ferocious energy had washed over me. A feeling I had never felt anything like before in my entire life.

I slowly sat up and opened my eyes. Everything seemed so bright, I could hardly stand it but slowly my eyes began to adjust. Then I realised I could hear conversations from people outside the park. I could hear a man's heartbeat from metres away. I could also detect a very slow heartbeat nearby and realised it was Lilith's.

She had collapsed beside me and hadn't yet stirred.

'Lilith.' I exclaimed, saying it softly but it sounded booming to me now.

I heard her groan but she didn't move so I decided to roll her over.

Slowly she opened her eyes and gazed up at me. I gazed down at her, a great big smile on my face.

'You saved my life.' I said.

'And yet I took it,' she whispered back.

I shook my head and felt at my side where the knife had gone in. There was no blood now, only a dried scar.

'It doesn't matter Lilith,' I said. 'Nothing matters now. I had already made my mind up to accept your gift before I was stabbed.'

Lilith sat up but I could see she was still weak. I held out my hand as I got to my feet. She grasped my hand with what strength she had left and I slowly pulled her to her feet.

'Get me home Alex.'

I lifted her with ease into my now powerful arms and strode towards the park exit, ignoring the glances of people passing by.

Chapter 9

I stood looking in my bedroom mirror, Lilith lying on the bed behind me. She was still weak from the blood exchange but was beginning to recover.

I couldn't see anything different about my appearance. But of course I could feel a pair of now elongated canine teeth. I lifted my upper lip and studied them.

'They don't look all that sharp.' I proclaimed, poking at first the left one, then the right.

'Sharp enough.' Lilith sat up and watched me.

I turned to her and smiled.

'I have a question for you.' I said.

'Go ahead.'

'I saw you sire Severin in that first vision you gave me. And yet with me you became so much weaker and have taken a lot longer to recover. Why is that?'

Lilith still looked far from fully recovered and sat there looking at me with very weary eyes.

'I gave you far more blood than I did with Severin.' Lilith answered.

'But why?'

'Because I wanted to make you as strong and as fast as I possibly could. The more blood a vampire gives their sired, the more powerful they become. That is why I am weak now. I will need to feed as soon as it is dark.'

I nodded and went over to her and took her hands gently in mine. I had to remember I now possessed the strength to hurt her.

'What is it like? Taking a victim I mean?'

Lilith smiled and touched my arm.

'I will show you tonight Alex. We will both feast.'

'How do you choose your targets?'

'I usually go for men. They tend to think with their dicks, no offence, so are much easier to lead astray to take some of their blood.'

'You say you don't kill any more?'

'No. I said I hardly kill any more. Usually I take only what I need as I have great control over my thirst. You however, will not. I'd be very surprised if your first victim survives the attack.'

As a human this would have appalled me. The very thought of taking another person's life would have devastated me. But that was the old Alex.

This Alex was now controlled by the vampire within. And to be perfectly honest, the mere thought of biting into someone's neck filled me with pleasure.

'Can we go now?' I asked. 'To feed I mean.'

'Patience, my darling. I took a great risk to sire you in the park but had no choice, for you would have died. But we cannot afford to get careless. We must go about in secret and with discretion.'

'But why? No man on earth could take us in a fight.'

Lilith glared at me and actually lashed out with her hand. Even in her weakened state the blow was powerful enough to knock me into the wall.

'What was that for?' I held my aching cheek but realised the pain was already subsiding.

'Have you already forgotten what happened to Severin?' she hissed.

I stared at her and cursed my clumsiness. I bowed my head to her.

'Forgive me Lilith.'

'Aye, I will but you must promise me not to think of humans as weak, and certainly not helpless. Maybe alone they don't have our strength, but in numbers they are very dangerous. Remember this, for it will prolong your life Alex. Mark my words.'

I nodded and looked out of the bedroom window. The late afternoon sky was still covered with cloud. I could hear a noisy motorcycle somewhere but could not see it. Then I was aware Lilith had come up beside me.

'You appear troubled. I can sense it. What is it Alex?'

I turned and looked at her.

Her eyes weren't their usual brilliant green but appeared dull in comparison, almost faded in fact.

'You told me Severin only lied to you once,' I said. 'When he went after Archer after telling you he wouldn't.'

Lilith sighed and nodded her head.

'His one and only time,' she whispered 'and it cost him his life.'

I nodded and held her. Her arms went around me and she lent her head into my chest. I sighed with happiness at simply holding this enchanting creature. I listened to our hearts beating as we slowly began to dance. Lilith was humming that Irish melody she had been singing earlier and we slowly moved to its rhythm. We turned in a circle, still holding one another until I felt something brush my head.

I had closed my eyes while we danced and now when I opened them gasped and laughed out loud for we were right up against the ceiling. Without even thinking we had floated upwards in each others embrace.

Lilith laughed too and then began to float back down again, taking me with her.

'Good job we weren't in a club doing that. We'll have to be careful,' she said.

I smiled and kissed her.

After a small meal of sausages and mash, Lilith and I hit the streets. Or rather we floated above them in the darkness. She wanted to show me how to perfect my floating skills. It wasn't exactly flying but came close to it. Even with our super natural powers we couldn't defy gravity for too long without having to return to earth.

We floated through a small cloud and came out the other side, holding hands.

'How did you discover you could do this?' I asked. It was so silent up there that I had no need to shout to be heard.

'Christiano taught me. He made my early life as a vampire a complete misery. But I had nowhere else to go so I kept following him, until he finally relented and started to show me, to teach me, as all sire's should do.'

'And that's what you will do? For me?' I asked

Lilith looked across at me as we continued to float and smiled.

'I will teach you everything I know. Take you places you would never have considered going to. You will see things that will astound and amaze you my dear sweet Alex.'

With those words we began to drop slowly back towards the ground.

We landed in an almost deserted car park and to my amazement, I realised where we were. We had floated almost twenty miles in just a few minutes.

'That was incredible.' I exclaimed, laughing out loud into the night and my companion laughed too.

'Yes, it is a good way to get around. No traffic jams.' She laughed again and then raised a finger to her lips and pointed.

I followed her finger to see a couple approaching one of the cars.

'Keep quiet and follow me,' she whispered.

Suddenly Lilith was on the move, keeping to the shadows of the car park's wall. I thought it would be hard to keep up with her but to my surprise and delight I managed it easily.

We had quickly closed to within a few feet of the couple. Lilith suddenly took me by surprise.

'Yes, my darling, it is a beautiful night,' she said quite loudly.

The couple looked over and slowed their approach to the car.

'Good evening.' I called out to them.

'Yes it is.' The man said and removed a set of car keys from his jacket pocket.

'We're going to the dance.' Lilith said happily.

The woman smiled.

'That's nice for you. What dance is that?'

We were now right by them. They were middle aged, man and wife, judging by the wedding bands.

'The dance of blood.' Lilith answered and before I could say or do anything, she had grabbed the woman by her hair and was pulling her towards the back of the car.

'Mary!' The man went to intercept but I quickly blocked him.

'Going somewhere?' I asked.

'What's she doing to my wife? Get away from her, you bitch.'

'Now, now, is that any way to talk to a lady?' I scolded him and gave him a gentle push. I must have misjudged my strength as he slammed into the car, rocking it with enough force to set the car alarm off.

'Fuck!' I shouted and grabbed the fallen keys. I quickly found the button for the alarm and stopped the harsh sound. They are bad enough to normal ears, imagine what a car alarm close up can do to a vampire.

Lilith came up from the back of the car, her mouth covered in blood. She looked at me and licked her lips.

'She will live. Your turn.'

I advanced on the still stunned man and drew him up to my height.

'That's it,' Lilith encouraged me. 'Bite into the pulse of his neck. Be quick and clean.'

I did as she instructed me and for the first time I felt someone other than Lilith's blood enter my mouth. Nothing had prepared me for the sensation. The incredible rich flavour and loveliness the blood made it hard to concentrate. All my mind could focus on was the delicious crimson liquid pouring into my throat.

'That will do.' I was vaguely aware of Lilith saying, but I ignored her and carried on drinking until she pulled me roughly away. I snarled at her and she struck me across the face, sending me flying over the car and into the wall.

I lay there stunned, unsure what had happened.

Getting to my feet slowly, I saw that Lilith had put the couple into the front seats of the car.

She shut the door and looked at me.

'They won't remember a thing but they will live,' she said.

'I, I …'

'It's okay,' Lilith came to me and held my hand. 'It was the blood lust Alex. I told you it's overwhelming the first few times.'

'I couldn't control it.' I admitted, shaking my head.

'It's over for now. You'll be okay.'

I looked at her and then remembered I hadn't closed the wound on the man.

'His wound, I …'

'I took care of it. All sealed up. Now let's get out of here.'

Still shaken by what had happened Lilith and I took to the air and left the car park far behind.

'It will get easier, I promise,' Lilith called to me. 'But until then I won't leave your side. Not while we feed at least.'

'No," I said. 'Please don't leave me.'

'I think it's time I showed you my home,' she smiled. 'Or should I say our home?'

Chapter 10

London. Home to approximately 7 million people. The 50 mile journey had taken only a few minutes, with little rest.
Now we stood outside a wonderful house. There were lights on downstairs and through the windows I could see dark red curtains.
'How old is this place?' I asked, admiring the brick work.
'It was built in 1742,' Lilith replied.
'It's been here all this time when so much of Camden has changed?' I asked, amazed at this piece of news.
'Indeed it has.'
Lilith took hold of my hand and led me up the steps towards the solid oak door. Like the curtains the door was painted dark red, in an otherwise white brick surround.
Lilith opened the door with a large dead lock key and pushed the door open.
I was expecting the door to squeak on its hinges as if from a classic horror movie, but it swung back without a sound. In fact the house was completely silent. Even to my now enhanced hearing, all I could hear was the sound of cars in the next street, for this house was alone beside the canal.
'How did you manage to find this place?'
Lilith closed the door and turned on the lights, which were simple wall sconces with black lace shades.
'I purchased it from the owner who met an untimely death at the hands of my beloved,' she explained.
'I see. So how long has the property been in your name?'
Lilith shrugged.
'This time around, about 22 years I think.'
I furrowed my brow. 'I don't understand.'
'I pay someone very well for keeping things in order. The house gets transferred to various members of the O'Shea clan, but I remain the sole owner.'
I shook my head in incomprehension.
'Vampires have to remain a myth to humans. But there is a law firm that specialises, shall we say, in vampire clients. Our elders had to move with the times and so knew the need for protecting ourselves against human laws.'
'Aren't you afraid the law firm won't rat us out?'

'Not really. And why would they? We pay them far greater sums of money than any human client would.'

I followed Lilith as she began to walk down a hall.

'You mean to say you are a rich woman?'

Lilith laughed then and glanced over her shoulder.

'I have shares and investments that continue to do very nicely. Besides, I come from a well off family. Money, my dear Alex, is not a problem to me. Nor is it to you. What's mine is yours.'

As if on cue, she flipped a switch on the wall, illuminating a fabulous lounge. My whole apartment would have fit in this one room. There were the red curtains I had seen from outside. On one wall was a large brick fireplace, and to my surprise logs were burning in the grate.

'Why do I get the impression we aren't alone?' I said.

'Before we left your apartment I telephoned ahead. I have a house keeper who takes care of the place when I'm away.'

'A house-keeper?'

'Yes. I change them quite regularly so they won't get suspicious. The current one has worked here for 2 years now.'

I nodded and gazed around, taking it all in.

On the far side of the room stood an upright piano. Various pictures of people I didn't know adorned the walls. The oak floor was covered by a deep, red rug. On either side of the fire stood two equally, red arm-chairs.

'May I?' I gestured to one of the chairs and Lilith smiled, nodding her head.

I sat down and stretched my legs out, enjoying the sensation of the oldest form of heat known to man. I turned my vampiric gaze towards the flames and smiled at the beauty of their dance.

Lilith went over to a large drinks cabinet.

'Would you care for a drink?' she asked.

'Yes please. I'll have what you're having.'

Lilith nodded and poured out two glasses of sherry. She handed one to me before sitting down in the other chair.

'So Alex, do you like the house?'

'Yes, what I've seen of it.'

'Don't worry. You'll see the rest of it before the night's out. But we can rest here for now. Floating above the earth is far more tiring than it looks, as I'm sure you agree.'

I concurred with her on that. But I smiled when I remembered our close encounter with another creature of the night. An owl had almost flown into

Lilith at one point, but no harm had been done.

'So who is in the pictures?'

Lilith shrugged and gazed at one of them from her sitting position.

'I do not know. They were a gift from Christiano.'

I nodded and sipped at the sherry. It was the loveliest I had tasted.

'When did you last see him?'

'Oh, God knows,' Lilith said. 'But we speak on the telephone sometimes.'

I couldn't help repress a smile.

'What?' she asked, quizzically.

'Nothing,' I said. 'It's just that the thought of two very old vampires chatting on the phone is kind of funny.'

Lilith smiled and bowed her head slightly.

'I suppose it is.' She agreed.

We continued to sit there, relaxing and enjoying the crackling fire. We made a bit of small talk about what we had seen on our journey here. I remarked I had never seen the night-lights of London from above and was amazed at the sheer amount of them.

Finally we had finished our drinks and Lilith led me through to a spacious kitchen. I wasn't sure what to expect but it certainly wasn't the modern kitchen that greeted me.

'It badly needed updating,' she told me, 'so no expense was spared last year. I like cooking as you know, and I am pleased with the results.'

All the units were white, as were the appliances. But I loved the black marble counter tops. I went over and opened a door, which belonged to an American style fridge freezer.

Inside it were stacks of steaks, various joints of meat, pizzas, and that was just what I could see. I closed the door and turned to find Lilith gazing at me.

'You seem a little overwhelmed Alex.'

'Well yes, I am.' I admitted.

'But why?'

'I don't know. I just wasn't expecting such a lovely house.'

Lilith shrugged in that now very familiar way of hers.

'Forget the horror movies my love. We vampires live in comfort. We move with the times. There is only one I know of who still lives in a castle. The rest of us own nice houses like this or hotels even.'

I nodded and went over to a door that led outside. I opened it and my eyes instantly picked out a fox standing in the middle of a large and immaculate lawn. He saw me and froze for an instant before running off.

I turned back and shut the door behind me.

'Come, let's see the rest of the house.' Lilith said, grabbing my hand. We walked back through the lounge and down another short hallway that ended in a door, which when opened revealed a small library and study.

'I spend a lot of my time in here,' she told me.

I could see why she would want to. Three of the four walls were lined with shelves of books of all sizes. Some of them looked extremely old.

The remaining wall had French windows that led out into another part of the garden.

'I had those put in.' Lilith said. I nodded and went to the large desk that was in one corner. On it was a state of the art flat-screen monitor. I looked under the desk and saw an almost brand new computer.

'You can use a computer?' I gasped.

Lilith smiled and nodded.

'I dated a computer genius for a while,' she said. 'He taught me.'

'Oh. So what happened to him?'

'I got carried away with a love bite and he didn't want to see me any more. Funny that.'

I laughed at that and Lilith saw the funny side too.

'Now let's go upstairs,' she said, taking my hand once more.

The staircase was an iron spiral one, painted in black. Lilith led me up as it was too narrow for us to walk side by side.

The first room we came to was the bathroom. Like the kitchen, it was very modern and had a power shower in one corner and a very large square bath in the other. Black tiles adorned an otherwise white wall and the towels and furnishings were stylishly monochromatic and subtly luxurious.

The next room along the hall was the spare bedroom. There was an unmade bed in there and a small wardrobe but that was all.

'No one comes to stay.' Lilith said, almost sadly I thought. But I let it pass and followed her towards the last room.

She opened the door to her bedroom.

'Oh wow,' was all I could say at first.

All the walls were painted black, the carpet and curtains were the same dark red as downstairs. A large double bed sat in the centre of the room, the golden headboard against the wall. The bedspread was dark red too, as were the pillows. Sensuous pictures of white lilies adorned the wall.

Lilith went over to the closed curtains and drew them back to reveal

French windows. She slid one back and stepped out onto a balcony.

The wind must have picked up because a sudden gust blew her raven hair across her face as she stood there, looking into the night.

Before I joined her I took in more of the room. Two built in wardrobes took up one entire wall. I took a peek in one and saw a variety of dresses all hung up neatly. Most were red, black and white. Clearly her favourite colours, I thought.

I looked in the other wardrobe and was surprised to see it empty.

'That is for your clothes Alex.'

I closed the wardrobe door and turned to see her staring at me, her back against the balcony railing.

'I can really move in with you?' I asked.

'Of course. This is your home now.'

'But what about my apartment?'

Lilith shrugged

'You can keep it if you wish. Might be a useful stopping off point for us. But you won't live there anymore.'

'And my work?' But I already knew the answer.

'Work for you, my dear Alex, is a thing of the past.'

Then she beckoned me to her and like a well-trained puppy I went. She held me to her and kissed me on the mouth, just as the nearly full moon came out from behind the clouds.

'Shall we make love out here or in bed?' she whispered.

'You choose.' I replied between kisses.

As her answer she unzipped her dress and let it fall to the balcony floor.

Chapter 11

I awoke that Sunday morning in Lilith's bed for the first time. She was dozing softly beside me, one arm draped protectively over my chest.

I saw that it was a bright sunny day outside, as a tiny beam of light had found its way through a chink in the curtains. I decided to try something and very slowly stretched out my left hand towards the sliver of sunshine. As it was, my arm felt heavier this morning, my movement seemed more sluggish. But as I moved my hand into the light, I immediately felt a burn.

I let out a hiss of annoyance and pain and looked at my smouldering hand. Already a blister had formed where the light had touched me.

The commotion had wakened Lilith and she opened her eyes.

'What did you do?' she gasped, immediately taking my hand into hers.

'I wanted to see what the sun felt like.' I replied meekly.

'Hurts like hell?'

'Just a bit.'

Lilith shook her head and then gently bit into my wounded hand.

'Your own blood will heal it,' she said 'minor burns aren't a problem for us, only major ones.'

I watched as she smeared my blood over the burn and I immediately felt the heat and sting of it subside. When I next looked the burn had gone completely.

'Thanks.' I kissed her.

Lilith smiled and slowly got out of bed.

'We will start going to bed later and later so that we are awake during night hours. It's simply something we have to get used to, especially in the summer months.'

I nodded and lay back in the bed, watching her examine herself in the large ornate mirror.

'So much for vampire's not having reflections.' I stated.

'Yes, just a myth. One of many.' Lilith made a dismissive sound and started to run a brush through her gorgeous hair.

'Do you have to cut your hair? Or does it stay that length?'

'No, it doesn't grow anymore. I can cut it but it would never grow again.'

I rubbed my jaw and realised there wasn't any stubble. Lilith saw me in the mirror and turned with a smile.

'And no, you won't ever have to shave again, Alex.'

I had to admit that was something I wasn't going to miss. But I realised I truly was going to miss the sunshine. Something I had taken for granted right up until yesterday and now I knew I could never again walk outside on a glorious sunny day.

Lilith must have seen my expression because she stopped brushing her hair and came back over to me.

'What's wrong my darling? You look very sad all of a sudden.'

I looked into her eyes. They had lost their shine from the night before. Perhaps this was a side effect of the sun too.

'I just realised I will miss the sun.' I answered softly.

Lilith nodded her understanding and took my hand.

'Yes my love. We all feel that way at the start but you'll soon learn to love the moon just as much, if not more.'

I suddenly gasped as I thought of something else.

'What is it?'

'My parents!' I almost shouted. 'They don't know what's happened to me.'

Lilith laughed and went to stroke my face but I slid away from her.

'I'm serious Lilith,' I said. 'How will I be able to see them again?'

'It's really not a problem. As long as you've fed before you are due to see them, they will still think of you as human. If they ever ask to see you when the sun is shining politely decline and say you have other plans.'

I was beginning to see she had a point.

'And they would really still think I was my usual self?'

'Trust me. They wouldn't know the difference.'

I nodded and stood to go and use the bathroom. As soon as I was on my feet I felt that lethargy feeling wash over me again.

Lilith noticed and stood with me.

'It's the sun Alex,' she said. 'It really weakens us on a clear day. At the height of summer we rarely venture out until at least two hours into total darkness.'

I nodded and walked nude down the hall to the bathroom.

'I will get us some breakfast,' Lilith called after me. 'And please don't make the mistake of opening any curtains when you come down.'

We enjoyed a coffee each and some scrambled eggs on toast. I hadn't seen a little alcove last night which was just around the other side of the kitchen. It was just a simple pine table and two identical chairs.

'You don't have many visitors then?' I enquired.

'No. I don't have many friends Alex.'

I thought about that statement and then about my soon to be ex-colleagues at work.

'I suppose it isn't prudent for a vampire to have human friends.'
Lilith nodded somewhat sadly and drank the rest of her coffee.
'It can get very lonely sometimes,' she admitted. 'And that is why I'm so glad I found you Alex. Neither of us ever needs to feel lonely again.'
I smiled at her and held her hand across the table.
'So how will I go about quitting my job tomorrow?'
'Just phone in to say you're never going back.'
'And when they ask for a reason?'
Lilith shrugged.
'Tell them you got another job. Or that you're going to travel the world. They'll be pissed at you but what can they do?'
I saw what she was getting at and to be honest I didn't think I owed the firm anything. They had, after all passed me over for a promotion and brought in some useless guy to do the job. But I was going to miss the office gossip, even though it was mostly about my love life. I was sure I was going to miss seeing Karen too, but wasn't about to admit that to Lilith. Could vampires get jealous? I didn't want to find out and certainly didn't want to be on the end of another of Lilith's right hooks.
'Now then,' Lilith said. 'You must have lots more questions about vampirism so go ahead. Ask away.'
It was true. I did have lots of questions I wanted answers to.
'Okay. You sired Severin and now me. What's to stop you from giving the vampire gift over and over again?'
Lilith shook her head.
'It's one of the most sacred of our vampire laws. Laws that have been set for centuries.'
'What law?'
'The law that states a vampire may only ever sire three times.' She explained.
This came as a bit of a surprise, I must admit.
'Why?' I asked.
'It is not to be questioned, only obeyed Alex. I can only sire once more.'
'Yes but who enforces the law? Vampire police?'
Lilith gave me the proverbial dagger look.
'Don't mock what you don't understand.'
I put up my hands and apologised.
'I'm sorry but you're right. I don't understand.'
'You will and you must. Your very existence depends upon it Alex. Break any of the sacred laws and you will be brought to justice very swiftly and painfully.'

'Okay, but by who? Who deals out the justice?'

'The council of the Morisakis.'

I shook my head, meaning I had never heard of it.

'Morisakis was the first of our kind. It is documented in the ancient scripts I have had the honour of seeing. His followers are all vampire kind's governing body. We obey the ancient laws or face the consequences Alex.'

'Followers? You make it sound like a religion.'

'Perhaps it was in ancient times. Now the Morisakis is just a council who enforce the original laws.'

'So what are the consequences?'

Lilith fixed her gaze upon me and answered quietly.

'Torture and death by sunlight.'

My eyes went wide at this piece of news, yet at the same time it all made perfect sense. Vampires had to remain a secret from human kind, so if there were too many vampires around it would be impossible to stay hidden. I saw the need for some such laws but punishment by such a devastating method?

Lilith stared at me as if trying to read my thoughts. But I knew she wasn't capable just yet, unless she had lied and I had no evidence she had lied so far in our short time together.

'What are you thinking?' she asked.

'About the laws. What other laws should I know about?'

Lilith stood up from the table and beckoned me to follow her. She made her way towards her study. Once there she went straight to a very old and dusty book on the bottom shelf.

'Here,' she said, handing me the book. 'All our laws are copied here for you. It may be an old book Alex, but the laws remain relevant.'

I nodded and sat down at her desk, opening the book.

But then I frowned for the book was written in a language I didn't even recognise, let alone understand.

'What is this?' I gestured towards the writing.

'Oh,' Lilith looked at me with a hint of amusement on her face. 'It didn't occur to me you wouldn't know Greek.'

I shook my head and Lilith sat on my knee and started to translate for me.

'Law one: the most sacred of all vampire laws. Human kind must never learn of our existence. Or the truth overall.'

It was my turn to frown.

'What does that mean? The truth overall?'

Lilith kissed my cheek before answering.

'The truth is this Alex. Vampires were once the dominant species of this planet. But the environment changed gradually. The darkened skies became clearer as the world evolved. Some vampires adjusted accordingly and began to only come out when it was safe to do so. Other's perished in flames because they didn't understand the power of the sun's lethal rays. Over time mankind took over and vampires could do nothing about it.'

'Because of law one.' I said.

Lilith nodded.

'There are some vampires living today that still resent human's taking over. They are the natural enemy to the Morisakis. They are rogue and are a danger to all of us.'

I couldn't picture a secret vampire war being raged but nothing was surprising to me any more.

'Are there many of these rogue vampires around?'

'No. And they call themselves the True Species. Or the Truest.'

'Very original.' I laughed but Lilith shushed me with a look.

'Take this seriously Alex.'

'I'm sorry. Go on.'

And so Lilith continued the lesson of my vampire heritage.

The second law states that no vampire may kill another vampire without the written and express permission of the Morisakis.

Law three is that a vampire may not sire more than a maximum of three vampires, to avoid the possibility of over-population.

I had discovered there was a lot more to this Vampire business than I first thought.

Chapter 12

Unfortunately we had to spend most of that Sunday marooned indoors as amazingly for October, the sun shone brightly in the sky the whole day.

Lilith used the time to explain more about what it meant to be a vampire. I had always assumed that if vampires were real then once you became one, you could do what-ever you wanted. This clearly wasn't the case, and the more I thought about it, the more I realised something wasn't quite right.

It was shortly before eight o'clock in the evening and we had just made love for the third time that day when it came to me.

Lilith had just finished a shower and was drying her hair while I sat on the end of her bed watching her.

'Lilith,' I said, 'you told me that vampires have to remain a secret. That they can't be discovered by humans or face destruction from the Morisakis.'

She turned rubbing her hair with a towel and nodded.

'So how did this Archer man know what you were and what Severin had done to his sister?'

For a moment I didn't think she had heard me or wasn't going to answer, for Lilith carried on drying her hair humming a tune to herself.

Then she walked back into the bathroom and a moment later emerged wearing a red dress. She looked truly gorgeous.

'Severin got careless,' she explained. 'We were both feeding; I on a servant and Severin on a woman who turned out to be Archer's sister. I heard men approach and told Severin to stop. He disobeyed me for only a few seconds but by then they were right outside the room.'

She began to pace the floor in front of me while I waited for her to continue.

'Two men came through the door and cried out for help. I should have killed them there and then but instead I grabbed my beloved and dragged him away from the woman. Archer began shouting for help and I instantly heard more men on the way. I could have killed him. Oh I wish I had. I could see Archer's sister was almost dead for Severin had taken too much of her blood.'

For a moment Lilith was quiet but then finished her tale.

'Anyway, Severin and I leapt through the glass window, landed three stories down in the back garden and made our escape. Of course, we discovered later that the woman didn't survive Severin's assault.'

I nodded but something was still missing. Then it clicked into place.

'But surely upon discovery, the Morisakis heard you had broken their most sacred law?'

Lilith turned with haunted eyes.

'Yes, and they began to hunt us, just as Archer would too. Oh my Alex, how I have broken our laws. Not only was I foolish enough to let us get caught feeding but I have also broken our second law.'

It took me a moment to realise what she was getting at.

'You've killed another vampire?' This time it was my turn to show shock.

'Five, actually.'

I gasped and stared at her, while Lilith looked down at her feet.

'Are they still hunting you?'

'Yes. They will never stop until justice is served.'

I glanced around at the room and immediately felt insecure.

'Is it safe here?'

'They wouldn't risk a full on assault Alex. Not here, in London with so many humans around.'

'So what are you going to do?' I went up to her and held her arm.

'What I've been doing ever since Severin and I were found out: keeping my wits about me. Trying to keep to populated areas as much as possible. That is why I rarely visit the countryside.'

I gazed at her and shook my head.

'How can you exist like that?' I asked. 'Forever wary of an attack and knowing that the Morisakis will never stop. Can they be bargained with? Is there nothing we can do?'

Lilith went over to her wardrobe and opened it.

'No. Their laws must be obeyed. Punishment for breaking those laws is death. One day, perhaps soon, my sins will catch up with me and my time will end.'

Lilith put on a pair of shoes that matched the red dress she wore. Then she stepped up to me and took my face gently in her hands.

'That's why we cannot afford to draw any more attention to ourselves Alex.'

I looked into those eyes that I knew would soon be full of life again, but until Lilith fed they would remain faded and almost devoid of life. Mine were probably similar if I looked in the mirror.

'I think you're wrong.'

Lilith stared at me and a look of anger flashed across her features. But she held that anger in check.

'Wrong? How so?'

It was my turn to stroke her face.

'My Lily, don't you see?' I smiled. 'The more attention we draw to ourselves, the more the Morisakis will be afraid to touch us. For fear of discovery themselves.'

Lilith pondered this but shook her head.

'You think like the True Species.' She turned away and glanced out of the window.

'Perhaps they have a point.' I said.

'What point is that?'

I went up to her and slid my arms around her from behind.

'We should join them,' I said, 'the True Species. After all we both share a common enemy now, the Morisakis.'

Lilith leaned her head back against me and sighed.

'Mankind would become our enemy too Alex. The True Species want to be discovered. They want to take the world by force and become dominant again.'

I nuzzled her neck and liked the faintly soapy smell of her after her shower, again being a lavender scent.

'I'm not saying we should join in with the taking over the world thing. But they can at least offer us protection against the Morisakis.'

Lilith turned in my embrace and looked into my eyes.

'You are as headstrong as Severin was,' she said, 'and yet, some of what you say makes sense.'

I nodded and we just gazed at one another for a few seconds, her arms enfolded around my waist. Then she kissed me and broke the embrace.

'I will think about all you have said. But now we will go out to feed.'

I nodded and looked down at my clothes.

'Am I dressed okay?'

'It will do until we can buy more clothing for you. We could go tomorrow if the sun doesn't come out. Failing that you could always order stuff online.'

'Really?'

'Of course. Vampires love the internet.' Lilith laughed and I did too.

Soon we were walking along Camden High Street, passing familiar shops I hadn't been in for sometime. The nightlife was as active as I remembered it. Bars and clubs were crammed to bursting point, despite it being a Sunday night.

People didn't pay us any attention as we strolled along, hand in hand, just like any other couple.

When we were clear of people for a few yards I stopped her.
'Can you sense other vampires around?'
Lilith nodded and looked at me.
'You can too if you know what to reach out for.'
'Sorry?' I asked, puzzled.
'Their auras, Alex,' she explained, 'vampires have far more powerful auras than humans. If you think of nothing but a vampire you will sense them.'

I concentrated my thoughts as she had directed me and immediately I became aware of a vampire feeding off a young woman in an alley just around the corner. He seemed about my age physically, but probably a lot older as a vampire. He must have sensed me because he suddenly looked up from drinking her blood and hissed. I gave a small nod and pulled my thoughts away.

Lilith was staring at me, a small smile on her lips.
'Well?' she asked.
'That was amazing,' I said. 'I saw what he was doing until he sensed me.'
Lilith nodded.
'I know him. His name is William. He sensed you but not me.'
'How come?'
"Because he is only 77 years old; with age comes more ability. Both you and he are incapable of shielding your minds. But come, I grow hungry.'

Lilith took my hand in hers again and began to walk towards a Chinese restaurant.
'We'll eat here and then find a different kind of food,' she smiled.

The meal was lovely. We ordered roast duck, which we shared and then a variety of other delicious dishes. I didn't know if my taste buds had altered since the transformation but the food was certainly among the best I had ever tasted. We shared a bottle of red wine too. To the unsuspecting eye, we were just another couple enjoying a meal together, when in reality we could massacre everyone in the entire building with just our bare hands.

We came out of the restaurant two hours later as places were beginning to close for the night.
'Where now?' I asked.
But there was suddenly a frown on Lilith's face as something grabbed me from behind and threw me to the ground, and a man's voice growled:
'Don't mess with my business again.'
'Cease this, William!'
I looked up and saw that Lilith had shoved the vampire I had seen before

up against a wall and was holding him without effort three feet off the ground.

'Lilith,' he frowned. 'I didn't know he was with you.'

She slowly lowered him to the ground and released her hold.

'He sensed you. That is all. I am teaching him our ways.'

William nodded and came over to me, holding out his hand.

'I apologise,' he said. 'If I had known you were Lilith's I would never have had introduced myself in such a rude manner.'

I took the offered hand and he pulled me to my feet.

'I'm William. And you are?'

'Alex.'

'Well, pleased to meet you Alex.'

We shook hands and both looked at our older companion.

'So how are things with you?' Lilith asked William.

'Can't complain. You?'

'Not bad.' She answered and they both laughed as if they were sharing a private joke.

'So how did you meet Alex?'

I was expecting her to tell the tale of me having Severin's soul etc but instead Lilith simply said I was someone she had had her eye on for some time.

'Ah, just like with me and Jodie.' William smiled.

'Yes. Exactly.'

They both looked at me and William nodded.

'You chose well,' he said. 'He's a handsome devil and no mistake. Strong too. Could probably take me if he wanted to.'

I didn't understand what he meant but Lilith spoke before I could.

'I gave him almost everything I had.'

William slowly nodded and then walked around me in a circle.

'I can sense his power Lilith. It flows off of him like a raging but beautiful waterfall.'

'Indeed.'

William glanced at the two of us before giving me another apology.

'I will leave you two lovebirds to it. See you around Lilith. Alex.'

And with that he walked away.

After he had vanished from sight Lilith looked at me and smiled.

'He was impressed with you Alex.'

'I agree,' I said. 'But what was that about me taking him? I don't understand.'

'William was sired by a vampire less than a hundred years old. He is weak compared to almost every other vampire I know.'

'Including me?'

She nodded.

'I gave you the blood of a 450 year old. That gives you far greater power and strength than he has. Why do you think he was so apologetic?'

I realised what she was saying and laughed.

'He's been a vampire for 77 years, and yet he's afraid of me?'

Lilith nodded again and smiled.

'He won't come near you again Alex. Only as a friend now.'

We began to walk on. The street was beginning to fill with people going home, finished with eating and drinking for the night.

'Who is Jodie?' I asked as we continued to walk, passing another couple heading the other way.

'She's William's love and first sire. Very weak. He made her when he was a mere 25.'

'You've met her?'

'Yes. Jodie is very wary of me but nice enough.'

'But you wouldn't harm her would you?'

'No but she thinks I will steal William away from her.'

'Oh so you and William are …'

'No Alex,' she said. 'William has always had a lust for me but I have never been interested in him. That's why I keep my distance from them both.'

I nodded and laughed.

'What's so funny?'

'I'm not surprised he lusts after you Lilith.'

Lilith laughed and playfully hit me on the arm.

Then she took my hand in hers again and we started to walk, just as the rain began to fall lightly upon us.

Chapter 13

I looked out at the night from Lilith's bedroom window. The rain that had started earlier was continuing to spatter against the window. It was late. I glanced at the clock and it read 2.45

Yet strangely, I didn't feel at all tired. I felt alive.

Lilith had gone out again. She had told me to wait there for her and that she wouldn't be gone long. I didn't know exactly where she was going but I knew she was going to bring back food for us.

I took the opportunity to have a closer look at the house. In an unlocked drawer of her study desk I found a very old photo album.

I carefully flipped open the pages and saw Lilith in some photographs. In others was a man I didn't know. And in yet more I found myself staring at pictures of Severin.

I removed the first picture of Lilith I found and turned it over, but there was nothing written on the back of it. All I could tell was that the photo was very old. Maybe even one of the first photographs ever taken. I also knew that looking at Lilith's smiling face, she had not altered one bit, at least, not in outward appearance. As a person I knew without doubt she had changed.

The man I didn't know looked big by anyone's standards. Tall and bald, he wasn't smiling in the picture, and there was an air of authority about the way he looked. I took what I assumed was the most recent one of him and again turned it over. This time there was a name and a date.

'Christiano' 17th November 1896.

Carefully putting the photo back into its sleeve, I looked at some more of Severin. We weren't completely different. I was just over 6 feet tall and Severin was a couple of inches taller, with fair hair rather than my black.

'Do I really have your soul?' I asked aloud.

Not getting an answer I put the photographs away and shut the drawer.

I made myself a whisky and even as a vampire I grimaced at the burn in my throat as I swallowed the liquid down.

Then I stood still in the lounge area and concentrated my thoughts. I only thought of vampires but I could not detect any nearby.

I was just about to return to the study to get a book when the front door opened and Lilith came in. She was laughing and joking with two other women, despite looking almost bedraggled, as it was still raining.

'Ah there you are,' she said pointing at me. 'Come here and meet my two new friends, Chloe and Emma.'

The girls were both in their early twenties and had obviously been out drinking at a club.

'Hi Alex. Lilith has told us all about you.'

I smiled and gave a little bow.

'All good I hope.' I said.

'Of course, my darling.' Lilith came up to me and kissed me. 'I've been bragging to these two what a great kisser you are. Why don't you show them?'

I hesitated, not sure what she meant, but both the women came over and started to stroke my hair and face.

'Yes, come on Alex. Show us.'

I looked at Lilith who stood to one side and she gave a small nod.

'Okay,' I said. 'Who's first?'

I chose the one I thought was the better looking of the two. She had short red hair and a short black dress on.

I began to kiss her. Slowly and softly at first, placing my mouth on hers and her cheek and neck. When I returned to her mouth I opened mine and she did the same. I felt her tongue collide with mine before she gave a little gasp when she caught one of my fangs with it.

'Hey, what's with the teeth?' she said, taking a step back.

'He's a vampire, stupid,' Lilith gave a little laugh and had moved closer to the other girl.

'Yeah, right!' Both girls started laughing while Lilith and I just stared at them.

I don't know if the staring un-nerved them but they exchanged looks.

'I think we'd better go,' the red haired one said.

But Lilith blocked their path.

'You will go when I'm finished with you.' She roared and was suddenly upon the one I had kissed.

'Chloe!' Emma screamed and tried to pull Lilith off her friend.

I grabbed her arm and swung her towards me. Without hesitating I sank my teeth into her neck and began to suck out the glorious red liquid of life. As I took her blood I glanced over at my beloved and saw her doing the same. All you could hear was the sound of slurping and the sucking of lips, until finally Lilith let Chloe fall to the floor of the hall. As soon as she stopped I reluctantly pulled my mouth away from Emma's neck and let her fall beside her friend.

'You know what to do next.' Lilith said, watching me.

I nodded and bit my thumb. With my blood seeping out, I ran it gently across the two puncture wounds in her neck, sealing Emma's wound and any trace that I had bitten her.

Lilith inspected my handiwork and nodded her approval before going over to do the same to Chloe.

'Grab her and follow me,' she said.

Soon we were running along by the canal, faster than human eyes could follow. I caught up with Lilith as she carried the woman's body through a gap in a hedge and out into a deserted street.

'They both live over there.' Lilith pointed and I followed her to a small house with a garden in need of some work.

Lilith placed Chloe on the step before fumbling through the girl's bag.

Next she withdrew a key and tried it in the lock. It turned first time and we then entered the house. Lilith dropped the unconscious Chloe onto a couch in a small living room. I did the same to Emma, placing her still form into an arm-chair.

'Let's go.'

And so Lilith and I shut the house's door behind us and made our way back home.

Once inside, we stripped out of our wet clothes and I actually threw Lilith onto the bed. I was on top of her before she could do or say anything and began kissing her breasts.

'Alex.' Lilith giggled but I continued kissing her and slowly made my way down to between her legs.

Lilith moaned and sighed beneath me and held my head to her.

Sometime after six a.m. we both fell asleep, having made love like it was our first time. I had never known passion like it. I had never known such feelings of utter love and attraction existed until I met Lilith. I now knew that I would do absolutely everything in my power to keep this extraordinary creature safe. And I knew she would do the same for me.

I awoke and a glance at the clock told me it was almost midday.

I slowly moved Lilith's arm to one side and got out of bed. She didn't stir and for a moment I was content to just stand and watch her sleep.

But then I remembered I had a phone call to make, and, not wanting to disturb my lover's rest, slipped into a tired looking shirt and jeans and made my way down-stairs to get my mobile phone. I quickly called up and rang the familiar number.

'I.T. department, how may I help?'

'Hi Karen. It's me, Alex.'

'Shit! Alex. Where are you?'

'I'm in London.'

'What? What the hell are you doing there?'

'I just moved here. I'm sorry but I won't be coming back to work for you guys.'

There was silence on the other end.

'You still there?' I asked.

'Yes. This isn't like you Alex. What's happened?'

'Nothing,' I lied, 'I've just had enough that's all and I got a better offer. Listen I have to go but take care, okay?'

I shut off my phone before she said anything else and I took a breath.

'It's over now honey.'

I looked up and saw my beloved coming down the stairs wearing just an oversized t-shirt. I took my eyes away from her lovely slender legs and nodded at her.

Lilith came to me and took me in her arms.

'It's not over,' I said, 'it's just beginning.'

Lilith hugged me just a bit harder before breaking away. She took a peek out of one of the windows and let the curtain fall back again.

'The sky is cloudy and it's a slight drizzle. We can go out and buy you some clothes,' she said.

'Good. I think I need some.'

'Yes.' Lilith laughed.

'What do I do with my old stuff?'

'We can arrange a removal firm if you wish. Easily done.'

'Won't they be suspicious?'

'Of what? A guy moving into his girlfriend's house. What's suspicious about that?'

'No, I mean the whole vampire thing.'

Lilith shook her head and led me over to a mirror.

'Look at yourself Alex.' She said.

I did so and realised I looked the same as always. I still had colour in my cheeks and my eyes were their usual colour too.

'See? You pass for human easily. Just don't flash your teeth, okay?'

I smiled at her and nodded.

Lilith went off to the study and made the arrangements for my clothes to be delivered in a couple of days time. That gave me plenty of time to get back and pack them up.

'We'll go back tonight.' Lilith said.

After we had properly dressed we were once again on the streets of London. I bought bags and bags of clothes. I had never bought so much in one day, but I had to admit I was finding it fun. And best of all none of the money I spent was mine. But Lilith kept reassuring me that it was fine, she was only too glad to pay.

We took a trip on the Tube, which was a bit disconcerting at first. Being crammed up together with so many living people, I felt all of their individual pulses calling out to me, tantalising me. Sure enough, I did feel my blood lust begin to rise at one point, but I think Lilith sensed this and her simple touch on my hand told me it would be all right.

We emerged from the Tube station without incident and made our way to Regents Park.

I kept glancing at the sky, almost as if I expected the sun to come blazing out at us any minute. But the cloud cover was thick and covered the entire sky as far as the eye could see. But the drizzle had stopped so we made our way to a park bench and sat down. The tree overhead had kept the bench dry.

'This is the life,' I sighed, looking at the swans and ducks drifting along across the pond.

'Yes it is,' Lilith agreed.

We sat there hand in hand and just let the minutes slip away. From time to time people would walk past but no-one took any notice of us sitting there.

'I was very impressed and pleased with you last night.'

I looked at Lilith, not knowing what she was referring to.

'You showed great control with Emma. For only your second victim you did excellently.'

'Thank you,' I said and grinned at her.

'Not at all. Give credit where it's due. It took Severin 3 victims before he got it right and didn't kill them.'

That surprised me.

'Why do you think that was?' I asked.

Lilith gazed at me and held my hand even tighter.

"I know why. It's because I didn't make him good enough. I didn't give him enough of my blood. That's why I gave you so much. Almost too much,' she sighed.

'Can vampire's die that way? By giving too much of their blood?'

'Yes. Even our bodies can't survive with not enough blood within.'

'Our blood flows the same?' I asked.

'Not the same, no. Much slower. Listen to my heartbeat, Alex.'

I didn't need to move my head nearer to her chest, and instead just concentrated upon that one, single sound. My eyes widened in astonishment.

'Your heart is barely beating at all,' I said.

'Only once in a while, that's why it's impossible for a vampire to have a coronary thrombosis.'

I nodded and saw an old man start to throw bread to the various birds that were slowly surrounding him.

'I love this park,' Lilith muttered and closed her eyes, leaning her head against my arm. 'I've always loved coming here.'

'I came here once. Many years ago.'

'We shall come here often my dear Alex,' she said.

I looked at her and felt yet another rush of love for this woman.

I turned my gaze back to the old man who had finished feeding the birds and was now walking towards us.

I smiled at him, remembering to keep my mouth closed.

The old man stopped and looked at us.

'Hello.' I said.

But the man didn't reply, instead he just continued to stare at us.

Lilith stirred beside me and opened her eyes. She had just sat up when the old man was suddenly standing right in front of me and glaring into my face.

'I know what you are!' he hissed, and with amazing speed left the park as if he'd never been standing there.

Lilith grabbed my hand again and pulled me to my feet.

'What is it? Who was that?' I asked.

'That was John Sebastian. A member of the Morisakis.'

Lilith was leading me out of the park towards the Tube station.

'Why didn't you sense him?'

'How could I? He's over 700 years old.'

'So what now?'

'What now? We go home, that's what.'

Chapter 14

We were back at Lilith's house within half an hour. Lilith was agitated and I was a little un-nerved to say the least. It wasn't the fact that I had met the Morisakis but more the fact that such a powerful enemy came in the shape of such a seemingly weak old man. I had seen Lilith move but not at the speed this vampire had.

'How many are there in this Morisakis?' I asked, watching her pace up and down in front of the fire.

The first thing she had done was to light the fire, as if the burning flames could offer her comfort in some way.

'I don't know. Not for sure. But there are at least 25 members in London alone.'

'They have members the world over?'

'Yes. The main house of operations is in Paris. It's where the high council are."

That surprised me. Being named after this legendary vampire, I assumed their main headquarters would be in Greece.

'If they knew what I was why didn't this John Sebastian do something other than get in my face?'

'Don't you see Alex?' Lilith stopped pacing and stood in front of me. I looked up at her from my chair by the fire.

'What?' I asked.

'This was a warning. They know that I created you and so they have another target.'

'I haven't broken any laws.'

'It doesn't matter. I should already be dead which means you wouldn't be here.'

I conceded the point and turned my gaze towards the fire.

Lilith finally sat down in the other chair and looked at me.

'Perhaps I'm wrong,' she said, 'perhaps we should leave and go somewhere else.'

'Perhaps, but this is your home Lily.'

She shrugged.

'It means nothing if I lose you. I lost Severin and my world was torn wide open. If I lost you too then my world would be torn completely apart, never to recover. Do you understand?'

I nodded and got up from my chair and sat on the arm of hers, stroking her hair.

'Let's stick to our original plan,' I said. 'Let's fly back to mine and spend the night there.'
Lilith gave me a small smile and hugged me for a moment.
'You are fast becoming my calming influence Alex.'
'As you are mine.'

We had dinner which was a delicious steak each and then we took to the air from her garden.
The evening traffic of London disappeared below us as we drifted on the wind. Again we held hands as we soared through one cloud and into another. It was cold but I guess vampires don't feel the cold quite as much as a human does. At least the rain held off until we began to descend back into my hometown.
I was about to unlock my front door when my neighbour came out of hers.
'Oh hello Alex. Not seen you for a while.'
'Hi. I've not been here much.' I admitted.
Old Mrs Greenacre had lived next door to me for the past 5 years. She was retired and lived on her own after the unexpected death of her husband George.
'And who is this lovely young lady?' Mrs Greenacre looked at Lilith standing there.
'Oh sorry. Mrs Greenacre, please meet my girlfriend, Lilith.'
'Nice to meet you ma'am.' Lilith gave a little curtsey which made my neighbour laugh.
'Oh no need for such formalities young lady. Lilith? We don't seem to hear of that name much these days.'
'No," she agreed. 'It's not very popular.'
'Pity. I've always loved the name myself. So is he taking care of you young Lilith?'
'Yes ma'am. He certainly is.'
'Good. Good. Well, I must get to bingo. Be seeing you Alex. Bye Lilith.'
'Goodbye.'
After I had shut the door Lilith burst out laughing.
'What a charming woman,' she said.
'Yes she is.'
'And she called me young.' Lilith laughed again and went into the lounge.
I followed her and put on some coffee.
'So what are we going to do?' I asked from the kitchen. 'About the damn Morisakis, I mean.'

Lilith came and stood in the doorway, her arms crossed.
'I don't know.'
I placed two cups on the counter top and faced her.
'Have you thought any more about the True Species?'
'I have but I'm not convinced they are our best option.'
I nodded and the kettle finished boiling. I poured out the two cups and handed one to Lilith.
Then we stood looking out of my lounge window. The town's lights spread out before us.
'Lily, may I ask you something?'
'Of course.'
I took a sip of my coffee and glanced at her.
'We've made love a few times now and never used precautions. Can you get pregnant?'
Lilith looked at me and shook her head.
'No. Vampire's can't reproduce Alex. They can only change humans that have already been born.'
I nodded and turned my gaze back to the window.
'Why do you ask?'
'Just curious,' I answered.
But Lilith saw through the lie.
'No, it's more than that. Tell me Alex.'
I looked at her again and gave a small sigh.
'I always wanted to be a father Lily. Guess that's not going to happen now though is it?'
Lilith looked at me sadly and touched my arm gently.
'You would have made a great father Alex. That's easy to see.'
'We could adopt,' I blurted out but Lilith shook her head.
'And how would we explain to our child why we didn't change and get older?'
I saw the sense of her words and didn't say anything more. I drank some more coffee and went and sat down. Lilith remained at the window.
'I had a daughter once.'
I almost dropped my coffee.
'What? When?'
Lilith looked at her finger-nails and then at me.
'Four years before I became a vampire. I called her Sofia.'
I got up again and walked over to her.
'What happened to her?' I asked softly.

'She died aged 3. A fever took her.'
I could see that even after 400 years + the subject still upset her. Tears had come to her green eyes. It was my turn to offer her comfort and yet struggled to find the words. All I could do was copy her touch of the arm.
'It's okay Alex. You'd have thought I'd have got over it by now.'
I nodded but said what came to mind.
'The death of a child is something we should never get over.'
Lilith gave me a small smile and I knew we could offer each other comfort just by simply being next to one another. Words weren't all that important. Not really. Not to Lilith and me.
'Were you married then Lily?'
'I was. To a very cruel man who beat me more than once. He was Sofia's father.'
'So what happened to him?'
Lilith actually gave me one of her full and genuine smiles.
'Christiano made me a vampire and he became my first victim.'
'Really?'
'Oh yes. I bled him well. I didn't waste a single drop and I enjoyed every fucking minute of it.'
I knew Lilith was passionate but up until that moment I hadn't really seen the passion for being what she truly was come through. And yet, her slaying her violent husband was something she was clearly proud of.
We finished our coffees and then embraced properly.
'Have you boxes for your clothes? Might as well get to it.'
'Yes. Follow me.'
I found some suitable boxes in my spare room and began to pack away my best and favourite clothes.
'What else do you wish to take?'
'Not sure. Some books. My computer would be nice.'
'Of course.'
When everything that I was taking was packed away I took another look around the place. How many more times would I step into the apartment I had called home all these years? Obviously I didn't have an answer to that question but I knew I would be very happy with Lilith in her Camden home. Yes, the threat of the Morisakis couldn't be ignored but what were we going to do? Or perhaps more importantly what could we do?
As we lay in each others arms in my old bed I realised we needed more information. Information not only on the Morisakis and the True Species but also what our options were.

Lilith moved her head onto my chest and I adjusted my arm around her.
'Darling.' I called
'M'mm,' she mumbled, half asleep.
'Where did you go to see these ancient scriptures?'
'China; why my love?'
'I think the answer might be in them. Would it be possible for us to see them?'
Lilith moved her head back onto the pillow and I could see her looking at me.
'Possibly,' she said. 'The guardians of the scriptures aren't anything to do with the Morisakis. They might let us see them.'
'Can we arrange it? The trip to China I mean?'
'Yes. I will make the right calls tomorrow. The numbers I shall need are back at home.'
'It can wait until we return there with my things.'
But Lilith shook her head.
'No, I think we should at least try this idea of yours and the sooner the better.'
'Okay. So what will you do?'
'I'll return home by myself tomorrow. I'm sure you'll be safe on your own here while I'm gone. Then you can travel with the removal company to Camden.'
'As long as you're sure?' I asked.
'I'm sure. Now is it my imagination or is your cock hard?'
I gave her a sly grin and suddenly she had rolled me onto my back and was on top of me.
Slowly she mounted me and began to slide up and down my shaft.
I gazed up at her in the darkness but of course with our enhanced vision, it didn't seem dark at all. Her body was still a perfect silhouette against the window and I reached up and cupped her wonderful breasts as Lilith began to quicken her rhythm.
I was still inside her when Lilith stopped momentarily and lowered her mouth to my shoulder. She kissed me at first and then I felt a sharp pain as she bit me hard. I grimaced at first but then the flow of my blood going onto her waiting tongue seemed to take the pain away.
'Your turn,' she said in an almost breathless voice. And as she began to move her hips again Lilith offered me her wrist which I kissed and then bit into. Her blood mixed with the sensations of the orgasm exploding within her was incredible. I felt Lilith's body shudder above me and I knew she had climaxed too.

She slowly withdrew her body off of mine and then lay beside me, stroking my face.

My shoulder was already healed and I saw that her wrist was almost complete too.

'Thank you Alex.' She whispered and kissed me on the mouth.

'For what?'

'For just being you.'

I smiled at her and we kissed again, deliberately slicing into each other's tongues with our fangs so we could share more of our blood.

Even though I had tasted Lilith's blood several times now, I found the sweet nectar just as intoxicating and extremely addictive.

I licked and sucked at her wrist, and while I did so, I fixed my eyes upon hers. Not only did I see her love for me there, I also saw trust. Trust that I wouldn't go too far and take too much of her precious life-force.

After a few more minutes, we finished exchanging blood and slowly fell to sleep, Lilith's head once more resting on my chest.

Chapter 15

We woke the next day to find it raining and windy. There was no chance that the sun would come out so Lilith would be safe to make her way back to London. I made us a coffee and with it we ate a couple of slices of toast.

'I've been thinking.' Lilith said, in between mouthfuls.
'What about?'
'How best for us to travel to China.'
This surprised me.
'Surely by plane.' I said.
But Lilith shook her head.
'Too risky, Alex. Even if we booked a night flight, there's every chance we'd arrive in sunlight.'
I hadn't thought of that. This rule about no direct sunlight was taking some getting used to.
'Okay, so what do we do?'
Lilith thought as she finished her toast.
'It's too far to fly by ourselves. Our only option is by boat.'
'China's a long way Lily. That will take ages.'
'Have you a better idea?' she asked
'Actually, I think I do. We don't need air to survive, correct?'
'No. Our supernatural powers prevent us from ever dying of oxygen starvation.'
'Good. Okay. Do you know someone in China? Any old friends?'
'Yes. I was going to call to ask if we could stay with them. Tai Ling and Sun Wong.'
'Do you trust them?'
'I do. I have known them over a hundred years.'
I smiled as the pieces to my plan were beginning to fall into place.
'Excellent,' I said. 'How about we get ourselves shipped over by a cargo plane? We could be put into a large enough crate and sent to your friends' address.'
But Lilith smiled and shook her head.
'I've got an even better idea my love.'
'What?'
'It means us going separately.'
'If that's what it takes.'
'We could be shipped in coffins,' she grinned.

'What?' I was startled by this idea.

'It's perfect. We get the right paper work drawn up to say two relatives of Tai Ling had died while over here and their bodies are being flown back to China.'

I frowned, not convinced.

'What if they open the coffins? They'll see we're not Chinese.'

'My dear Alex, if the paper-work is drawn up correctly and the fees are all paid, they would have no reason to open the coffins. Plus an x-ray at the airport would reveal exactly what they'd expect to see, a body.'

I nodded and finished my coffee.

'You really think it will work?'

'Yes. And the best thing about a coffin is it's completely safe from the sunlight.'

I had to take her word for that.

'But how will we travel back?'

'Probably the same way but we'll see. And anyway, once we are over there there's nothing to stop us from staying or travelling to other places.'

I had always wanted to travel and see the world but never thought I would get the chance. Evidently; that was no longer the case.

'Okay. You set things in motion. And you're sure these friends of yours will help?'

Lilith smiled again and nodded.

'They owe me, so yes, they will help.'

It was settled then. This was the way we would get to China. Not my chosen method but if the needs must and all that.

'I need to teach you another vampire trick.'

I washed the cups and plates up and felt Lilith's arms around me.

'What trick?' I asked.

'Finish that and come into the lounge with me.'

A few seconds later I joined her in the middle of the room.

'I'm going to show you how to truly fake being dead.'

'How do you mean?'

'It's a useful ability that only vampires can achieve, without the aid of a drug. Listen carefully: I want you to clear your mind. Think about darkness, complete and total darkness.'

I did as she told me and closed my eyes. I imagined myself deep under ground in a cave, with no light source of any kind. I pictured myself trying to see the hand in front of my face but not seeing anything, not even a vague outline.

'All is completely dark,' Lilith whispered beside me. 'You cannot see a single thing. Now slow your breathing right down. Go on.'

I slowed my breathing, all the while still imagining the dark all around me.

'Good. Now as your breathing slows, take control of your heartbeat and slow it down too. Humans cannot do this, only we can. It's a natural impulse to fight it but in fact, you can stop your heart completely. So stop your heart beating Alex. Go on.'

But I panicked at what she was asking me to do and broke the concentration. I opened my eyes and my breath came rapidly.

Lilith looked at me disappointedly.

'I can't do it Lilith,' I said. 'How can you ask me to stop my own heart?'

But my lover hushed me by placing a finger on my lips and told me to look into her eyes.

'Okay, I'm looking.'

But she shook her head.

'No Alex. Really look. Look me in the eyes like you've never looked before.'

I did so and I gradually felt a wave of dizziness and then drowsiness come over me.

'I now have complete control over you my love. The vampire's stare is all powerful and none can resist. Go back to that dark place you were at before Alex.'

Without any hesitation I found myself back in the cave, back in complete darkness.

'Now in your dark place slow your breathing.'

Again I did as she asked.

'Now once your breathing has slowed, you can slow the beat of your heart. You can and you will slow the beat of your heart.'

No part of me resisted the command. All I heard or even felt at that moment was Lilith's voice. It was everywhere, in my mind, in my ears, in my very blood.

'Your heart is slowing to a complete stop Alex.'

It was the weirdest sensation of my life. Basically my heart stopped at her instruction, although I didn't know anything about it. Such was her power and control over me.

'You have stopped your heart Alex.'

I was vaguely aware of her hand slipping through my now open shirt and caressing my bare chest.

'You have no pulse. No heartbeat. There is not a single sign of life within your body.'

Still, all I could focus on was Lilith's voice.

'You are dead Alex.'

Lilith told me later that at this point I was just standing stock still in the centre of my lounge while she went to the window. I wasn't breathing or moving. In fact in Lilith's words anyone could have given me the smallest of pushes and I would have fallen over.

'Your heart will not start beating again until twenty minutes has passed.'

In that twenty minute period I did nothing but stand there, staring blankly into space. And yet I wasn't aware of anything going on around me. As long as Lilith remained quiet I would have remained like that for.... Well, who knows how long? But finally the command came:

'Start your heart and breathe again Alex.'

I did as was told and slowly withdrew from the darkened cave.

'My hold on you is terminated.' Lilith said and suddenly I saw and could think again. She had her back to the window, gazing at me.

'What happened?' I asked dumbly.

'I caught you with my stare Alex.'

'I thought that was a myth.'

Lilith smiled and shook her head.

'It's one of our most powerful weapons,' she said.

'Like mind control.'

'Exactly, but complete mind control. Impossible to resist once you've caught a victim with your gaze.'

'I know my heart stopped,' I said, 'and I know it stopped for twenty minutes. Why?'

'It's a useful ploy sometimes. To be able to fake death is one of the talents we have at our disposal. I know it has successfully fooled doctors with the highest of qualifications.'

'Okay. I can see how it could come in useful but why stop it for twenty minutes?'

'Because any longer than twenty and the blood hunger automatically kicks in. Don't ask me how, it's just the way it is.'

'And you wouldn't be able to control the thirst?'

'No. It's almost as if the magic blood rebels against being used in that way. It's something else that Christiano taught me.'

'I see and while I was held in your gaze you could have done anything to me? Had me do anything?'

Lilith nodded and walked towards me.

'Try it for yourself.'

'I don't know if I can.'

'Yes you can. You have all the same powers I do. I gave them to you, remember?' she smiled.

'Okay.'

'So go on then Alex. Capture my gaze.'

I looked into those beautiful green eyes of hers and thought of....Her. Nothing happened.

'I don't know how.' I shrugged.

Lilith took my hand in hers, gave it a gentle squeeze and then released it again.

'It's really easy. To capture someone's gaze all you have to do is look into their eyes and think of a prison. Or chains.'

'I'll have a go.' I muttered and took a step back from her.

'Lilith,' I said quietly, but with authority. 'Look into my eyes.'

As soon as her eyes were on mine I thought of Lilith bound tightly in thick, unbreakable chains.

And suddenly I knew I had done it. I don't know how exactly, but I knew she was under my power.

'Lilith, walk to your right two steps,' I told her.

She did as I said without comment.

'Lilith, tell me you love me,' I commanded.

'I love you Alex.'

That response was interesting. It told me she was not only under my control but also she knew who was controlling her.

'Lilith, I want you to fight my control over you.'

'I cannot,' she replied simply.

'Try Lilith,' I ordered, 'try to break the control I have over you.'

'I cannot,' she said again.

This was weird stuff, but all the same, yet another plus side of being a vampire. The plus points were far outweighing the minus points now.

'Lilith, undo your shirt,' I said, with a grin.

Without hesitation Lilith unbuttoned the shirt she was wearing.

I knew we had things to do, so I didn't take that particular fantasy any further. And besides I was feeling the blood lust nagging at me for attention.

I remembered how Lilith had ended her control.

'Lilith, my control over you is terminated.'

My beloved blinked a couple of times before her focus was on me.

'You did it Alex. Well done.'

I nodded and smiled at the view her newly opened shirt was revealing.

She looked down at herself and let out a little high-pitched shriek.
'I can't believe you got me to do that!' she laughed.
'Hey, it's every guys fantasy,' I protested.
'Fair enough.' She quickly buttoned up the shirt again and glanced at the clock.
'I really should get back to London.'
'Okay.'
'You'll be alright here?' she asked.
'I'm sure I'll be fine.'
'This will be a big test for you Alex. I can feel your thirst. See if you can feed with control without me around. If you can, then you've come along way in a very short space of time.'
I nodded and kissed her.
'Stay safe Lily,' I said.
'And you.'
I went down with her to the ground floor and as soon as the coast was clear, Lilith took to the air and was quickly out of sight.
I knew it was time for me to feed so I went off into town, realising that this was the first time as a vampire I was on my own. My Lilith wasn't there to help me or offer me guidance.
It was an afternoon I shall never forget.

Chapter 16

So for the first time in a few days I was on my own. My beloved had gone back to London to make arrangements for our trip to China and I was left to while away the time. I wasn't entirely sure what I would do but I did know one thing, I had to feed and pretty soon.

With the poor weather it was safe for me to go out and soon I found myself back in familiar surroundings. I was once again walking in the local park, where Lilith had made me a vampire.

I was marvelling again at my heightened senses. I could smell and hear things I had never known were there before. As I walked past a flower bed, with no other noise around I clearly heard a butterfly's wings beating as it circled the flowers.

With my superior speed and reflexes I easily placed my hand over the butterfly and, cupping it gently, I brought it up to my face.

It didn't even try to fly away but instead seemed happy enough to stay in my palm as I looked at it. I didn't know its name but the butterfly was a nice mix of purple and brown in colour. I loved the way the pretty colours sparkled in the rain, and I then realised I was holding one of the most exquisite creatures I had ever seen.

I opened my hand and let it fly away, watching it as it fluttered back to the same place to suck at the flower's sweet nectar.

I walked on, my thirst growing.

I didn't stop at the children's playground. Usually I liked to watch the children playing and laughing, having a great time with no cares in the world. But not today. Not with my thirst building within me. The demon wanted to be fed and I feared what might happen if I hung around the play area too long.

I made my way through the park and was about to cross the road when I spotted the youth who had stabbed me. He was standing in a group of troublemakers outside a bike shop. They were taunting an old man who had dropped his bag and was trying to bend down to retrieve it.

I crossed the road and went up to the man.

'Let me get that for you,' I said and plucked the bag off the ground for him.

'Thank you,' he smiled, and with a shaking hand took the bag from me.

The youths all jeered and shouted names at me until I turned round and faced them.

The one who had stabbed me was ashen faced, clearly recognising me.

'You!' he stammered, 'I did you! I did you in the side. No way should you be walking around.'

His friends all looked at him and laughed. One of them gave him a shove.

'This the guy you said you'd done in? Looks like it!' he roared with laughter and the others joined in.

The youngster who had stabbed me pushed him out of the way and took a step towards me.

'I'll do you again,' he growled, sliding a knife out of his jacket pocket.

It was my turn to laugh, which un-nerved him even more.

'Do you really think you can possibly harm me with that?' I taunted him.

He took another step forward, but he seemed uncertain now.

I began to walk away from the front of the shop at a brisk pace, and went down a quiet alley. I knew a confrontation was about to happen and didn't want an audience, but I was confident in my vampire abilities. Just as well as I had never been one for fighting when I was growing up.

Of course I could have easily taken flight and left them far behind but I wanted them to catch up. I wanted the confrontation. I wanted to teach them a lesson they would never forget.

I heard them running after me as I reached the end of the alley and turned into a dead end. Other than the alley entrance, high building walls surrounded me. I leapt onto the highest one without effort and hid myself from view.

I listened to the gang arrive from my squatting position.

'Where the fuck is he?' I heard one ask.

'He came down here. I know he did.' I recognised the voice of the boy who had stabbed me.

'So where did he go?' another voice asked.

'Up here boys,' I said, standing up.

They all looked up at me with startled expressions on their faces.

'How the fuck?..' exclaimed one lad.

But I didn't let him finish. I jumped off the roof and landed the twenty feet below right amongst them. I grabbed my attacker and with a firm grip on his jacket I leaped back onto the roof where I'd just been.

I gave him a light shove and watched as he fell to the roof's surface.

Glancing over the edge, I saw the others running off. Either in fear or to get help, I didn't know, and I didn't care because I knew I had my blood source in front of me.

'What are you?' the youth slowly got to his feet, the knife still in his hand.

'What do you think I am?' I asked. I gave him a smile and showed him my fangs.

'No way, no fucking way!' he shouted as he lunged at me and I easily sidestepped him.

'Believe it fucker.' I snarled, batting the knife away as he came at me again. It went sailing over the edge of the roof and I heard it hit the ground below.

The youth threw a punch at me, which I easily caught in my hand and twisted, satisfied to hear the bones in his wrist snap like dried twigs.

He cried out in pain and I let go of his hand. He immediately began to cry as he cradled his wrist with his other hand.

But I had no sympathy for him. No pity. He had shown no regard to me or Lilith in our first meeting. He had deliberately stabbed me on our second encounter and had even bragged about it to his mates.

I could see he was looking at me through his tears. Now there was nothing but fear and pain on his face. It was pathetic to see.

'Stand up and I'll let you go,' I hissed, 'lie there and I'll rip your lungs out.'

Slowly he got to his feet, still crying and holding his shattered wrist.

'You know what I am and you know what I want,' I said, 'give me your blood willingly or I shall take it by force. And believe me, you wouldn't want that.'

'Please mister. Please don't kill me.'

I beckoned him to me, and slowly the adolescent moved forwards.

'Tilt your head to the side,' I commanded him.

The boy did as he was told and I realised I had captured his gaze without even trying. This was going to be too easy. I actually hesitated.

Question was, because it was so easy could I go through with it? Did a sadistic part of me want the fight? Want him to struggle? I smiled and bit deep into his neck anyway. Was it my imagination or did I literally taste his fear as I drank my fill from him? I'm not sure to this day but I remember quenching my blood thirst and afterwards not only sealing the wound but also placing him back on the ground, instead of leaving him on the roof.

I had just stood up from him and was about to walk out of the alley when I heard the approach of running feet.

I saw the troublemakers coming back. Only this time, there were more of them.

'What have you done to him?' The biggest one slowed to a stop a few yards away from me.

'He'll live,' I said with a great deal of pride. I had taken his blood without my Lilith's guidance and yet I knew the youth would survive.

'Surround him,' the leader ordered and I watched as the gang began to fan out around me.

'You should have walked away,' the leader said and from his jacket he withdrew a monkey wrench.

'Walk away or fly?' I asked innocently, gently floating off the ground.

'Jesus!' The leader swung the wrench, but I was already out of his reach.

But another of the youths behind me threw a knife, which hit me between my shoulder blades. And, vampire or no, it hurt like hell.

I hissed in pain and landed again a few yards away, my back to a wall. I reached around and yanked out the blade.

'Get him!' The ringleader yelled and suddenly Lilith's warning about strength in numbers came into my mind. I shrugged off the pain, for I could feel the wound already closing and launched myself at two of the youths. I didn't know any fighting techniques but instead just used raw power and speed to get in my blows.

I sent one youth flying backwards into another wall where he lay still. Another of the gang, quite a pretty girl, I grabbed and held from behind, putting her between me and the rest of my attackers.

'Back off or I swear I'll break her neck,' I snarled, gripping her jaw to show I meant my threat.

The rest of the gang hesitated but stopped their movements.

The leader looked at me and then over at the one I had thrown ten feet into the wall.

'Your move, superman.' he stood there, wrench still in his grasp and itching to be used.

'I'm unarmed,' I said, 'why don't me and you fight this out? Just the two of us.'

The leader mulled this over, while I kept my hand on the whimpering girl's neck.

'Deal,' he finally said, 'fuck off you lot, it's me and 'im.'

The gang didn't retreat far I noticed, just down to the entrance of the alley. I slowly released the frightened girl and told her I meant her no harm.

She ran off and joined the others, leaving their leader face to face with me.

'Let's get this over with,' I said. 'Take a shot.'

The youth smiled and swung with all his might. With my enhanced reactions the swinging wrench looked like it was coming at me in slow motion. I flicked out my right arm just before it would have hit me in the chest. Instead, I caught the wrench and with a quick twist of my wrist, bent it in half. Smiling, I dropped the now useless tool to the ground and looked at my assailant.

'No way!' the leader backed away. 'That's impossible!'

'Like me flying is impossible?' I taunted him and then laughed as he ran off to join his mates.

I turned at the sound of a groan and realised the one I had thrown into the wall was coming around. I quickly checked the pulse of the youth I had drank from and satisfied he would live, floated out of the alley and across the roof tops.

Looking back I know I could have killed him. Could have slain them all, especially the girl, whose slender neck had been in my powerful grasp. And yet I let each and everyone of them live to tell tales of a strange super-man to anyone who cared to listen. Lilith was teaching this monster very well.

I hadn't been in long when my doorbell rang. I wasn't expecting anyone so when I opened the door I was surprised to see Karen standing on the mat.

My former work colleague looked at me and smiled.

'Hi Alex. Can I come in?'

'Er hi,' I said and allowed her to walk past me and on towards the living room.

She had only been to my flat once before and that was with a couple of the others.

'I've been worried about you,' she said, as she took off her coat, and laid it over the back of a chair.

Beneath she was wearing a well cut blue blouse and a slim fitting skirt and, unusually for her, high heeled shoes.

'I'm fine, really,' I said and stood there looking at her. I had to admit, she looked great, especially with her hair tied up.

'Aren't you going to offer me a drink?' she asked.

I nodded and apologised, going into the kitchen to put the kettle on.

'So tell me why you left. And without saying goodbye,' Karen said from the living room. 'I've been worried. That's why I'm here.'

'I'll be with you in a moment. I'll make us some tea and then I'll explain.'

But the truth was I didn't have a clue as to what I was going to say to her, in fact, I was racking my brain to think of a reasonable excuse.

I heard her mutter okay and then fell silent. I looked out of the kitchen and saw she had sat down.

I finished making the tea, all the while trying to decide what I was going to tell her.

I took the cups into the lounge and set one down in front of her on the coffee table.

'I'd forgotten what a nice place you have here, 'Karen said, glancing around the lounge. I noticed her crossed legs were bare and remembered all the times I had thought about stroking them at the office.

'Yes, I still like it here.'

'Then why leave? Why London?' she asked, plaintively.

I shrugged and tried to smile but found it difficult.

'To be with Lilith,' I admitted, eventually.

'Lilith. The woman you've known all of five minutes?' Karen was incredulous.

Again I shrugged and realised how pathetic it must have looked.

'It seems totally irrational to me Alex. Not like you at all.'

Of course she was right, and she should know; Karen knew me better than almost anyone.

'Please Karen,' I said, 'I have to do this. I have to leave.'

'But why? I don't understand.'

I went over to her and placed my hand on hers.

'Please don't ask me why,' I said, looking into her eyes pleadingly. 'I can't really answer that. I have my reasons and please leave it there.'

But Karen withdrew her hand from mine and glared at me.

'Why the secrets, Alex? What's going on? Has this Lilith done something to you? Got you on drugs or something?'

I shook my head and turned away, partly in shame and partly in anger.

'I can't say,' I muttered.

Karen got up and then I felt her arms around me.

'You can tell me Alex, I care about you,' she said softly. 'You know I do.'

I turned in her embrace and saw there were tears in her eyes.

'Don't cry Karen. It's okay. I'm okay.'

She shook her head and buried her face into my shoulder, holding me tighter.

This was completely unexpected and I wasn't sure what to do. I placed my hands on her back, lightly patting her shoulder in an effort to comfort her.

Suddenly I felt Karen's lips seductively kissing my neck.

'No Karen,' I said, astonished and gently but firmly pushed her away.

'Oh come on Alex,' she murmured, 'I know you want me. You've always wanted me.'

'No Karen. It isn't right,' I protested, shocked at this turn of events.

But she wasn't listening; instead she was undoing the buttons on her blouse.

'Please Karen. Don't do this. I'm your friend.'

'Yes Alex, I'm your friend too. But you know what? I've had these dirty fantasies about you for ages now, and when you told me you weren't coming back...Well, let's just say it hurt. It hurt a lot, Alex. And I'll be damned if I'll let some five minute wonder lay steal you away from me. I mean it. I want you to fuck me.'

Now she had removed the blouse completely and I was staring at her white bra-clad breasts, nipples clearly hardened beneath the lacy material.

'No Karen,' I said, putting up my hands. 'I'm with Lilith now. You should go home to your husband.'

But she fumbled with the button on her skirt and I backed away and went into the kitchen, shutting the door.

'Alex!' she wailed, banging on the door with her fists.

'Go Karen. Go now.' I called to her, still in shock at what was happening. I couldn't understand or get to grips with Karen's behaviour towards me.

I simply could not comprehend that, in all the time I had known her, Karen had not in the slightest shown any physical interest in me. I didn't know why she was acting this way but I was finding it extremely hard to resist.

'I'm going into your bedroom Alex. I'm not leaving until you've joined me,' she said firmly.

The pounding on the door stopped and I heard her walk away.

What was I going to do? I paced around my kitchen and thought of my lovely Lily. I fancied Karen, hell I'd fantasised about this scenario for years, and having sex with her would be amazing I was sure, but I wasn't about to cheat on Lilith. Then suddenly I had an idea and knew exactly what to do. A voice in my head was telling me this was wrong. That if I was meant to be with Karen, it would have happened while still human.

I opened the door and made my way to my bedroom, where I found Karen lying naked on top of the quilt looking up at me. Her tears had stopped and she was smiling.

She really was extraordinarily enticing and I had to swallow hard to control myself. Her body really was stunning; almost as beautiful and as slender as Lilith's and just for a moment the obvious question popped into my head. Was I mad to turn her down?

But I already had my answer and looking her in the eyes I smiled at her.

'Karen,' I said, 'you don't want me.'

'Yes I do,' she answered. 'I want you in this bed with me right now.' As she said this, she slowly slid her hand along the length of her right leg which I found disturbingly erotic. 'Come fuck me, Alex.'

But I continued to stare into her eyes and I saw them slowly lose their focus and knew I had her gaze.

'No Karen,' I said. 'it is time for you to go. Get dressed and never come here again. Forget that you wanted to fuck me. Do you understand?'

'Yes,' she said in a strange monotone. 'It is time for me to go. I will not come here again.'

I nodded and with some regret watched her slip her white lace underwear onto her undeniably lovely body. Then without further prompting, Karen passed me and went into the lounge where I watched her put the rest of her clothes back on.

This reverse striptease was hard for me to bear. Though I would never forsake my beloved Lilith, I found myself taking a deep breath as Karen slipped on her high heels and stood once again, all lady like and pristine. Only moments before, she had been wantonly naked on my bed, thoughts of which I quickly shook from my mind.

'Now Karen,' I said, 'I want you to remember what I'm about to tell you. I want you to remember that I left the firm to travel and that I won't be coming back.'

'I will remember,' she said in a voice that wasn't really hers any more.

'I also want you to remember that you have a loving husband at home and that you love him dearly. That you love and want only him.'

'I will remember,' she said again, standing in front of me. Her only movement was her breathing. Her eyes weren't blinking at all. This vampiric power was still new to me and was truly amazing to behold.

''Good Karen,' I breathed a sigh of relief. 'Now then; my control over you is terminated.'

As soon as I'd said that she blinked and looked at me.

'Well Alex, I really should get going.'

I nodded, rather sadly because I knew it would be the last time I would see her.

Karen looked down and saw her un-drunk tea on the table and then picked the cup up.

'I'd forgotten all about this.' She giggled in the way Karen always did at work. She almost downed the tea in one go, before putting the cup back down.

'Take care Karen. Was nice seeing you.'

She nodded and lent in for a kiss to my cheek.

'Take care Alex. Have fun on your travels.'

'I will.'

And with that she was gone.
Perhaps a golden opportunity lost but my conscience was clear.

Chapter 17

The next day I travelled to Camden with the removal van. Luckily it was another miserable day, weather wise. Driving the removal van was a middle aged guy called Raymond, his co-worker being a younger man, Kenny. Both were quite chatty and wanted to know why I was leaving a nice, quiet and small town for the big noisy city. Luckily, it was a miserable day, weather wise.

'Oh you know,' I said, 'it's what my girlfriend wants.'

'Damn!' the one called Kenny said, 'she must be something special for you to move there, that's all I can say.'

'Trust me, she is,' I smiled.

An hour later we pulled up outside Lilith's home. The grey afternoon sky hadn't changed much from the previous day, so Lilith came out to greet us. She looked stunning in a short black dress that belonged in a nightclub. Her hair was tied up behind her. It had only been just over a day since I had last seen her, but the moment I saw her I realised I'd missed her.

I smiled at her as she approached the van. I got out, as did Kenny, while Raymond turned off the engine and got out his side.

'Hi Alex.' Lilith said simply and kissed me on the mouth.

I noticed Kenny and Raymond exchange glances but neither said anything.

'Hi Lily. Good to see you,' I said, wrapping my arms around her.

She smiled and looked at the van as Raymond unlocked the back doors.

'Did you remember everything you wanted?' she asked.

I nodded and stepped to one side as Kenny reached in for the first box.

'Where do you want this stuff?' he asked.

'Oh just put it down in the hall thank you. We'll sort it out later.'

'Okay.' Kenny grinned, and hefted the box out.

I really hadn't brought much of my things with me, just most of my clothes, my computer and some of my books. I really didn't think I would have much need for all of it.

Soon the van was unloaded and the two guys sat down in our arm chairs while we stood.

'Nice place you have here,' Kenny remarked.

'Thank you,' Lilith said, 'we like it.'

We all drank coffee in relative silence. I took a wander out to the back garden and stood on the small patio, watching as two crows landed not far away from me and began to peck the ground at the bread Lilith had thrown out.

'You were right.'

I turned and saw Raymond come out of the door.

'Right?' I asked.

'She is special,' he laughed.

'Oh yes. She is,' I laughed too.

'Is she one of those gothic girls?'

'I guess so,' I said, 'she likes everything dark.'

'Yeah, I noticed the lack of light in there,' he said.

I shrugged and finished my drink.

'Well we'd better get going. Got another job to go to.'

I nodded and followed him in but stopped dead at what I saw, as Raymond froze too. Lilith had Kenny pinned against the wall, his feet inches from the floor. She turned as she looked our way and hissed, letting the removal man fall.

'I'm sorry. I couldn't help myself,' he stammered.

'What's going on?' Raymond asked, and I wanted to know the same thing.

'This little cretin thought it would be funny if he grabbed my arse,' Lilith snarled.

I hadn't seen her so angry and I too felt it grow within me.

Raymond glared at Kenny.

'This true?' he demanded.

'Yes I'm sorry,' the culprit answered, hanging his head.

'Get out my house,' Lilith roared, pointing towards the front door.

'Of course,' said Raymond, and with that the two men beat a hasty retreat. I left Lilith alone and followed them out.

'We're so sorry sir,' Raymond muttered as he opened his door.

'I've a good mind to call your boss,' I said.

'No please don't do that sir. Kenny didn't mean any harm by it. He's young and foolish. It won't happen again.'

'No, I should think not,' I glared at the younger man as he got into the van.

'I never knew she was so strong,' I heard him mumble.

I started laughing as they drove off.

On going back inside I found Lilith standing looking into her mirror, her arms crossed. Her body language told me she was still furious.

'Sometimes I curse myself for looking the way I do,' she said.

'How do you mean?' I asked, placing my hand on her shoulder and looking into the mirror too.

'Oh I just know Christiano would never have bothered siring me if I hadn't looked like this.'

I laughed softly and Lilith glared at me.

Before she could do or say anything I put up my hands and looked into her eyes.

'You honestly think your beauty is a curse?' I was incredulous.

'What would you call it?' she replied bitterly.

'A gift,' I said, 'maybe not from a god you don't believe in but a gift nonetheless.'

'A gift,' she muttered and looked into the mirror again.

'Yes. You are without doubt the most beautiful woman I have ever laid eyes on Lily.'

In the mirror I saw a small smile emerge.

'Really?' she asked.

'Yes. And the most beautiful woman is all mine.' This time while we looked at our reflections I kissed the back of her neck.

'Yes Alex,' she sighed. 'I am all yours.'

I was filled with a longing right then, to make love to her right there where she stood, but I was also eager to learn if she had been successful with the travel arrangements.

'Did you make your calls?' I asked, walking away from her.

'Yes,' Lilith answered, following me back to the lounge. 'William and Jodie are bringing the coffins tomorrow night. They will see that we are transported safely to the airport.'

'You trust them?'

'Yes. Neither would dare cross me.'

I nodded and began to put some logs into the fireplace.

'I will personally go and collect the paperwork and documents tomorrow.'

'Where will you get those?'

Lilith sat down in her chair and drew her legs up.

'A vampire works the twilight shift at the mortuary,' she said. 'I have had dealings with him before.'

It sounded like the plan was in full operation and that nothing was being left to chance.

'Now tell me, how did you manage without me yesterday?'

After I had lit the fire and had sat down in the other chair, I began to tell her all that had happened. I didn't leave out any detail, even when Karen had tried to seduce me.

'And you say you captured her gaze with ease and were successful with your commands?'

'Absolutely,' I said, 'she wasn't even aware that anything untoward had happened.'

Lilith nodded slowly and looked at me.

'I must say you have surprised me Alex.'

'How come?'

'You seem to have taken to being a vampire like a duck to water. I have known of many tales where newly turned vampires have struggled to cope with the new sensations and powers given to them. And yet here you are, almost like you've been one for as long as I have.'

I shrugged and looked at the fire.

'Perhaps having Severin's soul has helped me,' I suggested.

Lilith pondered this in silence for a few seconds. All I could hear was her small intakes of breath and the crackling of the fire.

'Perhaps but after the initial fight at the castle right after I had made him, Severin struggled to cope. He especially hated the sensation of floating.'

I didn't know what to say, so said nothing. I just let my gaze wander into the dancing flames.

'I am especially proud you managed to drink from that youth without killing him,' Lilith said, 'very impressive for only your third victim.'

I glanced at her and nodded.

'You know something Lily?' I said, 'we will have to get a proper couch so we can cuddle up together in front of this fire.'

Lilith gave a small laugh and nodded.

'I agree.'

Later that evening we decided to go the cinema. Really it was something to do while choosing who to feed off but I think we both enjoyed the romantic comedy we had chosen to see. A part of me kept forgetting that this magnificent woman beside me had been alive long before cameras were even invented. I made a mental note to ask her if she had ever met anyone famous but back to the business in hand, for we were silently following a young couple along a quiet street.

They were about to go through a garden gate when two men grabbed the girl.

'Well what do we have here?' one of them sneered. 'Real pretty aren't ya sweetheart?'

With my enhanced vision I saw one of the men draw out a gun. It was a pistol of some sort.

'Please, don't hurt us. Take my wallet,' pleaded the girl's companion, drawing out a wallet from his coat and throwing it at the man holding the gun.

'Why thank you,' he said nastily. 'But we might just take her too.'

The men slowly backed out of the gate and towards a parked car.

Lilith glanced at me before moving forwards. I followed silently.

'Come on sweetie. We're going for a ride.'

The man holding the gun opened the car door and then lashed out at the girl's companion. I saw blood fly from his shattered nose as he went down.

The girl was struggling and the man holding her couldn't get her into the car.

'Hey, give me a hand will ya?' he snapped.

'Delighted to.'

It was Lilith who had spoken and leapt into the air, landing on the car's roof.

'What in fuck's name?' the man holding the girl staggered back and lost his grip on her after Lilith had smashed her foot into his shoulder.

The girl had just run back to her still down boyfriend when I flew at the gunman.

He was about to aim a shot at Lilith, still standing on the roof when I hit him full speed, taking him off his feet and up into the air. I carried on floating up and up, all the while gripping the man by his arm.

'Hey, let me go. What's going on?' he wailed.

He tried to turn in midair and actually fired a shot at me. I felt the bullet whistle past my hair.

'Fire again and I will drop you,' I snarled.

The man looked down to see we had climbed high above the roof tops of the terraced houses.

'No way man. Don't drop me. I'm sorry.'

'Let go of the gun. Play nice and I will too.'

'Yes, yes. Okay.'

I smiled with satisfaction as I saw him release the gun, and watched it tumble away into the night.

I remembered an old clock tower we had passed earlier in the evening going to the cinema and now made my way there, the man still in my grip and helpless.

I made a gentle landing on the clock tower and left the man lying in a startled heap as I stood looking at the clock's hands.

I tutted and glanced at my watch.

'Don't you hate it when clocks run slow?' I asked and with no effort I pushed the big hand forward by two minutes, hearing gears crunch and grind within the tower.

'Much better,' I said and turned to look at the man. He was shaking with either fear or cold, probably both and what was he more afraid of? Me or the fact we were so high up? Again, probably both.

'Well?' I said. 'Got nothing to say?'

'What the fuck are you? What are we doing up here?'

I rolled my eyes and shook my head.

'I can see I'm going to have to have a little name tag or maybe a bat logo put on my jacket.'

'What?'

'Nothing,' I glared at him. 'I am a vampire and I'm going to drink your blood.'

'You're fucking crazy man. No way.'

I cocked my head to one side and laughed.

'Oh yeah and who's going to stop me?'

'You kill me and you're no better than me.'

'Perhaps,' I said, 'but who said anything about killing?'

And before he could say or do anything else I was on him. I pulled him to his feet and he'd just had time to cry out before I sank my teeth into his neck. Oh it was a truly glorious feed. And once again as the blood seeped into my mouth and on down my throat, I was convinced I could taste the man's fear.

After my thirst had been sated I returned with the man to the same deserted street. Lilith was sitting cross-legged on the same car roof, licking her lips like a cat with excess cream.

'Where's the other guy?' I asked, landing beside the car and dropping the now sleeping man in a heap.

'Over there.'

I looked to where she had pointed and couldn't help the gasp that escaped my mouth.

For there lying in three pieces was the same man who had grabbed the young woman. His legs had been ripped off and his upper chest was ripped wide open. Bits of shirt were embedded into the hole that exposed his shattered rib cage. As for his head it was further along the road, as if it had been kicked there.

I turned back to my beloved who was studying me intensely.

'You killed him?' I said. It probably sounded silly but this was the first time I had ever come across a dead person, especially considering the state of the body.

'Yes,' Lilith sighed and looked at her finger-nails.

'But why?' I asked, 'I thought you said you didn't kill any more.'

'He deserved to die,' was all she said and was then silent again.

I shook my head and turned away from her. I couldn't explain it but I simply couldn't look at her at that moment.

'I don't understand,' I shook my head again.

'What's to understand Alex? I killed him,' she said coldly. 'He deserved it so I did it. End of story.'

'Why did he deserve it? Tell me.'

And without even thinking, I was suddenly dragging her off the car roof by her feet.

'Let me go Alex or I will hurt you.'

'Answer me! Why did you kill him?'

I shoved Lilith against the car; luckily it was old and didn't have an alarm fitted. The car rocked all the same and shifted the back end towards the middle of the road. I also knew I had hurt Lilith with the shove for she cried out and slumped to the ground.

'Lilith?' I crouched down beside her and saw that she was crying.

'You don't know what it's like,' she sobbed. Her hand was on my arm but there was no strength in the grip.

'Tell me.'

'You don't know what it's like to be a monster Alex. You haven't killed anyone yet. Until you do, you will never understand.'

And suddenly she shoved me out of the way and took to the air at an incredible speed.

I was hurt and relieved at the same time. Hurt that we had had our first fight but relieved I hadn't caused her any harm by pushing her against the car.

I gazed around the awful scene and decided I'd better leave too. There was no sign of the young couple, so I assumed they had fled before Lilith's murderous assault. As I took to the air to head back to Camden, the wail of approaching police sirens began to hurt my ears.

Chapter 18

When I got back home, there was no sign of Lilith. No sign that she had returned at all.

After I had made another fire I poured myself a scotch and slumped down in one of the arm-chairs. I was content to watch the flames licking away at the small logs I had placed in the hearth but I was also secretly worried about Lilith.

I had never seen her so upset. I didn't think she was especially upset with me but something clearly was going on with her that she hadn't spoken to me about. That much was evident.

I took a sip from the drink and swirled the liquid around in the glass. Normally a whisky would be ideal for a cold night such as this one but I wasn't enjoying the drink at all. In fact I decided to get up and pour the rest of it down the sink in the kitchen.

I was about to go back into the lounge when I heard a commotion outside in the garden.

Opening the door, I gasped when I saw Lilith lying on the grass in the middle of the lawn. She was absolutely still and I ran to her.

There were blood and bruises on her face. Her left eye was swollen shut and her right arm was bent at a strange angle.

'Lilith.' I called but there was no response. I picked her up in my arms and carried her back to the house, where I laid her down gently in front of the fire.

She muttered something and her good eye slowly opened.

'What happened to you?' I asked, looking down at her poor ruined face.

At first her eye failed to focus on me but after a moment it finally did so.

'Give me your blood,' Lilith said without preamble.

Without a moment's hesitation I bit into my wrist and offered the wound to her waiting mouth.

I winced slightly as she drank hungrily from me, biting me again when the wound began to heal itself.

After a few moments she pushed my arm away and slumped back to the floor.

'Thank you,' she said and then turned her head towards the fire.

'Tell me Lily. What happened?' I asked gently.

'I don't want to talk about it.'

But I wasn't going to give up that easily.

'Please Lilith. Talk to me. I hate this silence between us.'

Slowly she turned her head back to me. She tried to sit up but winced and held her chest.

'Damn. I think they cracked a rib or two,' she gasped.

I shook my head and eased her back to the floor.

'Who are they? What happened?' I asked again, fearing that the Morisakis had been involved.

From her prone position Lilith looked up at me. I saw that her left eye was back to normal again, the swelling gone. I had no doubt the rest of her injuries would heal soon.

'I insulted a couple of drunk men and let them beat me up.'

I looked at her and shook my head.

'But why?' I asked, genuinely shocked.

'Because I deserved it after what I did to that man earlier.'

Again I shook my head and began to pace around the living room.

'What is the matter with you Lilith?' I asked. 'It's almost as if you hate being a vampire.'

'Yeah? Well, sometimes I do.'

'Fine. Well, when the sun rises tomorrow and it's a bright sunny day why don't you walk outside and fry yourself?' I snapped. Confusion and frustration had brought those harsh words to my lips.

The moment I said it, I regretted it. But I was hurt and angry at her. Maybe it was because I was still new to this but I simply didn't understand why she was acting the way she was, saying the things she was saying.

'You really want me to do it? Walk into the sun's rays?' she glared at me.

I shook my head and knelt down beside her. I gently took her hand in mine, although she was resistant at first.

'Of course not Lily, I love you.'

It was the first time I had said it and I realised I absolutely meant it.

'You love me?' she gazed at me.

'Yes. And I hate it that we're fighting and going through this. I hate it that you're not talking to me about what's upsetting you.'

I felt her squeeze my hand and this time she managed to sit up without wincing with pain.

'It's the anniversary of my daughter's death. And I regret not being a vampire back then because the blood would have saved her from the damn fever.'

I nodded and squeezed her hand back and pulled her into my embrace. My poor Lilith, the pain and loss of Sofia still so fresh to her, even after all the centuries.

'Come here,' I said softly.
'Hold me Alex,' she said and I knew she was crying.
We just stayed in that same position by the fire for a few minutes. She clung to me like a child while I soothed her and gently stroked my hand through her hair and across her back.

A little while later we went to the bedroom and made love and things were back to normal. It was almost as if the events of the past few hours had been forgotten or simply hadn't happened. Naturally Lilith's injuries had completely healed, even her broken arm. After making love we lay in the darkness in each others arms, her head resting on my chest.
'Tomorrow, before we go to China, I want you to do something for me.'
'Anything,' I answered.
'Don't be so sure,' Lilith whispered and ran her hand across my thigh.
'What do you mean?'
Lilith brought her head up so that it rested next to mine on the pillow.
She kissed me and looked into my eyes.
'Tomorrow Alex, I want you to kill someone.'
My eyes went wide at her request.
'Kill someone? Who?' I asked.
'Don't worry,' she smiled. 'He is a violent man who runs a small drug cartel. You need to make a kill Alex. Believe me, you need to.'
'I don't understand.'
I was about to say something else but Lilith placed a finger to my lips and shushed me.
'Every vampire needs to kill. It appeases the demon that dwells within us all.'
'Why are you only telling me this now?'
Lilith closed her eyes for a moment but then looked at me again, with a sigh.
'Because you weren't ready. I brought you over to my world at peace. The shock of making a kill straight away to a vampire made that way can be too much, even devastating. You may have suffered psychological effects my darling.'
'Vampires can have mental disorders?'
'Of course. Especially if they aren't nurtured correctly when they are first sired.'
Slowly it dawned upon me. Her words were sinking in. I remembered her tale of how Christiano had made her, how he had filled her head full of

violent images as the change occurred.

'You have those problems don't you?' I whispered.

Lilith blinked and slowly nodded her head.

'I do Alex. I cannot control the urge to kill sometimes. The demon within me is too strong to be held in check for long. That was why I lost control tonight, why I destroyed that man.'

I suddenly felt sorry for her. Certainly not afraid although of course a seriously pissed off Lilith could more than likely kill me.

I touched her face and offered her a small smile.

'It's okay Lily,' I said. 'I understand.'

And I did understand. I now knew what she was going through, not just with her daughter's anniversary but the whole rage issue as well.

'You can help me control it.' Lilith said.

'I shall try, of course, but how?'

'I know the signs when I have to kill. I shall let you know in future and you can make sure it isn't anyone innocent,' she explained.

'You mean you will only kill criminals?'

Lilith nodded.

'It shouldn't be a problem Alex. Crime is everywhere.'

I had to agree with that sentiment but was concerned about finding a criminal to order.

'What if we don't find one in time?'

'Then I shall just have to fight it for as long as I possibly can. But the demon always wins in the end Alex, mark my words.'

I kissed her and held her just a bit tighter.

'So I will need to kill on occasions?' I asked.

'Yes my love. It may save your life one day.'

'Okay but why tomorrow?'

'Because the sooner we get your first and most difficult kill out of the way the better.'

'Most difficult?' I asked, confused again.

'The first is always the hardest Alex. After that it gets much easier.'

'Alright but why this guy you mentioned?'

'He is a target I have had in mind for myself. He thinks nothing of destroying young lives by selling his drugs. He even has his own son working for him,' Lilith explained, a look of distaste crossing her lovely face.

I took this information in and realised the truth of her words.

'So we could be some kind of vigilante team,' I laughed.

Lilith smiled and laughed too.

'Yes. I suppose so.'

We kissed and I felt her hand slowly squeeze my cock.

'And you have no regrets or feelings of remorse afterwards?' I asked, surprised.

'Sometimes, sure. But then I think how poor the justice system is and if we are helping the long term cause then so be it.'

Lilith grabbed my hand and guided it down between her legs.

'Now then,' she whispered, 'no more talk.'

After we had made love for the second time Lilith fell asleep but I lay awake deep in thought.

I thought about all she had told me. About the fact our inner demon was too strong to resist and that eventually we would have to kill. I wondered if this was true of serial killers and other sociopaths. Did they too have some kind of demon inside them that they could only fight for so long? Of course with our vampire abilities it would be far easier for us to kill than a mere human could. But even so, the thought of actually taking a human life appalled me, despite taking the blood of a few victims already. But what my beloved was asking me to do, or just about ordering me, was to kill someone. End their life. I wasn't sure I could go through with it.

Lilith had also said that the first kill is always the hardest to do. I could see the logic in that but was it ultimately true?

I glanced at the sleeping beauty beside me and planted a kiss on her naked shoulder. There was clarity in that one look. With that single look at my beloved I knew there wasn't anything I wouldn't do for her. In that moment I knew I would do anything she asked of me, and if that meant taking a human life, then so be it. Tomorrow was only hours away.

Chapter 19

The next morning I awoke to find myself alone in our bed. I yawned and listened for any sounds of Lilith in the house. Sure enough I heard her pottering around in the kitchen.
I decided to grab a shower and after I had put on fresh jeans and a shirt, joined her.
To my pleasant surprise Lilith had made us a huge breakfast each, which consisted of bacon, eggs, fried bread, sausages, mushrooms, toast and baked beans.
'This kind of breakfast is bad for you Lily,' I laughed as I broke the surface of one of my eggs with a slice of toast.
'Makes no difference to our arteries,' Lilith winked and swallowed down some of the strong coffee she had brewed.
'I'm still getting used to this domestic vampire thing,' I admitted.
'Why? You surely didn't expect us to just survive on blood did you? How silly!'
I conceded the point and ate hungrily. I had never been one for eating much in the way of breakfast so this made a really nice change.
Afterwards I helped her clean up and then we sat down in the lounge with more coffee.
'What time are they coming with the coffins?'
'Not until midnight,' Lilith answered.
'What can I expect from this Jodie?'
Lilith looked at me with amusement in her eyes and a smile played across her sensuous lips.
'She is as timid as a vampire can possibly get. Why William didn't wait before he sired her I'll never know.'
'Love makes people do the craziest things.'
Lilith didn't reply but merely nodded, her gaze drawn to the window.
'Damn it!' she hissed, 'why is it so sunny today?'
I shrugged and went over to her.
'I'm glad you opened up to me Lilith. Last night, I mean.'
She looked at me then and raised her hand to gently touch my face.
'I should have done it sooner. I'm sorry.'
But I shook my head.
'No, it's fine. You were protecting me and I'm grateful for that.'
Lilith smiled and beckoned me down to her so that she could kiss me.

'But no more secrets, Alex, I promise you. If we are going to spend eternity together then that's the way it has to be. For both our sakes.'

'Agreed.'

We kissed again and then suddenly the doorbell went. We looked at one another.

Lilith frowned and slowly got to her feet. She edged her way to the door.

'Who is it?' she called.

'Postman. Got a parcel that needs signing for.'

She gave me a look of surprise, and after checking through the peephole, she slowly opened the door. Luckily the sun was around the back of the house so she was able to stay in the shade of the doorway.

'A mystery parcel,' Lilith smiled at the postman, managing to keep her fangs hidden.

'It's from the area so it hasn't come far.'

Lilith frowned again and nodded, quickly scribbling her name onto the postman's pad and thanking him, before closing the door. She brought the mystery parcel over to the table. It was a cube in shape and wrapped neatly in brown paper.

'Whatever could it be?' she asked.

'Do you recognise the address it came from?'

Again I saw her frown and shake her head.

'No I don't.'

Without further talk, Lilith sliced her nail through the brown paper and opened the box.

Whatever was inside made her gasp and she dropped the box and took a step back.

'No!' she cried.

'What is it?' I asked, moving closer from where I had been leaning against the wall.

'Look at it,' she whispered, turning away.

I stepped up to the box and peered inside and couldn't believe what I saw. For there in the box, a terrible expression on his face, was the severed head of William.

'But how?' was all I could think to say at that moment.

Lilith just shook her head and didn't reply.

I looked in the box again and then noticed a single piece of white paper lying behind the head. I reached in and plucked the paper out, unfolding it carefully.

'You'd better read this,' I said and handed her the note.

Lilith took it from me and read it out loud.
'To Lilith O'Shea. Soon.'
'It's from them isn't it? The Morisakis.' I said.
'Yes,' she sighed and dropped the piece of paper onto the table.
I had read about stories of intimidation but this surely took first prize.
'They killed him for just knowing you?'
But Lilith shook her head and looked at me.
'No. They would only have killed him if they'd found out about our plan to get to China.'
In the horror of the moment I had completely forgotten that we were depending on William and Jodie for safe transportation.
'What do we do now?' I asked.
Lilith didn't say anything. Instead she picked up the box and marched through to the lounge. I followed her and then watched in silence as she pulled out William's head by the hair and walked outside with it.
"We will bury it. It's all we can do for him now. That and see if poor Jodie is still alive.' She explained.

I suddenly felt terrible sorrow for someone I hadn't even met. The love of her life was gone forever. The man who had sired her and taken care of her was not coming back.

I nodded and watched as Lilith, using just her powerful hands, quickly dug a hole deep enough for the head to fit. After she had covered it back up, I saw my lover bow her head as if offering a prayer to a God she didn't believe in. Finally, she stood up again and came over to me.
'This changes things Alex,' she said.
'In what way?' I asked.
'We cannot go to China now. I won't risk something happening to you or someone else I care about.'
'Then what shall we do?'
Lilith looked at me, a new and determined look on her lovely face. Her eyes had become almost feral, a rage I hadn't seen before.
'We make contact with the Truest and damn the consequences.'

After scrubbing her hands clean, Lilith spent some time in her study making phone calls while I lit a fire that would somehow, I hoped, bring warmth into a suddenly very cold world. I had only met him the once but a part of me regretted the fact we would never become friends. I was beginning to realise that for creatures who lived such long lives, friendships were indeed a problem. And yet in William's case it shouldn't have been so, for he'd been a vampire too and therefore should have lived forever. Why had the infamous Morisakis acted so cruelly? Why did they seem to take such pleasure in this game they were playing? Not just with Lilith but me also.

Lilith came out of her study, that same determined look still there.

'We meet them tonight. Tower Bridge.'

I nodded and beckoned her over to me. She came into my arms without hesitating.

'What shall we do about Jodie?' I asked, kissing her hair.

'As soon as this infernal sun has gone down we'll go to their place. See if she's there.'

'And if she isn't?'

'Then we'll look for her. If she's still alive I know where she hunts. She might take her anger out on any man who crosses her path.'

'I thought you said she was weak.'

Lilith broke our embrace and looked at me.

'She is weak, for a vampire. But still more than a match for your average man.'

I nodded and watched as my beloved checked the fire. The smell of the burning wood was acting as a strange comfort to me and the flames doing their dance was always compelling.

'That's the second head I've had to dispose of,' she muttered.

'Yes.' I said softly, recalling the vision of her throwing Severin's head onto the fire at the farm.

'And once again it's my fault,' she shook her head.

'No Lily,' I said. 'These are sadistic bastards we are dealing with. You weren't to know they'd do that to William.'

'Maybe but I should know by now what they are capable of.'

'So what did the Truest have to say?'

'Not much. They didn't give me any information of where they are based. They were reluctant to talk let alone meet with us.'

'They know why we want to see them?'

'Yes. They know of me and my fight with the Morisakis, but they refuse to say if we can join them or not. Hopefully we can convince them at the meeting.'

Something about that was troubling me. And then I knew what it was.

'Why Tower Bridge?'

'I don't know. Why do you ask?'

'It's out in the open. Surely for a secret meeting we would be better off inside somewhere?'

Lilith thought about that for a moment, and then nodded.

'You're right. Wait there.'

And with that Lilith went back into her study.

I went and stood by the door and the next minute I heard her on the phone again.

'Listen to me,' she said. 'I'm choosing where we meet okay? There's a club called Twilight. Do you know it?'

She waited a moment.

'Good. I know the owner. We can trust him. We both have trust issues so this way both sides can relax. Eleven o'clock?'

Again she waited for the person on the other end.

'Good. We have an understanding. Don't be late.'

Lilith replaced the receiver and glanced up at me.

'I'll feel much better in a place I know well,' she said.

'Twilight Club?'

'Yes. I worked there for a time, as something to do. Nothing more.'

I smiled and Lilith stood up from behind the desk.

'What?'

'Nothing. I was just trying to picture you working, that's all.'

Lilith smiled too.

'It was fun for awhile. But I got sick of being hit upon night after night.'

I allowed her to walk past me and through to the kitchen where she put on some more coffee.

'So who owns Twilight?' I asked.

'Jacob. He's probably the only vampire I can truly call a friend.'

'How long have you known him?'

'About sixty years now, before he bought the club he worked at the docks.'

'For a vampire he seems to enjoy working.'

Lilith nodded.

'Some of us like to keep busy. He loves the club and says it's a great way to meet chicks.'

We both laughed at that remark.

'So how old is Jacob?'

Lilith thought about that for a moment.

'Actually I'm not sure,' she said. 'But he must be over 500. He's older than I am.'

'Don't you have some way of knowing? Some kind of vampire intuition?'

Lilith smiled and nodded.

'Yes we do. I've just never used it on him before. We will meet him tonight. Why don't you have a try and determine how old he is?'

I shrugged at the suggestion.

'I'll try but I'm not sure how I'd go about it.'

'Jacob has nothing to hide and is proud of being who is he. He won't shield himself against you. He'll let you read his mind I'm sure.'

This confused me.

'I thought you said we couldn't read each other's minds?'

'Only to a certain extent, Alex. I can't for instance read yours and tell you what you are thinking. But I can look deeper and discover things hidden away, given enough time to concentrate.'

'So it's like a partial power then? Not full-on telepathy or empathy?'

Lilith nodded.

'It's a power that is useful but could be better,' she said. 'It grows with age so that's why the oldest among us can read minds in their entirety.'

I nodded and saw this made sense.

'So it's the same with all vampire abilities. The older you are the more powerful you become.'

'Yes,' Lilith answered. 'In every sense of the word.'

She finished making the coffee and, returning to the comfort of the lounge, we sat down again.

'Try me Alex.'

'I'm sorry?' I put down my cup.

'Try to gain something from my mind. I won't resist you. See what you can find out from my past.'

'But how?'

'Concentrate. Think of nothing but me. Think of my mind as segments in an orange. You slowly have to peel them away one by one to eat.'

I shrugged and did as she asked. And suddenly I was in. I wasn't sure what happened exactly but I was suddenly aware of seeing her as a little girl running through a meadow.

'I see you as a child,' I said. 'Your hair is long and flowing behind you as you run through a meadow. There is another little girl beside you. She has long fair hair and a little blue ribbon tied within it. You are both laughing in sheer delight. Now I see a haystack in a field. You both run to it and start to throw hay at one another. You are having such fun. Your little blue dress is covered in hay and straw, so is her brown dress.'

Then the image was lost and I saw Lilith gazing at me from across the kitchen table.

'Very well done Alex,' she smiled and took my hand in hers. 'That was amazingly accurate.'

'That was an actual event from your childhood?'

'Yes. I remember it so well. It was one of my happiest moments. She was my best friend.'

'Who was she?'

'Clara.'

I nodded and drank some more coffee.

'We were best friends for 15 years, until she got married and moved away. I never saw her again.'

'I'm sorry Lily.'

But Lilith smiled and shook her head.

'It's okay. A very long time ago.'

'How old were you in that memory?'

'Nine I believe.'

'And where was it?'

Lilith again shook her head.

'I can't remember. Somewhere in the Irish countryside.'

'So your hair has always been raven black?'

Lilith smiled and nodded.

'Yes, which was always considered odd because both my father and mother had brown hair.'

I remembered a question I had wanted to ask her.

'Have you ever met anyone famous?'

'For sure. You can't really live for 450 years and not bump into celebrities on occasions.'

'Like who?'

Lilith laughed and swallowed some more of her coffee.

'I've met several musicians over the years. And no, I haven't fed from any of them. Actors too. The odd politician here and there.'

'Such as?' I prompted her, laughing.

She laughed too.

'Winston Churchill was very down to earth. He called me bewitching with the beauty of heaven itself.'

We both laughed.

'You really met Winston Churchill?'

She nodded and chuckled again.

'He remarked I was a splendid maiden, and he had no idea what I truly was.'

We continued to make small talk through out that sunny day, knowing full well we daren't venture out until the sun had gone down.

We were also very aware of the dangers that the night might bring, with the forthcoming meeting with the Truest. But of course first we were going to determine if Jodie was still alive.

Chapter 20

As soon as the sun had kissed England goodnight, Lilith and I made our way swiftly across London by air. Lilith was a woman on a mission for I could barely keep up with her flight speed.

Minutes after taking off from her garden, we circled over one more office-block before starting our descent.

'William's place is just over there.'

My beloved pointed at a run down-block of flats, just as we landed in a small park area.

All was quiet as we made our way towards the block. It seemed almost too quiet, as it was still early evening. I thought there should be at least some people wandering around but I kept this to myself and followed Lilith into the building.

'They live on the fourteenth floor so we'll take the lift.'

As soon as Lilith pressed the call button the lift door slid open with a bit of a creak.

We entered the lift without a sound and the door slid shut.

'This could be a trap,' I said as the lift began to move.

'Maybe, but I have to see if she's alright.'

We stood in uneasy silence as the lift continued it's upwards journey, creaking all the way as old lifts tend to do, but we got to the fourteenth floor without interruption.

'Where is everyone?' I asked.

'Only drop outs and drug addicts doss here now,' Lilith said and moved through the opened lift door.

'Yeah but we still haven't seen or heard anyone,' I was nervous.

'I don't know Alex.'

I followed Lilith along a short corridor until we reached a door in need of paint. The number on the door read 112 and it was ajar.

'Wait here,' Lilith whispered.

I nodded and watched her slide silently inside the flat. The first thing I saw when the door was fully opened were poorly decorated walls, the blue and yellow paper peeling and torn.

'Jodie,' I heard her call. 'Are you here? It's me, Lilith.'

No answer.

I looked further into the hallway and saw Lilith go into the first of the rooms. Moments later she came out, saw me, and shook her head.

Then she went into the next room of the flat and suddenly I heard a hiss followed by a loud crash.

I charged into the same room and saw my beloved face down on the wooden floor. Standing over her holding a metal chair was a young blonde woman. She was small and petite, no more than five feet tall.

'Who the fuck are you?' she hissed and came at me, the chair still in her grip.

'I'm a friend,' I just managed to say before she threw the chair at me. I was able to see it coming and batted it away, although it still sent a small shockwave up my arm.

I turned to face the woman but she was suddenly on me. Her nails dug deep into my cheek and neck and we both fell to the floor. It was all I could do to stop her scratching my eyes out.

Suddenly the woman was lifted easily off of me and thrown across the room where she landed with a crash into a wardrobe. Lilith had thrown her so hard the doors were in splinters and our attacker lay in a heap inside, unmoving.

'Are you alright?' Lilith asked me.

'Yes,' I said, taking her hand and she pulled me to my feet.

Lilith stepped in closer and actually ran her tongue over my bloody cheek.

'Who is she?' I asked.

We both looked towards the wardrobe where the woman was slowly coming round. She gave a pathetic little groan and started sobbing.

'That is Jodie,' Lilith said, stepping away from me and towards her.

'Okay, so why did she attack us?'

'She's irrational Alex,' my lover said, sadly. 'Her life, as she knew it, has gone. We might act the same in similar circumstances.'

I saw no need to argue the point and stayed where I was, watching Lilith slowly approach the grief-stricken vampire. In human terms I would have placed her at no more than twenty years of age.

'Jodie,' my beloved spoke gently as if to a child. 'It's all right now. Things will be okay, sweetheart.'

And suddenly it occurred to me that perhaps this was how Lilith looked upon Jodie. Not just as a child but perhaps even as her lost daughter.

Jodie was still giving little sobs as Lilith knelt down beside her and gently touched her knee.

'Come on Jodie,' she was saying. 'I won't hurt you again. No one will hurt you again, I promise.'

'You, you promise?' Jodie stammered, blinking through the tears.

'Yes,' Lilith offered her a smile and reached out her hand for Jodie. The young vampire took the proffered hand and slowly and gently Lilith pulled her free of the wardrobe.
'Come,' Lilith said, 'I want you to meet someone.'
She led her over to me and Jodie wiped her eyes and hair from her face.
'This is Alex. He will take care of you just as I will.'
I simply nodded as Jodie looked at me.
'I'm sorry for attacking you,' she said quietly, 'both of you.'
Lilith shook her head and smiled.
'Think nothing of it,' she said, 'besides, not many vampires have knocked me down. That was a good shot with the chair.'
For the first time I saw Jodie smile and it completely changed her face. She was very pretty. I could see why William had loved her so.
'Really?' she asked and my beloved nodded.
'Yes. Very good hit.'
Then Jodie looked at me again.
'But I didn't manage to knock you over,' she said.
'No,' I agreed. 'But it hurt all the same.'
To emphasise the point I held up my arm and gave it a little shake.
Jodie laughed and so did Lilith and I.
'Come, let's get out of here. Grab what you need Jodie, you're coming home with us,' Lilith declared.

Jodie didn't have much in the way of possessions and managed to pack it all away in one battered suitcase. Once we were free of the building, Lilith carried her and took to the air. I followed carrying the case.
As we soared high over London I couldn't help but wonder what it was going to be like having another person in the house with us. But I had no objections; as Lilith had said, Jodie had lost everything she had held dear to her. Her world was gone and Lilith and I were going to have to help her build a new one.

We got back to the house without incident and the first thing Lilith did was to run a bath for Jodie.
'Enjoy your soak. We'll be downstairs.'
Jodie just nodded and padded into the bathroom and shut the door.
I followed Lilith into the spare room.
'In that cupboard should be some bedding.'
I followed to where she had looked and sure enough, there were some

fresh sheets and blankets.

I helped Lilith make the bed up and then followed her back onto the landing.

'Jodie?' Lilith called through the bathroom door. 'I'm going to leave you some clothes outside the door. Tomorrow we'll go out and get you some more.'

'Okay, thanks,' was the reply.

Satisfied, Lilith beckoned me to follow and we went into our bedroom.

'You're very quiet Alex. Is everything alright?'

'Yes. I'm fine,' I replied.

'It doesn't bother you that she's here?'

I shook my head.

'Not at all, besides she needs us.'

My sire nodded and went over to a chest of drawers.

'These should fit her.'

She pulled out some clean underwear and a couple of t-shirts. In another drawer she found a short skirt and a pair of trousers.

'What do we do about the meeting?' I asked.

Lilith thought about the question and finally shook her head.

'I think we need to postpone it Alex. We can't leave Jodie alone, not tonight.'

I agreed and took the clothes from her.

'I'll finish getting her room ready. You make the phone calls.'

Lilith nodded and with a quick kiss she went downstairs.

In another cupboard I found a couple of pillows and some pillow cases. I finished making the bed and then placed the small pile of clothes outside the bathroom door.

After I had done this I made my way downstairs and found Lilith in the study.

'I know we said tonight but I had business elsewhere,' Lilith was saying into the phone.

I lent against the wall and watched.

'It can't be helped. I have a very young and distraught vampire here and it's my fault she's become that way. Give me one more night.'

Lilith sat down in her chair and cradled the phone between her shoulder and ear, while scratching her leg with her other hand.

'Thank you. Same time, same place tomorrow,' she said and hung up.

'They weren't impressed I take it?' I asked.

'You could say that,' Lilith then punched in another number.

'Who are you calling now?'
But Lilith held her hand up.
'Jacob? Hi, it's me. Listen, something's come up. The meeting will be tomorrow now. Okay?'
She listened for a moment and then laughed.
'Of course. It will be good to see you too. Bye for now.'
Lilith put the phone down and then came around her desk.
'Let's make a fire and the place more welcoming,' she said.

I had cleaned the hearth before we had gone out and so the fire-place was all ready for putting new logs on. While I got the fire lit, Lilith made us all a drink each.
'Jodie loves sherry,' Lilith said as she put three glasses of it on the table.
'How old is she?' I asked.
'William sired her on her 19th birthday.'
'Why so young?'
'I have no idea. Perhaps he felt it was the right time.'
'What about her parents?'
Lilith shook her head.
'They died in a car crash when she was a child.'
'She really hasn't had much luck in life,' I muttered.
'Exactly. So we shall try to do our very best to make things better for her. It won't be easy my love, but we have to try.'
'What do we say about William?'
'I think we should allow Jodie to talk about him when she's ready to.'
'I agree but we must find out exactly what happened. And why for one thing, the Morisakis let her live.'
Lilith nodded.
'I've been thinking about that.'
'And?' I asked.
'They probably allowed her to live out of spite. It would be typical of them. They know she'd be completely lost without him, the bastards!'
I shook my head in disgust, realising my beloved was probably correct.
The more I learnt about this group the more I hated them and everything they stood for. Their rules made perfect sense to a degree but their methods for upholding them left a lot to be desired.
We were sitting in our chairs by the fire when we heard Jodie come down the stairs. We turned as she entered the lounge, wearing the short skirt and one of the t-shirts Lilith had provided. Her blonde hair had been brushed,

and she looked like a very different girl.

'My,' Lilith smiled, 'you look a picture.'

Jodie rewarded us with that amazing smile of hers and I got up from my chair.

'Have a seat,' I waved at it, 'make yourself cosy.'

'No, it's your chair,' she said, shyly.

'I insist,' I smiled at her.

Jodie smiled again and sat herself down, drawing her legs up and obviously enjoying the new warmth the fire was providing.

'And here's a sherry.' I handed her the glass and she took it with thanks.

'While we get you some clothes, we'll also buy another chair or two.' Lilith said.

'I don't want to be a bother,' Jodie said, sipping some of the drink.

'Nonsense,' Lilith smiled. 'This is your home now. Isn't that right Alex?'

I met her gaze with a smile of my own.

'Of course. What is ours is yours Jodie.'

'Thank you,' the young vampire said, 'both of you.'

We spent hours talking and drinking until well into the next day. Jodie wanted to know all about me and where I had come from. Lilith gladly told her about why she had chosen me. What we didn't talk about was William but we knew Jodie would do so when she was ready to. Vampires, after all, had plenty of time for patience!

Chapter 21

The following day I awoke in Lilith's arms and glancing at the clock I saw that it was well into the afternoon.

My movements had stirred my beloved and her eyes opened too.

'Hi,' she smiled, stroking my face.

'Hi,' I kissed her.

But as I pulled my face away from hers I looked up in shock to see Jodie standing in the doorway.

'Hello,' I said.

Jodie just nodded and then I realised she was crying.

Lilith turned over and beckoned her to the bed. Jodie came without any more prompting and sat down on the edge.

'It's okay Jodie,' Lilith put her arm around her, not caring the quilt had slid down baring her breasts.

'I miss him so much,' Jodie wailed and buried her head in Lilith's shoulder and hair.

Lilith gently stroked her back.

'I know you do honey,' she said, soothingly. 'And you will for a time.'

They stayed in that position for a few seconds. I just lay there watching but offering Lilith support by grasping her other hand and she smiled gratefully at me.

'I want the bastards who killed him,' Jodie snarled. 'Will you help me Lilith?'

My beloved nodded.

'Yes. Tonight we will be meeting the True Species. Hopefully they can offer us some protection while we plan our next move.'

Jodie broke the embrace and stood away from the bed.

'Can you trust them?' she asked.

'I'm not sure, but we need all the help we can get.'

Jodie nodded at this remark and then glanced at me.

'I'm sorry for disturbing you.'

'Not at all,' I offered her a smile.

'We're here for you Jodie. Please believe that,' Lilith added.

Jodie gave a small smile before leaving the room.

Lilith sighed and leaned her head on my chest.

'Are the Truest interested in taking on the Morisakis?' I asked.

'I doubt it. They just want to live how they want. But I don't think they want all-out war.'

'Okay.' I was thinking.

'Why do you ask?'

'Well, perhaps an all out assault is the last thing the Morisakis will be expecting.'

Lilith looked up at me, her eyes growing wide.

'Are you serious?'

I smiled and traced my finger along her nose.

'They expect us to run and hide Lilith. You know it and I know it.'

My beautiful Lily took my finger and gently bit into it, making it bleed just enough for her to have a small taste.

'What do you have in mind Alex?'

'I think we should attack one of their lesser houses. Drive home the message we are not afraid and will be remaining here.'

'But no one knows where their members dwell.'

'We don't, but perhaps the Truest might.'

Lilith lay back and stared up at the ceiling.

I didn't say anything, just merely contented myself by playing with her hair.

'You're right,' she finally said. 'I think it's time we fought back.'

And suddenly I was grasping nothing because Lilith was on the other side of the room, putting on her black robe.

'It will be dark in an hour. I'm going to have a shower. We will go out and get some clothes for Jodie. And while we do we'll feed too.'

And so within half an hour the three of us hit the streets. Our first stop was Camden High Street where we bought some nice tops and skirts for Jodie. She rewarded us with one of her biggest smiles. She was doing well to hide her pain and we were both proud of her. It was strange, because I had been a vampire for far less time than her, but I was already seeing her as the daughter I never had. I suppose the human element was coming into play, me being made a vampire at 36 while she was only 19.

Our next stop was a coffee shop where the three of us sat and drank lattes.

Lilith and I were slower at drinking ours, and Jodie suddenly pointed across the road.

'Can I go and try those on?'

We looked to see her pointing at a shop window with biker type boots in the display.

'Of course,' Lilith laughed and handed her two hundred pounds in twenty pound notes. 'If you need more just shout.'

Jodie smiled and almost skipped across the road, leaving us to finish our drinks.

'What are her limitations?' I asked, 'as a vampire, I mean.'

'She can't fly and she certainly can't look into people's minds. Her strength, though strong compared to human, is a lot weaker than yours or mine. Her speed is pretty impressive but not overly so.'

I nodded.

'So if it came down to a fight with another vamp, how would she get on?'

Lilith shook her head.

'Depends on the vampire of course. Against the very oldest, she would have no chance. We wouldn't have much chance either, but given the element of surprise she could do some damage.'

I nodded and remembered the way she had knocked Lilith to the ground in her flat.

We finished our coffees and started to make our way towards the shop our companion had gone into.

'When do I have to kill this man?' I asked.

'Tonight, before we meet the Truest.'

'And you think I'll be all right? That I won't hesitate?'

Lilith stopped on the pavement and faced me.

'I'm sure you'll be fine Alex. I have faith in you.'

I wasn't so sure but I let it pass.

'So what's his name?'

'His name is Milan Bortov.'

'Russian?'

'Yes. He's a bad, bad man Alex and won't be missed.'

I nodded.

'Where does he live?'

'I don't know but I know he has a warehouse at the docks.'

'So I just wait there for him? What if he doesn't show?'

Lilith sighed.

'He will. He always does business there.'

By now we were standing outside the shop. Peering through the window I saw Jodie lacing up a pair of long black biker boots that went well with her short black skirt and jacket.

'She looks happy enough,' I smiled.

'It's only a mask, poor child, but it's a good mask,' Lilith said, her eyes clouding over briefly, perhaps with her own memories of loss and pain.

Two hours later I stood and watched as my Lily and Jodie fed. Their victims were two brothers, only too glad to be alone with two such beautiful women. Lilith watched and nodded with approval as Jodie sealed the wound on her victim's neck.

'Very good,' she commented, letting her victim slump to the ground behind the pub we had met them in.

With a last lick of her lips Lilith sealed her victim's puncture marks and then walked over to me.

'You sure you don't want to feed yet my love?'

I shook my head, having decided I would feed off Bortov before killing him.

'Very well, come. Bring Jodie and follow me to the docks.'

I took to the air after Lilith, Jodie clinging to me tightly.

As we flew she spoke to me.

'Will I ever be able to do this?'

'I don't know,' was my honest answer, 'perhaps Lilith knows.'

'I mean I know I'm weak Alex. Very weak for a vampire.'

'So I'm told, but you have other qualities instead Jodie,' I said, encouragingly.

'Like what?'

'You have a speed that is at least equal to others. I also know you are a good person at heart.'

Jodie tilted her head at me as we flew on.

'Really?' she asked, 'You really think I'm a good person?'

I glanced at her as we took a turn to the right and smiled.

'Yes. And of course Lilith thinks so too, otherwise she wouldn't have come and found you.'

Jodie thought this over as we passed by a water tower.

'I was afraid of her,' she admitted. 'I was scared Lilith would take William away from me.'

I looked at her and shook my head.

'That was never going to be the case. Lilith never thought of William in that way.'

'But he liked her. He told me more than once.'

'Yes, but it was you he loved Jodie,' I reminded her.

'Perhaps, but maybe I was always second best. Second choice.'

I didn't know what to say to that, mainly because I had a suspicion it may have been true.

Luckily I didn't have to say anything more because ahead of me Lilith was landing on the roof of a warehouse. I landed beside her and Jodie withdrew her arms.

'This is the building. See? They are already here.'

I looked to where Lilith was gesturing and saw five parked cars at the waterside. All the cars were new BMWs, except for one Mercedes.

'Nice cars,' I muttered.

'All from drug money Alex.'

I nodded and glanced at Jodie, who waited in silence.

'So what do we do now?' I asked.

Lilith smiled and kissed me.

'Let's knock on the door.'

And with that she dropped over the side of the roof and landed by the main large door.

Jodie and I quickly followed.

Lilith started banging on the huge door with her fist. In the silence of the evening the sound was like thunder.

Inside, we heard the men go silent from their chatter. I tried to picture their confusion as to who was paying them a visit. My bets were on a drug bust by the police but how wrong could they be?

With a sweep of her arm Lilith swept the massive door to the side where it crashed off its runner and fell with a thud onto the concrete floor.

One man stared at her while the others panicked, scattering to various parts of the warehouse. They quickly disappeared behind pallets of boxes of all shapes and sizes.

Lilith's black dress flowed behind her as she marched into the warehouse, straight towards the one staring at her.

'Milan Bortov, your time has come,' her shout echoed around the warehouse.

'Says who?' The man was suddenly holding a small machine gun.

Without further words or warning he pressed the trigger. Jodie and I dived for cover behind more pallets while Lilith leapt into the air as the first spray of bullets flew past us and out into the night through the broken door.

Car alarms went off and I realised the bullets must have hit one or more of the cars parked there.

Lilith landed, her skirt flying behind her as she did a perfect cartwheel, followed by a double somersault that brought her on top of the gun-man. He tried firing again but his aim was off as Lilith hit him with her right leg. The kick sent the gunman flying into the wall where he then lay still, blood trickling out the back of his head.

Then more shots ran out as the men returned. I saw my beloved jump onto a narrow beam high up in the ceiling and knew the men couldn't see her in the dark shadows.

I decided to make a move. I ran out from behind the pallet I was hiding behind and saw the nearest man reloading his pistol. I hit him full speed and watched with satisfaction as he flew backwards into another pallet. He hit it with sufficient force to dislodge the boxes that were neatly stacked there. The gun sailed high and was lost in the shadows. Before the man could recover Jodie was upon him, biting deep into his neck. She didn't need to feed but she did so anyway and savagely. She used her fangs to tear the man's throat to shreds, blood spraying everywhere including into Jodie's face and hair. She didn't seem to notice or care.

I looked up in time to see Lilith launch herself at another man. She tripped him up first and was pleased to see him drop his gun.

As the man struggled to get to his feet, Lilith stamped hard on his arm. Even from where I stood I heard the bones crunch. He screamed with the pain of the action but Lilith quickly bent down and snapped his neck like a candle-stick, silencing him forever.

I glanced to my right and saw a man making a run for the entrance. I intercepted him and grabbed him by the jacket. With as much force as I could muster I hurled him into the wall. He hit face first, and the man's head literally exploded from the impact. Brain, bones and blood were all that were recognisable, his face completely destroyed. I had made my first kill. And I felt….Nothing. No pity. No remorse. I remember looking up from my handy work and seeing my beloved nodding with approval, a lovely smile on her face.

That left two more men but they had hidden away somewhere.

Jodie came to join Lilith and me; together we stood in silence, waiting for the slightest sound to give their location away.

Suddenly we heard the familiar electric hum of a forklift starting up. We separated again as the truck came into view from around another line of pallets.

The driver lent out of the cab and started firing his revolver. Lilith and I moved safely away from the bullets but one caught Jodie square in the shoulder spinning her around and into the forklift's path. Just before the truck's deadly forks could rip into her, I managed to dive in its path and swept my injured friend out of the way.

The truck crashed into another pallet and the impact was enough for the driver to drop his gun.

'Goodnight,' Lilith said as she stepped up to the forklift and smashed her fist into the driver's face, breaking his nose and more than likely his jaw too.

Jodie was crying from the bullet wound and I remembered she was weaker than Lilith and I. This obviously meant she couldn't heal as fast either, which was why the blood was still flowing from the hole in her shoulder.

I bit into my wrist and gave it to Jodie, who, despite her pain, fed eagerly from my offered arm. Then with my other hand I pulled her jacket away from the injured shoulder and sealed her wound for her.

'Thank you Alex,' she said and, to my surprise, she kissed me.

Lilith frowned when she saw this but didn't say anything. Instead she turned her head the other way.

I saw what she was looking at. The last gunman was trying to sneak along the side of the warehouse towards the door.

'Allow me,' I said.

Lilith nodded and I was off, running and leaping into the air at our final foe.

My two-footed jump kick caught the man square in the back, sending him skidding across the concrete into another pallet.

He tried to turn over but I knew my kick had shattered his spine.

'Fuck, it hurts! Help. Help me!' the man was shouting.

I stepped up to him, slowly and deliberately. I was the hunter and this was my prey.

I knelt down beside him and watched him gaze up at me with a mix of hatred and fear. Oh yes, the fear was most definitely there with this one.

'Hi,' I said. 'How are things?'

'End it, you fucker,' he snarled, but there was no strength to his words.

'Gladly,' and then I bit deep into the back of his neck. He was bald so there was no hair in my way, just pulsating flesh. His blood flowed thickly and strongly into my mouth and throat. I drank hungrily until I literally felt his life pass away.

I stood up and licked my lips one last time before turning back to see Lilith and Jodie watching me.

'How do you feel?' Lilith asked me.

'Like a vampire,' I laughed and my companions joined in.

Chapter 22

The very next evening the three of us were at last meeting members from the Truest.

We had arrived early, Lilith first talking to Jacob. I assumed they had some catching up to do so grabbed a drink and stood off to one side. I watched Jodie seemingly enjoying herself, dancing with the crowd.

I had never been one for nightclubs. I had always found them either too crowded or expensive. I certainly found the music not to my taste and it was always played at an intolerable level.

I took a sip from my vodka and then saw Lilith beckon me over.

'Alex, I want you to meet Jacob.'

I shook hands with the club owner.

His grip was very strong but he smiled pleasantly enough.

'Nice to meet you, Alex.'

His voice was surprisingly soft for such a big man. Jacob was way over six feet tall and heavily built. His plain white shirt didn't really fit very well.

'Hi,' I said simply.

'Nice grip,' Jacob laughed, holding his hand with the other one after we had broken the handshake.

'Thanks. You too.'

Jacob turned to Lilith and gave her a wink.

'I can see why you chose him.'

Lilith smiled and gave me a playful smack on the arm.

'It's more than that old friend,' she said. 'Come here.'

Jacob leant over the bar at Lilith's request and she spoke quietly in his ear. Even with my enhanced hearing I couldn't hear her words.

When Jacob stepped back I could see the surprised look on his face.

'Really? That is intriguing,' he gazed at Lilith thoughtfully for a moment.

'Absolutely,' was my beloved's reply.

Suddenly Jacob grabbed my head between his strong hands and looked into my eyes. I tried to pull back but couldn't move. I was a bit confused as to why Lilith wasn't helping me.

'Yes,' Jacob said, his voice low. 'Yes. I see it.'

'What's going on?' I asked.

But Jacob ignored me, instead turning his gaze to Lilith, but his grip on my face hadn't changed.

'You do realise what this means my dear?'

Suddenly I twisted my head free and lashed out, my right fist connecting hard with Jacob's cheek. He flew backwards and smashed into the bottles and glasses behind the bar.

Lilith gasped and immediately grabbed my arm.

'Alex, no!' she hissed.

But I shook her off and leapt over the bar and grabbed Jacob by his shirt.

'What's your problem?' I demanded.

Jacob held up his hand, his other rubbing his cheek gingerly.

'Forgive me,' he said. 'I meant no harm.'

Lilith stood at the bar, an anxious look on her face.

'Please Alex,' she said.

Two security guys ran up beside her but Jacob waved them off.

'Just a little misunderstanding. We're fine.'

'You sure boss?'

'Yes. Go back to the door.'

They hesitated but then made their way back through the crowd.

I let go of Jacob's shirt and allowed him to stand.

'Is anyone going to tell me what's going on?' I asked, looking at him and then at Lilith.

'Follow me,' Jacob said and walked towards a door down the side of the bar.

Lilith nodded and we both followed Jacob into a back room. As we entered two more staff members took his place behind the bar and started to clean up the mess.

Jacob ushered us to some chairs around a table and closed the door behind him. The music from the club was greatly reduced, which came as a small amount of comfort.

'Let me tell you something Alex,' Jacob said sitting down opposite. 'I have been a vampire for over 500 years and I have never come across or even heard of a vampire with the strength you possess, for one so young.'

'What he's saying is you should never have been able to break his hold, Alex.' Lilith added.

I shrugged and folded my arms.

'Do you know what Lilith whispered to me out there?'

I shook my head.

'She told me you have Severin's soul.'

I glanced at Lilith, who nodded in response.

'Yes, I know I have his soul. So what?'

Jacob smiled and rocked back in his chair.

'Somehow, your strength and his have combined. This is the only explanation I can think of.'

I looked to Lilith who took my hand in hers.

'It's true Alex,' she said. 'And perhaps in some way, the fact I created both of you has made this happen.'

Jacob got up and started to pace around the room.

'Yes, it's the only answer. I've heard of the transference of souls but not two souls combining in this way. Yet somehow, your vampire master has made this happen. Truly remarkable.'

'So what are you saying?'

Lilith gave my hand a small squeeze and kissed my cheek.

'It means my darling, you are unique! That I sired both you and Severin has created a vampire a lot more powerful than your average fledgling.'

Suddenly there was a knock on the door and one of Jacob's staff put her head around it.

'Jacob, your guests have arrived.'

The three of us stood as the girl allowed three figures to enter. One was a striking woman with flame red hair, her slender figure hidden beneath a floor-length red gown. Her companions were both male and dressed in black suits.

The woman immediately stepped up to Lilith.

'Speak,' she demanded. 'Why do you wish to join the Truest?'

'We want the same as you, to be rid of human kind,' Lilith lied smoothly.

The woman gazed at her and then looked at me.

'So you say and yet I smell a very young vampire.'

I avoided her gaze, which made her give a little laugh.

'He may be young but he is strong,' Lilith answered.

'Oh really?'

The words were barely finished before the woman attacked me. Her nails raked down my face and before I could react, she threw me to the floor.

'He is weak!' she hissed. 'No use to us.'

Lilith smiled as I got to my feet.

'Excuse me?' I said.

'What?' the woman snapped, turning back to me.

I back-handed her across the face, sending her sprawling over the table.

The two men in suits snarled and moved forward but Lilith and Jacob blocked their path.

'Cease this,' Jacob said. 'We all want the same thing.'

'He dare strike Cecilia,' growled one of them and made another step towards me.

'Wait!' the woman slowly straightened up and looked at me.
I crossed my arms and stood in silence.
'You are not all you seem,' she said.
'Cecilia, please. Listen to me.'
The woman turned and faced Lilith.
'I know of you Lilith O'Shea. I know of your struggle with the Morisakis.'
'Yes,' my beloved said, 'we only seek to join you.'
'No. I cannot allow it.'
Jacob came forward.
'Cecilia. I know you. I know your power and respect it. Please think about this.'
The woman stared at Jacob and then turned back to me.
'You intrigue me, what is your name?'
'Alex.'
Cecilia cocked her head as if taking the information in.
'It has been longer than I can remember since someone dared strike me.'
'You attacked me. I was defending myself.'
Cecilia gave a small laugh and was suddenly at my side, her fingers stroking my cheek where she had injured me earlier.
'You heal remarkably fast for one so young.'
Before I could say anything Lilith stepped forward.
'Please Cecilia, don't hurt him.'
The woman removed her hand from my face and stared at Lilith.
'You made him?' she asked.
My Lily nodded.
'I have no quarrel with you Lilith O'Shea but alas, I cannot help you. The Truest have a difficult enough time dealing with the Morisakis as it is without adding your little feud into the bargain.'
'But please, we…'
'The answer is no.'
And with that, she and her two companions left the room.
'Fuck!' Lilith swore.
'I'm sorry,' Jacob said. 'I thought she would help you.'
'What do we do now?' I asked.
Lilith looked at me and for the first time ever I saw fear in her eyes.
'I don't know Alex. I really don't know.'

After we had said goodbye to Jacob, Lilith and I left the club.
'Will Jodie be okay?' I asked.

'She's probably off feeding. She knows where to find the house.'

We had looked for her but had found no sign until one of the bar staff told Lilith Jodie had left with a guy a few minutes earlier.

We stopped by a burger outlet and grabbed some food.

'Any thoughts?' my Lily asked, biting into a cheese-burger.

'Maybe Cecilia will change her mind,' I suggested.

Lilith thought this over while chewing her food but eventually shook her head.

'Unlikely.'

'Do you know her?'

'Oh yes. Everyone over the age of 300 knows Cecilia.'

'Why?'

'She's a legend. She was the one who reformed the Truest. Cecilia is over 1200 years old.'

'I hit a 1200 year old vampire?' I asked, almost dropping my French fries.

'And lived to tell the tale.'

That was a plus, I had to admit.

Lilith had lapsed into silence and just finished her meal, so I did the same.

Afterwards we walked hand in hand along the street and felt the first few drops of rain.

'You know, I don't think we should give up just yet. Cecilia seemed fascinated by you. Perhaps we could use that to our advantage.'

I didn't know what Lilith meant by that but kept quiet.

'And I know Jacob won't have given up. Not yet.'

We walked towards the Tube station only to see it was closed.

And then the rain began to fall more heavily. With no one else around, Lilith and I took to the air.

Hand in hand we flew up and up until the capital was spread out below us, millions of lights all shining in the darkness.

'You're very quiet Alex.'

'Just thinking.'

Together we flew on, some inner instinct driving us forwards to our home.

'I'm not going to make promises to you I can't keep.' Lilith said.

With my free hand I wiped the rain from my eyes and looked at her.

'What promises?'

Lilith stopped her forward momentum and just floated there in front of me, still holding my hand.

'I can't promise we will be alright Alex. You know? I can't promise that one day, maybe soon, the Morisakis will kill me.'

'Don't say that,' I pleaded with her, but Lilith shook her head.
'You know it's true my love. All things must end eventually.'
'But we've only just begun.'
I gripped her hand tighter and pulled her towards me.
There, high above London we embraced in the dark. The driving rain falling still, soaking the two of us through and yet neither of us caring. We were simply two creatures of the night, completely and utterly in love, our focus only on one another.
The embrace lasted a few more seconds until Lilith broke it by kissing me on the mouth.
'Come my love, let's go home.'

Despite all our worries and the disappointing meeting, when we got home, Lilith and I made love almost as if it was our first time together. The hunger and the passion was total and afterwards we lay in one another's arms, listening to the continuing rain spattering against the window.
'I hope Jodie is alright.'
Those were Lilith's last words before we both drifted off to sleep.

Chapter 23

I was now getting used to sleeping in daylight hours. Of course, the time of year was probably helping. It would be interesting to see how the summer time would affect my sleeping, if indeed, I lived that long.

What my beloved had said to me the night before was playing on my mind. It was late afternoon and Jodie still hadn't returned.

Lilith was sitting by the fire reading. I, meanwhile, was restless, so took my hot cup of coffee out into the garden.

I stood out there in the cold air, although the icy wind no longer bothered me.

'Everything comes to an end,' Lilith had said.

For some reason, those words really bothered me. When I remembered how she had said them I felt numb. Empty.

I was in no doubt her words were true. But at the same time I was also in no doubt I could no longer imagine my life without her by my side.

I felt her presence long before she slid her arms around me from behind, a waft of her lavender scent slipped into my nostrils on the gentle breeze.

'What's wrong my love?' she asked tenderly.

I lent back against her, sighing as her lips brushed the back of my neck.

'I can't imagine a world without you my Lily,' I said truthfully.

'And I you,' she murmured, her hands running up my chest.

I turned in her embrace and we kissed deeply, gently biting one another's lips as we did so.

Then we heard a shriek of laughter. Breaking our kiss, we turned to see Jodie stepping from the shadows, a young man of similar age with her.

'Jodie. You're safe,' Lilith said with relief.

'I am,' she replied simply. 'Lilith, Alex: this is James.'

'Hi,' the new-comer smiled.

'Hello.'

Jodie gripped his hand and without another word, marched into the house.

'Interesting,' Lilith said, glancing at me.

'What do you mean?'

'He's human. I hope Jodie doesn't want to sire him.'

I shrugged.

'Why not? Perhaps she needs a companion.'

'He'd be so weak, Alex.'

'Yes, but who's going to tell her not to do it?'

Lilith nodded and touched my arm.

'You're right. I need to talk to her.'

I stayed in the garden looking out into the night. I saw a bat fly past as I stood in silence; of course to my enhanced vision it looked as if it was flying in slow motion.

I turned at the sound of the door opening as James came out.

'Why is she talking to Jodie?' he asked.

I smiled.

'It's for your best interest.'

He gave me a confused look.

Then we heard raised voices and Jodie came storming out of the house.

'Come on James. We're going,' she said.

'Don't be foolish,' Lilith snarled, following her.

'I don't need you,' Jodie spat, 'and you don't want me around while you and lover boy fuck.'

I saw Lilith's eyes narrow and was expecting her to lash out but instead she put her hands on her hips and glared at the girl.

'It's not safe Jodie. The Morisakis know of your involvement with me. They will kill you.'

'Good. I have no life anyway! They already took that away from me,' Jodie snapped, her voice reaching a high pitched wail.

'You don't mean that,' I said.

Jodie glared at me and pointed.

'How would you know? You have her. You have each other.'

'Yes we do,' Lilith said. 'But we have you too. You're our family now Jodie. Please believe that.'

'So? We have threesomes now? Is that it?'

Lilith shook her head and glanced at me.

'That's not what I meant.'

'Whatever. Let's go,' Jodie marched up to a bemused James.

I stood in her path but Lilith shook her head.

'Let her go Alex.'

'Lily?'

'If she wants to go, we can't keep her here,' Lilith said, quietly.

I reluctantly stepped aside and Jodie grabbed James' hand and walked past us without another word.

Lilith came and stood by me.

'I hope she'll be alright,' I said.

'She's made her choice,' Lilith said. 'It's just the two of us again.'

The next night, on Lilith's advice, we went to visit my parents. After all, they must have been wondering where I had got to.

'Mum, Dad. This is Lilith,' I was proud to introduce them to one another.

Then we all sat down in my parents lounge.

'You haven't been answering your phone,' my mother said.

'No, I've been spending a lot of time in London,'

'With me,' Lilith added, smiling.

'Well, it's about time you met someone,' my Dad said.

Mum ordered us a Chinese take away and soon we were all sat down to dinner.

'Lilith is quite an old-fashioned name,' Mum stated.

'Yes, I come from an old-fashioned family,' Lilith smiled, keeping her fangs hidden. I knew I had to do the same.

'So what do you do?' my father asked, picking up a spare rib.

'I work in a bar,' my beloved lied smoothly.

'And was that how you met?'

Lilith glanced at me and nodded.

'Yes, Alex is one of my regulars.'

'And how's your job, Son?'

'Fine. Still busy especially with Christmas fast approaching.'

We continued making small talk while we finished the meal. Then my Dad suggested we all walk up to the local pub.

Lilith and I walked a little way ahead but overheard everything my parents talked about.

'She's a striking looking woman,' my Mum said.

'Yes. A beauty. Not Alex's usual type either,' Dad replied.

'No. I always thought he'd get together with that woman from work. What's her name?'

I smiled to myself and Lilith noticed and held my hand that bit firmer.

'They are nice people,' she kept her voice low.

'Yes they are,' I agreed.

'And they adore you Alex,' Lilith added, warmly.

I smiled again and nodded.

'Yes and I have no idea why,' I laughed.

Lilith laughed too and then we entered the pub.

The four of us sat down with our drinks and soon we were talking about anything and everything.

'So have you heard from that sister of yours?' Mum asked.

'Not in a while. I keep meaning to phone her.'

'She's busy with the museum, putting on a new exhibit.'
'Really? What's Monica doing this time?'
'Why don't you go and see her? She'd love that.'
I nodded and agreed.
'I'd love to meet her,' Lilith admitted.
'We'll go and see her tomorrow,' I said.
'What about work?' My father asked.
'Oh I have a few days off,' I lied.
'Lucky devil; I never used to get as much time off as you seem to.'
My mother gave my father a sharp dig in the ribs with her elbow.
'Oh be quiet George. Lilith doesn't want to know about ancient history.'
Lilith laughed and shook her head.
'No it's fine,' she smiled.
'See, Amanda? She wants to hear me out. Good for you love!'
And so the rest of the evening in the pub was spent with dad talking about his working days as an engineer. He also talked about lots of events that had happened in his life time. I was thankful that Lilith didn't do the same because we would have been there all night.

My parents invited us to stay the night and since neither of us needed to feed, we agreed.

We had just crossed the road in front of my parent's house when we heard the screech of brakes and the squeal of tyres. A car came hurtling around the corner and mounted the pavement, crashing into the hedge just behind my walking parents.

'Mum!' I shouted out.

My parents were shaken but unhurt.

A youth got out from behind the steering wheel. He seemed uninjured but I could see his passenger was badly hurt.

'Call for an ambulance, Dad,' I said, going round to the passenger side of the crashed car.

'Of course.'

My parents went inside the house while Lilith stayed with me.

'What are you looking at, bitch?'

The youth glared at Lilith but she ignored him.

I, meanwhile, had wrenched the car door open.

'I'm out of here,' the driver said, beginning to run away, but Lilith appeared as if by magic in front of him further up the road. Only I had seen her actually move.

'Leaving the scene of a crime, huh?' she asked.

'What? How?' he stuttered.

But that was as far as he got because Lilith grabbed him by the collar and yanked him off his feet, dragging him back towards the car, just as my father came back out.

'Ambulance is on the way,'

I nodded in response and took another look at the crash victim.

There was still no response from the lad; he was out cold.

The struggling driver cursed Lilith but she held him without effort until the ambulance and a police car showed up a few minutes later.

The police took our statements and then took the driver away for questioning. His companion was whisked away by the ambulance, while the crashed car was towed away by the local garage service.

'Well, young lady. I'm impressed,' my Dad said.

We were all now seated back in the lounge, hot drinks sitting in front of us on the coffee table.

'How do you mean Mr King?'

'Oh call me George. I was impressed by your strength my dear. You held onto him as if he was a doll.'

Lilith gave my father a small smile but didn't say anything, instead just taking a sip from her coffee.

'Lilith used to be an athlete at school,' I explained. 'She was very good.'

My father nodded and glanced at my mother.

'You okay dear?' he asked her.

'Yes. Just a little shaken still.'

'Only natural,' Lilith said. 'It will pass.'

Shortly after my mother went to bed and to my surprise Lilith did too, leaving me sitting up talking with my father.

'She's quite a girl,' he stated.

'Yes she is.'

'Beautiful and strong too.'

'Yes.' I agreed again.

'Where did you say you met her?'

'Where she works: a bar in Camden.'

'And are things serious between you?'

'Yes Dad. I love her.'

'But why haven't you mentioned her before? How long have you known this woman?'

'Not long,' I admitted. 'But it just feels like it's meant to be, you know? 'Like she's the one?'

My father nodded.
'Like it was when I met your mother. Sometimes you just know.'
'That's very true.'
My father finished his tea.
'And this Lilith feels the same way about you?'
But before I could answer my father placed his hand on my arm.
'What am I asking that for? Of course she does. I've seen the way she looks at you.'
'Really? How does she look at me?'
My father shrugged.
'Like you're the last man on earth.'

I can't tell you how much I wanted to tell my father then. How much I wanted to tell him the truth about me no longer being just a man. And yet I couldn't bring myself to do it. My father and I had always been close but this was something I was never able to tell him.

The following year he was to die suddenly of cancer and it remains my biggest regret to date that I never confided in him about my transformation into a vampire. I did tell my mother my secret a couple of years later, but it isn't the time for that part of the story.

Chapter 24

Luckily for us, the next day the weather was very poor. The wind had picked up during the night and had brought with it skies full of dark and heavy rain clouds.

Lilith and I were free to move around outside like any normal couple. Any normal couple who liked walking in the rain that is.

And so, after saying goodbye to my parents we made our way across town to the museum where my sister Monica had worked for many years now. She was widely expected to take over as the director one day. Her showcase on ancient Egypt had won her much acclaim the previous year, bringing in tourists from all over Europe, quite an accomplishment for a small town.

We found her in her small office off to the side of a display that was dedicated to minerals and rock samples.

'Hello Monica,' I greeted her with a smile and a hug. 'This is Lilith.'

My sister was a lot shorter than me but other than that we were pretty much alike. Her short brown hair was cut neatly and her clear blue eyes shone brightly behind her glasses. She was dressed in a long lilac skirt and cream coloured blouse.

'Alex. Haven't seen you in ages,' Monica said. 'Nice to meet you,' she smiled at Lilith and my beloved gave a slight nod.

'Alex is very proud of you,' Lilith said. 'He talked about you all the way over from your parent's house.'

Monica laughed and playfully hit me on the arm.

'My brother always did look out for me.'

This was true. I was two years older than her and had always kept an eye on Monica at school. But I needn't have worried. Monica had always been the smart one, not only clever but artistic as well.

'Come with me,' Monica said. 'I want to show you the new exhibition I'm working on.'

We followed her out of her office and down a short corridor that came to a wall with double doors. My sister unlocked them and pushed her way into a large room. She flicked on the light switches and Lilith and I audibly gasped in shock at what we saw.

'Welcome to the world of the supernatural,' Monica said cheerfully, waving an arm at the display cases.

Lilith and I were amazed to see displays on werewolves, ghosts, goblins and land monsters. There was a case with a life sized mermaid sitting on a rock by a pool of water. Another display case held a small oak tree.

'Watch,' my sister said.

She stepped up to the case and pressed a button on the side of it. Suddenly the tree faded to black as little pricks of coloured lights began to swirl around its branches. The pricks of light began to grow until we could clearly see they were actually little fairies dancing and flitting about. We could also hear soft flute music being played as the fairies continued to dance and play.

Monica pressed the button again and the lights went out and the tree was just a tree again.

'Wow Monica! That's amazing!' I clapped her on the back.

'Truly stunning,' Lilith added.

'Thanks. Took a lot to work out, but I'm pleased with the results.'

We moved away from the fairies case and then came face to face with another. This one housed a Count Dracula type of figure, in the process of biting into a female victim's neck.

'Behold the mighty vampire,' Monica laughed. 'We've obviously caught him at a bad time.'

Lilith glanced at me with a small smile but didn't say anything.

'This is amazing work Monica,' I said.

'Thanks. I've still got a fair bit to do yet before it's ready for viewing though.'

'How much work?' Lilith asked.

'Well, for one, I want the mermaid animated. I want to work it so that she brushes her hair and a small fish leaps out of the water and goes back in again. You know? A continual loop.'

'Sounds good,' I exclaimed.

'I also want the werewolf to howl and bare his teeth as people walk up to the display case. It's all about motion sensors. Not cheap, but I've been given a generous budget so…' Monica trailed off and we followed her over to a seating area. We all sat down and I felt an immense new respect for my sister. I knew she worked hard, but to see it close at hand was really amazing. At that moment I was truly proud to be her brother.

'If you need more sponsorship please let me know,' Lilith said. 'It really isn't a problem for me. Money I mean.'

Monica smiled and looked at me.

'It looks like my brother fell on his feet with you then, Lilith. You're beautiful and rich!'

All three of us laughed and glanced around the room once more.

'I know a fair bit about the supernatural too,' Lilith again spoke and stood up, hands on her hips. 'You could say it's a hobby of mine.'

She smiled and to my amazement she actually revealed her fangs to my sister.

Monica's mouth dropped open in surprise.

'What? Are you into vampires and stuff then?'

Lilith inclined her head as a positive response.

'You could say that.'

'Oh cool. I mean, any input would be greatly appreciated," Monica stood up and took a few paces away.

'You know, I have always found female vampires to be just as much, if not more popular, than male ones,' my beloved said.

Monica spun on her heels and nodded.

'Yes, you're right. I argued that point with the director but he was adamant that we should have a Dracula figure.'

Lilith walked over to that particular cabinet and gazed at it through the glass. I saw a wry smile on her beautiful lips in the reflection.

'Well, I've always found the Count to be over-rated,' she said.

My sister went over and joined her at the case.

'Any ideas?' she asked eagerly.

I have to say I was finding this very amusing; my artistic sister taking advice on a vampire display from a real vampire. I was struggling not to laugh.

'I have been told by many admirers that I have the looks and poise for a perfect female vampire. I could be your authentic life model if you wish?'

It was my turn to gape in shock. My beloved was offering to stand in full public display, showing off her vampirism.

'Lilith?' I asked, incredulous at this turn of events.

She turned to me, a smile on her face.

'Just imagine it Alex,' she said. 'A life model is so much better than a mannequin. Every time.'

My sister clapped her hands in delight.

'Are you sure? That would be amazing. I'm not sure we'd be able to pay you though.'

Lilith shook her head and gently touched my sister on her arm.

'No need. I will be happy to do this for you.'

'Well, thanks, but can I do something in return?'

Lilith considered this for a few moments.

'Only that you allow me to provide my own clothes. And maybe have Alex in the display too?'

Lilith surprised me once again

'You want me in there too?'

'Yes my love. As my victim.'

I did laugh then, but my sister jumped up and down on the spot in girlish delight.

'That would look really good. And blood? Can you provide imitation blood, Lilith?'

'I think that can be arranged,' Lilith smiled, glancing at me.

'When is the exhibit due to open?' I asked.

'Next Saturday is the grand opening,' Monica told us.

'We will be ready,' Lilith said and opened the display case.

She stood still for a few seconds before suddenly sweeping her arm in an arc dramatically outwards, sending the figures of Dracula and his victim, flying across the room.

'Step aside Count. It's my time now.'

Chapter 25

Lilith told my sister that we would do one performance for the opening night and then see how it went. Monica readily agreed and was even more stunned when my beloved handed her a signed blank cheque.
'Whatever the cost,' Lilith had told her, 'just fill in the amount.'
The two of us had returned to London and we were curled up on the brand new black leather sofa that Lilith had had delivered.
'What are you thinking?' Lilith asked.
I kissed the top of her head and my Lily laced her fingers through mine.
'This all seems so utterly perfect, yet if our enemies had their way we would be destroyed in the blink of an eye.'
Lilith squeezed my fingers just a little.
'I have had to face that possibility for years now, Alex. And yet still I live to tell the tale.'
I shook my head and brought her face around to look at me.
'I don't understand Lily. If the Morisakis were truly determined to kill you, why haven't they already done so?'
My beloved sighed in that all too familiar way of hers.
'I don't have an answer for you. Perhaps they like to bide their time. Perhaps they think the endless waiting game will be my downfall? Who knows?'
'And there's nowhere we can go to be safe from them?'
'None I can think of.'
We kissed and held one another for a while longer but both knew we needed to feed.

So within the hour Lilith and I took to the air and made our way swiftly over the twinkling lights of our capital. The night air seemed soothing somehow.
'Where are we going?' I asked.
'I've heard rumours that the Morisakis own a small Italian restaurant. I want to check it out, to see if it's true or not.'
'But I thought we were going to feed.'
'Patience, my darling,' she said.
After another two minutes of flying Lilith paused in mid air and scanned the area below us.
'Yes, this is the right district.'

And with that, she began to float downwards, so I followed.
We landed on the roof of a carpet shop, opposite a restaurant.
'Why have we come here?' I asked.
'I've decided to take the fight to them Alex,' she replied, grimly.
'For what purpose?'
'To show I'm done with waiting. This ends one way or another soon.'
I had yet to see my beloved so determined and from one glance into her eyes I knew she was going to go ahead with whatever idea she was planning.
'Well, whatever you decide, I will be with you,' I smiled.
Lilith smiled too and gave me a quick kiss before resuming her watch on the restaurant.
'It's almost closing time. We'll wait for the last customers to leave then we'll strike.'
'But surely if the Morisakis do own this place, there will be a vampire or two in residence?'
Lilith looked at me.
'Open your mind and scan the building Alex.'
I did so as I had done that ill-fated day when I had met William, my vampire senses telling me there were three vampires inside.
'Well?'
'I count three vampires in there,' I told her.
Lilith nodded.
'Good. And your senses may have also told you that only one is over a hundred years old, no match for me.'
'Okay. So what shall we do?'
'We wait,' was the firm reply.

Ten minutes later, we saw a couple leave and the waiter who showed them out turned a sign on the door to say it was closed.
'Let's go, Alex.'
Lilith dropped from the roof with me in pursuit. We quickly crossed the deserted street and without preamble my Lily charged through the glass front door, sending shards of mini projectiles flying inwards.
'What the..?' cried the waiter, but he didn't finish his sentence because Lilith was on him, biting deep into his neck. A male vampire rushed at her but I intercepted him and drove my fist into his face, sending him sprawling over a couple of tables.
Lilith jumped up from the still-bleeding waiter and hurled herself at a

female vampire, who had just come from the kitchen area. They both crashed through the doors of the kitchen out of sight.

Meanwhile, my opponent was back on his feet and it was then that I realised this wasn't going to be as easy as fighting an ordinary man.

'Who are you?' he hissed, licking blood from his cut lip.

'Your enemy,' I said as I stood calmly, waiting for the attack.

It came, but not from him. Another vampire had crept around the side out of sight and I cursed myself for not using my senses properly.

I didn't have time to react as the force of the man's blow sent me flying across the room into a large mirror. I landed in a heap on the floor, glass shards all around and over me.

I didn't have time to reflect on seven years of bad luck because both vampires came at me again. I managed to get to my feet and block one punch but the other assailant got a kick into my chest that hurt like hell. I crashed with the impact into the bar, knocking over glasses and bottles.

I was quite stunned by the kick. My breath had been driven out of my body and knew I was probably in for a lot more punishment.

But then I looked up to see my two attackers stop their forward movements. They were looking beyond me towards the kitchen.

'You are a vampire! You don't need air to breathe!' A voice in my head suddenly made things clear to me. I don't know where the voice had come from but I raised my head and saw my darling Lily standing there. It wasn't the fact she was standing there that had got the men's attention. It was more to do with the fact she was holding the severed head of the female vampire, blood dripping from the neck onto the carpet. In her other hand, blood also dripping, was a large lethal looking meat cleaver.

'You! You killed Rachel!' my first attacker screamed.

I saw Lilith smile and hurl the head to the floor.

'Want to join her in death?' she grinned, showing her fangs.

And before anything else was said Lilith took to the air, her left boot connecting solidly with the chin of the one who had spoken. He cried out as he sailed across the room and landed with a crunch among other tables. Furniture and cutlery went everywhere as he came to a halt unconscious against the wall.

I slowly got to my feet as the last vampire attacked Lilith. He managed to knock her legs from under her and was immediately on top of her, his fingers squeezing at her neck.

Lilith tried to kick him off but the vampire was strong, his choke hold was clearly having an effect.

That was until I decided to intervene.

I charged at him and with all the power I could muster, ripping the creature off of her and hurled him through the front window of the restaurant. Glass and blinds littered the pavement outside. Not stopping to help my Lily up I jumped through the window and grabbed the vampire again.

'You had your chance,' I hissed, driving my fist into his stomach. I followed this up with a punch to his jaw which sent teeth and spittle flying from his mouth. His head snapped back and collided with the brick wall. The vampire slumped unconscious to the ground and yet I did not halt my attack. Instead I unleashed the fury of the demon that dwells within me. I gripped his hair and smashed his face into the wall again. And again. And a third time. His face and nose were ruined, nothing more than a bloody mess. I knew he would probably heal from the wounds but I didn't care. The monster had tried to kill Lilith and that made me so angry, I wasn't really thinking any more. I was about to do it a fourth time when I felt Lilith touch me on the shoulder.

'Alex, it's over,' she said softly.

I looked at her, the vampire's hair still in the grip of my powerful right hand.

'Over?' I wasn't sure what she meant.

'This battle,' she clarified for me.

I let go of the vampire and he fell silently to the concrete.

'Bring him back inside.'

I shrugged but did as she asked. Once inside, Lilith grabbed hold of the meat cleaver again. I then stared in shock and astonishment as she proceeded to hack the legs off of both vampires. It didn't take much effort on her part; just a few swings of her powerful arm, and when she was done, Lilith threw the cleaver across the room.

'Right. Get clear Alex; I'm going to torch the place.'

'But Lilith I…'

'Go!'

I did as she told me and left by the ruined front entrance. I made my way back onto the roof of the carpet shop and waited.

A few minutes later Lilith joined me. The first tell-tale signs of a fire were evident as smoke began to pour out of the front.

'I ripped out the sprinklers,' Lilith said. 'The whole fucking place will go up like a Roman fucking candle.'

I didn't answer, instead I just watched as the fire quickly took hold.

'Lilith I, I don't know what to say,' I stammered.

'Shssh. It's alright Alex. We'll talk about this later.'

But I was far from happy. I don't know why, but I was shocked and even a little bit appalled by her coldness, by her remorseless and cruel actions.

'Talk to me Lilith! Why this extreme?'

My beloved glanced at me and for a moment I saw the fury in those eyes. But it was quickly gone, to be replaced by a shining light of steely determination.

'This is the only way, Alex,' she said. 'You were right! We have to take the fight to the Morisakis.'

'But won't this make them even more determined to destroy you?'

'Of course, but we have to do something. I'm not prepared to just wait for the coming attack. We'll keep drawing as much attention to ourselves as we possibly can. All of vampire kind will know of us soon my darling. And we will make it impossible for the Truest not to help us. You'll see.'

I stared at her but her attention was back on the now raging fire. No alarms had gone off so I assumed she had destroyed those as well.

When she was satisfied with what she saw, Lilith turned to me, a serene and most beautiful smile on her lips.

'Now my dear Alex, are you hungry?'

After the fight with the vampires I had to admit the bloodlust was boiling beneath the surface. It needed quenching and fast.

'Yes my Lily,' I answered.

'I fed on that waiter as you saw but I'm sure we can find you some tasty morsel or other,' my beloved's smile broadened, flashing her fangs.

Only a few minutes later we happened to come across a robbery in progress. A man was trying to force his way into a locked house with a crowbar.

Lilith stood off to one side watching as I approached him in silence to stand behind him.

The man grunted with the effort and managed to force the door open.

'Somehow I don't think you live there,' I said.

The man almost dropped the crowbar in panic but managed to keep hold of it and turned to face me.

'This doesn't concern you, so sod off,' he growled.

I stood there looking at him from the shadows, hands behind my back.

'It concerns me greatly that you don't show me any respect.'

The robber laughed and took a step forwards, the nearby streetlight glinting in reflection off the crowbar.

'Come again?' he asked.
'It's really rather simple,' I said. 'Either you respect me or face the consequences.'
'Oh really? And just how will that happen? You'll take me to court? I'm the one who's armed here pal, not you.'
The robber took another step forward but I stood my ground.
'End it Alex. I want to go home,' a familiar voice broke the tension.
The man then saw Lilith behind me and stopped moving.
'Hey, now that is a nice piece of woman. Maybe I'll have some of that before I do this place.'
I sighed and took a step towards him.
'You don't respect me and now you insult the love of my life. What are we to do with you?'
Lilith gave a small giggle and suddenly the man swung the crowbar at my head. Compared to the speed the vampires moved earlier this was too easy. Again it was like watching the man move in slow motion. I easily ducked under the blow and avoided a jab at my ribs, by leaping to one side.
'I can avoid your blows all night my friend,' I taunted him. 'But can you avoid mine?'
He tried once again to smash me with the bar but this time I grabbed it and twisted it from his grip. Then with the bar in my hands I drove it as hard as I could through his left thigh. The man screamed in agony and collapsed to the ground. With my vampiric vision I could see the straight end of the crowbar sticking out the other side of his leg.
'That was careless of me, I do apologise.'
'Drink, Alex and let's get home,' Lilith hissed.
I had to admit I enjoyed toying with the man. After my battle with the vampires this was what I needed, a nice easy opponent who offered no threat at all. But Lilith was right. It was time to end it so I dipped my head in and bit the side of his neck. He offered almost no resistance as I took his blood and then sealed the wound.
I knew fully well he would probably die if I left him there, unconscious with the crowbar still embedded in his leg and yet I simply could not bring myself to care. So I left him where he lay and took to the air with Lilith, to head home.

Bloodlust satisfied, I still had another hunger in me and grabbed Lilith once we had entered our bedroom and threw her onto the bed. Before she could protest I was on her, ripping at her dress and taking a nipple in my mouth.

Our love-making was the most violent to date and yet utterly stupendous. We switched positions three or four times until in the end I took her from behind, cupping her breasts as I thrust deep within her until finally we were both sated and happy at the release.

I collapsed onto the bed beside her, breathing deeply. Lilith lay on her back, staring at the ceiling, also breathing deep and sustaining breaths.

Once I had recovered I lay on my side and placed my hand onto her cheek, stroking that perfect skin. I traced my finger from her nose up to beneath her eye and back onto her lips, where she briefly sucked on it.

'May I ask you something?'

Lilith turned then, her gaze locking onto mine.

'Of course,' she said, 'anything.'

I ran my fingers over her breast and circled around the nipple, which was still hard. Sweat still glistened in her cleavage but the scent of her remained intoxicating.

'Why did you chop their legs off?'

Lilith sighed and took my hand from her bosom and kissed each of my finger-tips.

'In case they woke up, Alex. I had to do something to stop them escaping the fire. I'm pretty sure they would have done.'

I saw the logic and yet still felt a little uneasy at her coldness; how easy it had been for her to do such a horrific thing. I guess the human in me was still protesting against the demon within me, something I was going to have to straighten out the longer I lived.

'I have a question for you,' Lilith said, her hand sliding up to stroke my face.

'Okay.'

'Why did you like tormenting that robber?'

I laughed and Lilith continued to gaze at me, her expression never wavering.

'Because I just did,' I replied.

'No. It was like you got a kick out of it.'

I smiled and knew she had seen through me.

'Yes,' I said. 'I enjoyed toying with him. He was completely pathetic after those vampires. Too easy. That's why I enjoyed teasing the man.'

Lilith nodded and ran a hand through her hair. It had become a bit tangled and untidy with the love-making, but she still looked absolutely stunning.

'Yes,' she agreed. 'I used to do that. Still do sometimes. It's true that in all walks of life the powerful always strike at the weak.'

'Human nature,' I added.

'Which apparently continues to live on after the vampire has taken over,' she said, archly.

'So where do we go from here, my darling?' I asked.

"Well, we could make love again or fall into a contented sleep. As for tomorrow who knows? Why don't we just take one day at a time?'

Chapter 26

We heard on the local news the next day of the 'mysterious' fire that claimed the life of a waiter in an Italian restaurant. Naturally there was no mention of the three vampires we had slain, for Lilith tells me that a vampire is literally reduced to mere dust when burnt. No teeth, bones or anything else remain.

My beloved turned off the television and I saw a satisfied expression on her face.

I was about to comment on it when there was a noise outside.

Lilith, dressed in a dark blue dress, looked out of the back door and then opened it. It was already getting late, for we had slept most of the day again. The sun had long since sunk in the sky.

'What do you want?' she asked.

'To talk to you. Please,' said a man's voice.

Lilith hesitated for a moment before stepping back and allowing a young man to walk past her into the lounge.

He looked vaguely familiar and then I realised it was Jodie's friend, James. He somewhat nervously sat on the sofa opposite the fire.

'I don't wish to disturb you but I come with a request.'

'Which is?' Lilith asked, coming to stand at my side.

'Jodie got into a fight last night. She was taken by some woman calling herself Cecilia.'

I glanced at Lilith who crossed her arms, staring at James.

'Jodie went up against Cecilia?'

James shook his head.

'No. No, she got drunk and started a fight with a vampire. Some guy. But then this woman turned up and all hell broke loose.'

'Where was this?' I asked.

'Covent Garden.'

Lilith studied her finger nails.

'And this concerns us how?' she said, after a moment's silence.

'What? She needs you! You have to help!'

Within the blink of an eye Lilith had James up against the wall, her right hand shoved hard into his neck. I saw that his feet were off the ground.

'We don't have to do anything!' she hissed. 'Jodie made her choice. She sired you and made you weak.'

James struggled uselessly in her powerful grip.

'On the other hand…' Lilith lowered him slowly to the floor and stepped away, glancing at me.
'What is it Lily?'
'Do you know where she was taken?' she turned back to James.
'Yes, I saw. They took her to apartments above a club there.'
I got to my feet and Lilith smiled.
'I think we should pay the True Species a visit.'

Soon James was guiding us to where the Truest were hiding. We had taken to the air, with me holding him. The journey didn't take long and soon we had landed outside the club, which wasn't open.
However two heavy set men stood outside the main entrance.
'Club's closed miss,' one of them growled.
Lilith offered him her best smile.
'You have a friend of mine here. I want to see her. And while I see her I want to have a talk with Cecilia.'
The man, who was human, stepped towards her.
'There's no one here. As I said, club's closed.'
His colleague took a step towards James and me.
'You're not going to give us any trouble are you?' he grinned, as if his shear size was meant to frighten me.
'That depends,' I smiled, standing my ground. 'Are you?'
The doorman frowned and made a move to place his hand on my shoulder. I flicked my arm at his wrist instead and with a slight twist sent him crashing to the ground.
'Hey!'
The other guard stepped towards me but then had his arm twisted savagely behind his back by Lilith, who hissed into his ear.
'Cecilia knows me. Take me to her. Now.'
The doorman I had thrown over glared up at me but didn't move. His companion tried to break my beloved's grip but couldn't do it.
'Struggle all you want, it will only hurt,' Lilith sighed.
'Okay lady. Just don't twist it anymore. Please.'
'And you'll take us to Cecilia?' I asked.
'Yes. Now let me go.'
I watched as Lilith relaxed her grip on the man's arm.
'Lead on,' she said determinedly.

The two men walked around the back of the club and up to a fire escape.

They began to climb it but Lilith didn't wait. Instead she leapt straight to the third floor and yanked open a door.

I quickly followed her through the door. The leap up was too much for James so he had to follow the two doormen.

'Cecilia,' Lilith called and suddenly there she was, stepping out of the shadows, wearing a gold dress.

'Lilith O'Shea.' She smiled but it was a cold and calculated smile.

The two women faced each other and then from another doorway, the two vampires we had met at Jacob's club came out, one of whom held a bound and gagged Jodie.

'So Lilith, you found our little hideaway,' Cecilia said. 'What is it you want? And please don't tell me it's the snivelling little girl.'

'That snivelling little girl is a friend of mine. The Morisakis killed her lover and sire. She's under my charge now.'

Cecilia cocked her head in a bird-like fashion.

'Under your charge? And yet you allow her to wander off to cause trouble? To pick fights with vampires far more powerful than even you? Come now, Lilith O'Shea, what example are you setting the poor child?'

I remained silent and watched as my beloved's eyes narrowed at the insult.

'You're right of course Cecilia,' Lilith told her. 'And for that I humbly apologise. But we had had a disagreement and she left my protection of her own accord.'

Cecilia stepped over to the trembling Jodie and gently stroked her face.

'A disagreement you say? Can hardly be serious if you willingly risk your own life to come and get her.'

Lilith shook her head.

'No. It was just a silly argument. I never meant her to leave.'

'And yet, she did exactly that. Curious.'

The powerful vampire suddenly bit into Jodie's neck and our companion cried out.

I didn't care how powerful she was, I wasn't about to let her kill Jodie without a fight. But before I could make a move, Cecilia withdrew her mouth from her neck and spat out the blood she had begun to suck.

'My god, she is weak,' Cecilia snapped. 'She is of no use to me. I can't even bring myself to kill the poor child.'

The vampire mistress stepped away from her and then glared at the two doormen who had finally caught us up.

'You two are worse than useless. Come here!' she demanded.

The two men glanced at each other before stepping forward.

'Lilith O'Shea. Would you care to dine?' Cecilia smiled and suddenly pushed one of the men over to my beloved.

'Gladly,' Lilith smiled in return and without further ado sank her teeth into the big man's throat. I watched as Cecilia did the same to her other doorman. Both female vampires drank hungrily until finally they both let their victims fall to the floor. Even from where I stood I knew both men were dead and glancing at Lilith I had never seen her look so radiant, so full of colour and life.

'Thank you,' she said simply to Cecilia, who gave a small bow.

Then the vampire mistress walked over to me and placed a finger to my lips.

'What is it you wish to talk to me about?' she asked Lilith, as she traced my mouth with the finger. I just stood still and said nothing.

Lilith hesitated, concern suddenly upon her features.

'I have come to ask you to reconsider allowing us to join you,' she finally said, her eyes locked onto mine.

'Have you now?' Cecilia said softly, her finger suddenly digging into the flesh of my cheek, drawing blood.

Lilith made no move to stop her and instead merely watched as Cecilia ran her tongue over my bloody cheek.

'Ah much better,' she said. 'You made him well, blood sister.'

Suddenly she pushed me away from her and turned her attention back to Lilith.

'And what makes you think I will change my mind?'

Lilith bowed her head for a moment and then looked up again, meeting her nemesis' gaze.

'Because we can be of use to you.'

Cecilia laughed.

'I hardly think so. I have more than enough followers, thank you.'

'But we have a common enemy,' Lilith protested.

Cecilia was about to reply when suddenly the whole building shook, almost as if an earth-quake had struck London.

'What in God's name?' she hissed, moving towards the door we had entered.

Suddenly half the wall and the door itself was blown inwards and once the dust had finally settled we all looked to see a solitary figure standing there.

Wiping the dust off of his finely made suit jacket, a Chinese man stepped forwards. He was quite short and only slightly built. He was in his 60's I would have guessed, but possibly older. And despite his fairly small stature, he carried himself as if he didn't have a fear in the world. I tried reading his mind but was met by a blank and dark wall. He glanced at me briefly and a small smile appeared, but then his attention was instantly drawn back to Cecilia.

'What is this?' he demanded in broken English. 'Why are two of the finest female vampires that ever walked the earth at each other's throats like dogs?'

To my astonishment my beloved sank to one knee and kissed the new-comer's hand.

Cecilia, on the other hand glared at the Chinese man.

'How dare you enter my property in this way?' she hissed and took half a step towards him. But with the merest of gestures, the new-comer waved his hand and an invisible force struck out at the mistress vampire, sending her flying backwards into a wall, knocking down pictures as she slumped to the wooden floor.

'Foolish child!' he snapped. 'Do you not know who I am?'

'I do,' Lilith said softly. 'I know who you are.'

The Chinese man looked down at Lilith and with the hand that she had kissed, touched her gently on the head.

I was still recovering, not only from the fact that had he sent a vampire as powerful as Cecilia flying with hardly any movement, but also the fact he had called her a child.

'Then who am I Lilith O'Shea of Dublin?' he raised her up by her chin but only gently, almost like a father getting the attention of his precious daughter.

'Why? It can only be you Zang Zing. My lord.'

Chapter 27

Cecilia's two vampire companions immediately made a move to confront the new-comer but the Chinese man waved his arm towards them and the same thing happened: both male vampires flew backwards and crashed into a wall. One of them smashed head-first into a large plasma screen.

Meanwhile, Cecilia had got to her feet.

'Zang Zing? That's just a myth,' she spat, glaring at the Chinese vampire.

Before he could answer, Lilith turned to face Cecilia.

'Think about it Cecilia. What more proof do you need?'

I watched as the two beautiful female vampires faced off once again while Zang Zing stood impassive, a bemused smile on his otherwise serene face.

Finally Cecilia bowed her head.

'I am honoured to have you visit my home,' she said softly.

Zang Zing smiled and stepped forward, taking Lilith's hand as he went towards Cecilia.

'You should not be fighting,' he told them. 'You are blood sisters. Kiss and make up.'

To my amazement Lilith and Cecilia did exactly that. They kissed one another on the cheek and as they separated I heard them both apologise.

'Good. Now let us talk.'

Zang Zing went and sat down on a red settee, the whole room being white with red furniture. Lilith glanced at me and made a follow me gesture with her finger. I sat down beside her opposite Zang Zing.

Cecilia sat in a single seat to one side, while her recovering companions stood at either side of her.

'Oh and before I forget...' With a slight wave of his finger, Jodie's bonds that had held her slipped loose and to the floor. Although slightly unsteady on her feet, Jodie made her way over to Lilith.

'I'm so sorry for leaving you,' she said, tears coming to her eyes.

'Hush now child,' Zang Zing said instead, 'come to me young one.'

Jodie hesitated but a slight nod from Lilith was enough to move her to stand by the mighty vampire.

'Lilith forgives you child. Now take some of my blood and become instantly stronger.'

Again Jodie hesitated but Zang Zing raised his wrist to her mouth and gave her a reassuring smile.

'Go on,' he whispered.

Jodie slowly kissed the offered wrist at first before biting into it. I watched Zang Zing close his eyes as Jodie began to drink the ancient one's blood.

After no more than a few seconds, Jodie staggered back and gazed in awe at the Chinese man before her.

'I feel... different,' she said, struggling for words.

Zang Zing bowed his head with a smile.

'You will,' Lilith explained. 'You've just fed from the most powerful vampire in the world.'

Jodie looked at her and her eyes narrowed. Then before any of us could stop her she threw herself at Cecilia's companion on her right.

'Bastard!' she snarled and dug her now very powerful fingers into the vampire's eyes. He cried out in pain and shock, and we all saw blood begin to run freely from the wounds Jodie had inflicted.

'Stop child!'

Those two words from Zang Zing were enough to bring Jodie back from her rage. She immediately jumped off of the fallen vampire and took a step back.

'I know what he did to you child. Believe me when I say, he will be punished.'

Jodie looked at Zang Zing and gave a small nod before sitting down next to him, once he had patted the settee.

'How do you know what he did to her?' I asked.

For the first time since he had entered in such dramatic fashion, Zang Zing turned his shining black eyes upon me.

'I know everything that goes on with vampire kind, Alex,' he said.

'You know me?'

'But of course! You are the only vampire with another's soul, truly unique and far more powerful than even your maker realises.'

I stared at him at this revelation but not understanding what he meant by it.

'Am I truly unique?' I kept the question to myself but as if reading my mind, Zang Zing smiled and gave me the answer.

'Yes, Alex. A part of Severin still lives within you. Or at least his demon half does. Somehow your own vampire spirit has merged with his, all set into motion once Lilith had sired you, as she did with Severin all those centuries ago. You will no doubt find your powers will grow at an exceptional rate. Severin's soul called out to Lilith from within you. Once she had created the vampire who stands before us now, she created a truly unique being.'

He turned his gaze on Lilith who shyly looked away, leaving me to ponder his words in silent amazement.

'This is all very interesting,' Cecilia said, 'but so what? What do we have to talk about?'

Zang Zing gave a little tutting noise and turned to her.

'I would have thought that after 1200 years Cecilia, you would have learned to be more patient.'

'Why are you here?'

Although I disliked her, I had to admire Cecilia's courage.

Zang Zing looked at her companion, the one Jodie had attacked.

'My question first: why did you rape this child?'

Cecilia's vampire shook his head, his eyes still hadn't recovered from the assault.

'I didn't. I didn't rape her,' he denied, shaking his head again.

'Liar!' Zang Zing roared and clapped his hands together.

We all looked in astonishment as the guilty vampire's head suddenly exploded. Flesh, blood and brain flew in all directions and the rest of his body crumpled to the carpet.

Jodie gave a small shriek of delight and clapped her hands.

Zang Zing gave her a gentle pat on the arm and turned his gaze back to a clearly shaken Cecilia.

'We have much to discuss. The night goes on and I grow tired of these games,' he declared.

It turned out that Zang Zing had decided to return to unite all of vampire kind. He told us he would not rest until the Morisakis and the True Species were all part of the one group, dedicated to keeping the peace.

'Fear not, Lilith O'Shea. You are under my protection now.'

'Thank you my lord, but what of the Morisakis?'

'Firstly, I am merely a vampire, same as you. I am not of noble blood so please refrain from calling me lord. As for your enemies, I will find them and make them see reason.'

'You mean, go to Paris?' Cecilia asked.

'Yes Cecilia. That is what I intend to do.'

'When will you go?' Lilith asked.

'Tomorrow night. Soon this war between our peoples will be at an end.'

'Why do this?' I inquired, still thinking about all he had told me.

'Because I am sick and tired of knowing of the petty fighting that is going on,' Zang Zing explained. 'The Morisakis enforce laws which they then break themselves! This madness has to stop.'

Cecilia shook her head.

'And what of the True Species? What will you do about us?'

Zang Zing looked at her.

'You will still have to abide by the laws. Humans are not ready to accept us, even you must know this Cecilia.'

'Accept us? Why should we give them a choice?' she hissed.

'Because there are far fewer vampires in existence than you believe. And it is for this reason, humans would reject you and ultimately destroy you.'

Cecilia glared at him but said nothing.

'Now, I will leave you,' Zang Zing got up as if to go.

'I have a question,' I blurted out.

'Yes?'

'Why am I unique? I still don't understand.'

Zang Zing smiled.

'All will be revealed young Alex. In good time.'

He turned to go, but stopped and placed a hand gently on Jodie's head.

'Fear no more little one, but be with Lilith. She is wise beyond her 450 years.'

And with that Zang Zing simply disappeared. I neither saw him walk or fly away.

Cecilia crossed her arms and looked at Lilith.

'Do you believe him? Do you believe he will talk to the Morisakis?'

'I do,' my beloved answered simply.

'And you truly think the Morisakis will leave you be?'

Lilith shrugged.

'Until today I wasn't sure Zang Zing was real. You saw his power. I believe he can do anything.'

Cecilia gave a small smile.

'I see. But what's to now stop me from destroying you myself?'

Before Lilith could reply Zang Zing materialized beside her.

'I will stop you,' he said, gripping Cecilia by the throat.

'What? How did?..'

'This is your last warning, Cecilia. If you two can't get along, I know who I will choose to keep alive.'

He squeezed a bit harder and Cecilia began to choke.

'I think she understands,' Lilith said calmly.

Zang Zing gazed into Cecilia's eyes and gave a slight nod.

'Yes, I believe she does.'

He let go and again blinked out of sight.

We decided to leave Cecilia to her coughing and her remaining companion and soon the four of us were back in Camden.

'Jodie, James can stay here with you for as long he wants okay?'

'Thank you Lilith,' Jodie gave her a hug and then the two of them went up the stairs together.

I crossed over to the fire and began to pile on some logs.

'You are very quiet Alex. Is everything alright?'

I glanced up at Lilith as she sat down.

'I guess I'm still a little in awe of Zang Zing's power.'

Lilith smiled and beckoned me to her once the fire was lit.

'As should we all,' she said, kissing me.

'You knew he was real though didn't you?'

'I had my suspicions, yes,' she answered, her arms snaking around me so that we were once again huddled on the sofa.

'How?'

'Oh things that Christiano mentioned to me. Jacob too.'

'And he really will help us?'

'I believe him Alex. You should too.'

I fell silent and watched the flames taking hold, relaxing with my beloved's gentle stroking of my arm.

'So just how powerful is Jodie now?' I wondered aloud.

'I have no idea, but you saw how much faster and stronger she was earlier. And she can fly now, don't forget.'

This was true. She had easily scooped James up in her arms and joined us in our flight home.

'I will remember not to cross her,' I said, and nuzzled my lips into Lilith's hair and neck.

'You have nothing to fear, Alex. Not from her and not from the Morisakis after tomorrow night. I am convinced of that.'

I nodded, believing her.

'And what of Cecilia?'

'I don't think she'd dare hurt any of us again,' Lilith replied before grabbing my and placing it upon her breast.

Chapter 28

For the next few days we didn't hear a word from Zang Zing. The four of us carried on as normal, sleeping, hunting and feeding.

Although much weaker than the rest of us, James learnt quickly and Lilith and I watched with satisfaction as he took down a big brute of a man around the back of a theatre. Meanwhile, Jodie was revelling in her new powers. She enjoyed flying and as soon as it was dark she would take to the skies at every opportunity. Unfortunately this would mean leaving James behind. Unless Zang Zing gave him some blood too, Lilith feared James would never be powerful enough to do the things that now came naturally to me.

As for myself I had killed another man, and if I'm honest, I enjoyed it. Did this mean I was becoming a blood-thirsty killing machine, the type I always despised in books and movies? Perhaps so, but I was only doing as my darling advised. To give in to the spirit demon within every once in a while, instead of fighting against its naturally evil nature. I enjoyed seeing the look of terror in my victim's eyes once they knew what I was and that they were about to die. It wasn't a sexual thing. Far from it, because my days with Lilith were filled with lust and sexual contact, more than I could ever have imagined. But I can't deny the killings did give me pleasure, and as far as I'm aware, each and every one of my victims had committed a crime of some sort.

As far as we were concerned the threat of the Morisakis was over so Lilith and I appeared as promised for my sisters exhibit opening.

I was dressed in a plain white t-shirt (to show the blood better) and Lilith was dressed in the same night gown she had worn when she had first come to me.

We looked out at the public from the big glass display box. Lilith flashed them her fangs and with a smile she bit into my neck. Monica stood applauding with the rest of the viewers as blood began to pour from my neck.

'That's amazing! However did you pull it off?' one man asked Monica.

'With a bit of help,' she had replied.

Lilith's funding had come through and Monica had made the changes to the other displays that she had wanted. The werewolf now gave a thunderous roar every time someone stepped on a certain carpet tile, even scaring me the first time I heard it.

The mermaid was now able to physically brush her hair while cascades of water would shoot up from the pool she was sat by.

The evening was a huge success for my sister and the press she received afterwards was full of praise. We went back from time to time to re-enact our vampires embrace as the press called it. Sometimes I would be the victim and other times I would bite Lilith. And the odd time Jodie and James would take our places if we were elsewhere.

Monica never discovered how we had accomplished our realistic display until a few years later, but I will come to that particular tale later.

I had just finished making coffee, when there was a knock on the front door.

Lilith went to answer it and Zang Zing was standing there with a huge grin on his face. He finished embracing my beloved and came towards me, his hand outstretched.

I put the mugs of coffee down and shook hands with the ancient one.

'I bring good news,' he said. 'And no, I don't wish for coffee thank you Alex.'

He smiled at me, having easily read my mind.

'Please sit down,' Lilith said.

Zang Zing sat down in one of the singular chairs by the fire, while Lilith and I sat beside one another on the leather sofa.

'You have a nice home Lilith O'Shea.'

'Thank you.'

Zang Zing glanced around the walls before turning his gaze back to us.

'I have just come back from Paris,' he said. 'I spent an enjoyable time in the company of the Morisakis. They asked me to give you this.'

He reached into his jacket suit and withdrew a plain white envelope.

My Lily took the envelope from him and pulled out a single piece of parchment. I watched as she unfolded it and saw her eyes go wide with amazement.

'What does it say?' I asked. All I could make out were beautifully scripted letters.

'To the vampire Lilith O'Shea of Dublin. We, the Morisakis, keepers of the ancient laws, now wish our destruction of you purged,' Lilith read.

She glanced at Zang Zing and handed me the letter.

I read it as well and saw in astonishment that Zang Zing had signed it.

'You wrote this?' I asked.

He gave a little shake of his head.

'No Alex. But I signed it only when the Morisakis made me their leader. The old one, shall we say, perished.'

'So it is finally over? For real?' Lilith clasped my hand, her gaze still on the ancient vampire.

'Yes my child,' Zang Zing smiled. 'You need fear them no longer. Or should I say "us" now?'

He gave a little chuckle and then laughed when Lilith was suddenly at his feet kissing his hand.

'So what exactly happened in Paris?' I wanted to know the whole story.

Zang Zing told us that on first encountering the Morisakis, they had shown nothing but hostility towards him. Battles had been fought in the very heart of the French capital. Zang Zing had destroyed three of their most powerful members before the rest had agreed to sit down to discuss matters.

On realising that Zang Zing would protect Lilith and myself from 'everything and anything you throw at them' the Morisakis knew it was futile to proceed with their little vendetta. After all, according to Zang Zing, he had demonstrated his full power by walking out into direct sunlight. No force on earth could harm him now. So who better to have as leader than the mighty Zang Zing himself? On seeing them turn against him, the Morisakis high ruler claimed that if he too could survive the sun walk then he would remain leader.

Zang Zing described to us how he and the Morisakis watched from the shadows as the high ruler marched confidently into the main courtyard and stood with his arms outstretched as Zang Zing had done.

'We watched as at first the high ruler smiled at us. The sunlight was shining down upon him. I smiled sadly back as I saw the first wisps of smoke rise heaven-wards.'

Zang Zing then described to us the agony on the face of his adversary as the sun's power took hold and flames began to break out all over his body.

'Still he resisted the urge to flee,' Zang Zing said. 'He had remarkable courage. I will give him that.'

But courage hadn't been enough, for the fires became too strong and quickly consumed the high ruler's body. Still he struggled to stay on his feet but after a couple of minutes, he had slumped to his knees, screaming in agony.

'He fell face down onto the earth and we all turned away as the flames devoured him.'

Zang Zing gave a little shrug and took his hand away from Lilith. She stood and rejoined me on the sofa.

'With their ruler gone, I was asked to take over. I agreed on the condition that the two of you would be free of the execution order.'

'How can I ever thank you Zang Zing?' Lilith asked.

'Hush now child. You have shown me nothing but respect and courtesy. That is thanks enough.'

Lilith gave a small smile and looked at me.

'Thank you Zang Zing,' I said simply.

He gave a little bow of his head and then stood up.

'Now I will go and see the fair Cecilia. I will see you again soon Lilith. You too Alex.'

And before our very eyes he disappeared again.

'How does he do that?' I asked.

'Perhaps we will know someday,' Lilith laughed and kissed me.

But our war with the Morisakis had one final and fatal twist in the tale.

We had all gone to a restaurant one evening a couple of months later. Jodie was walking ahead of Lilith and me, her hand clasping James'.

'What a beautiful evening my love,' Lilith said to me, her arm snaking around my back, hugging me close.

I did the same to her.

'Yes it is, Lily.'

We stopped and kissed one another.

Jodie had stopped too and looked back at us as we broke apart.

'Not again,' she laughed.

'We like kissing,' Lilith said, laughing too.

And it was then the attack came. From seemingly out of nowhere a black and white blur smashed into James, knocking him off his feet and headlong into a brick wall.

'James!' Jodie screamed.

Immediately Lilith and I went on alert, scanning the area with all our vampiric senses.

'Jodie, watch out!'

Lilith's shout came too late as the blur came back and smacked our companion across the face, sending her flying over two parked cars, landing face down in the road.

Suddenly the blur came to an abrupt halt and stood facing us.

'John Sebastian,' Lilith hissed, her eyes filled with a hate and fury I had only seen once before.

'Your time on earth ends this night Lilith O'Shea,' the old man pointed a finger at her with a smug expression on his face.

'The execution order has been revoked, you fuck!' she screamed.

'I follow the orders of no one.'

And suddenly he was on the move again. This time he flew straight up. I made a move to follow him but he was out of sight before I'd barely reached roof top level.

Lilith meanwhile picked Jodie up from the road and carried her back to the pavement.

'Jodie? Can you hear me?' she was saying frantically.

I dropped back down and went over to the very still form of James.

I crouched down and saw that his neck was broken and half of his head was caved in from the wall's impact. A stronger vampire would have survived the assault but James had been so terribly weak, he hadn't stood a chance.

I stood up and went back to join Lilith.

'Jodie?' she called again, trying to wake our friend.

There was still no response and Lilith gently shook her.

I softly touched her shoulder and my beloved looked up at me, tears in her eyes.

'I can't wake her,' she said quietly.

'James is dead,' I replied with genuine sadness in my voice.

Lilith picked Jodie up and immediately took to the air.

I was about to do the same when I was blasted off my feet and landed with a crash into another parked car.

I sat up against the car, trying to clear my vision when I suddenly saw a pair of shoes standing in front of me.

'I told you I knew what you are boy.'

I slowly looked up and met the hateful gaze of John Sebastian.

I struggled to get to my feet, as he suddenly gripped my chin and thrust my head back into the car door again.

'I'm going to enjoy playing with you,' he spat, eyes narrowed to slits. Then he lifted me off the ground and hurled me across the road, narrowly missing an on-coming car, which swerved to avoid me. I heard the blast of its horn before crashing through a wooden fence of someone's back garden.

I tried desperately to get some air back into my lungs, again forgetting I didn't need oxygen to live, but the old vampire was upon me again before my mind told me this information.

This time I screamed in agony as he thrust a splintered piece of the fence into my stomach. He withdrew the shard of wood and then pinned me to the grass with it by driving it through my shoulder.

I had never known agony like it. To this day, I still haven't felt pain quite the same as John Sebastian inflicted upon me that night.

I tried to move my other arm to pull the shard out but my enemy then stamped hard on my arm, shattering the bones within. I was in shock and completely at his mercy.

Perhaps it was because I was in such pain and misery, that I failed to notice that my adversary had gone.

I remember just lying there helpless, unable to move. I was crying, I do remember that, and wishing I could see my Lily one last time.

I had closed my eyes, for I opened them again at the sound of footsteps.

I half expected to see John Sebastian coming back to finish the job. What I didn't expect to see was Cecilia walking towards me, looking radiant through my tears. Her beautiful red dress split down one side of her left leg.

She carried a huge sword and just for a moment I had this horrible notion that she was going to kill me. But as she placed the sword down beside me, I noticed there was blood already on the blade.

'Don't try to talk. I'm here to help you,' she said softly.

I cried out in pain again as she pulled the shard of wood from my shoulder and gently lifted me to my feet in her powerful arms.

I was still unable to move either of my arms and as I looked hopelessly at my right one, it was then that I noticed a fallen body. As my vision cleared I also saw a head lying a few feet away. John Sebastian's head.

'I killed him,' Cecilia said calmly, not that it was needed.

I nodded slowly and took a couple of steps away from her. Then I remembered she had saved my life.

'Thank you Cecilia.'

She tilted her head to one side and smiled.

'You're welcome.'

I didn't walk any further and instead looked at her.

'Why?' I asked.

'Why?'

'Yes,' I said. 'Why did you help me?'

Cecilia gave a small laugh before picking up the sword again.

'Zang Zing and I had an engrossing chat,' she said. 'He did as he said he would, in Paris. I had to respect that.'

I looked at her and then I realised my shoulder had healed. The broken bones in my other arm were going to take a while longer.

'And what of you? What of the True Species?'
Cecilia looked away for a moment and then back at me.
'Zang Zing wants me at his side. All vampires belong as one. He made me see the truth of that.'
'Oh really? I got the impression Zang Zing didn't like you. Not as much as Lilith.'
Cecilia laughed and shook her head.
'I said the very same thing. And you know what Zang Zing said?'
I shook my head.
'Lilith is too much of a free spirit. And besides, he knows she'll never leave her beloved London.'
'And you will?'
Again Cecilia laughed.
'Yes. I leave for Paris tomorrow.'
Cecilia narrowed her eyes at me then and took a step forwards. Before I could stop her she had grasped my injured arm and was studying it.
'There is no way this should have healed this quickly,' she said thoughtfully, before letting go.
'Yes, it feels fine now.'
I flexed the arm and knew it was fully healed.
'Zang Zing is right about you. I sensed it too. I know of vampires far older than you who take a lot longer to heal. Curious.'
'Perhaps but I don't know why.'
'No. That's clear. I think only Zang Zing knows the answer.'
'He said it would become clear in time.'
Cecilia nodded.
'You should go Alex. Lilith needs you.'
'What about him?' I pointed at John Sebastian's remains.
'Don't worry about that. I shall take care of it. Now go!'
And with those words, I thanked her again and took to the air.

I made my way back to our home and found my beloved comforting a crying Jodie.
Part of me was delighted to see she had survived John Sebastian's assault. I knew she had Zang Zing's blood to thank for that. But part of me was sad for another loss in her young life. I knew she and James had become so in love with one another.
And yet, I knew with the passing of time she would come through it. Again.

A few hours later, Jodie had gone off to bed. Lilith and I were lying next to one another, just enjoying the silence of the early hours. Dawn was only an hour away and knew we would soon be sleeping again.

'I'm sorry I left you,' Lilith whispered, stroking my chest.

'It's okay Lily. You did what you had to do.'

'But I thought he would come after me. That's why I took off for Cecilia's place. I knew it was close by.'

I smiled in the darkness and kissed her.

'She saved me, so all's good.'

'I will thank her tomorrow.'

'You'll have to be quick. She's going to Paris.'

'What? Why?'

So I explained to her what Cecilia had told me. When I had finished Lilith hugged me just a bit harder.

'I asked her to go and help you. I never thought she would.'

'We underestimated her, I guess,' I said.

'Yes. But as Zang Zing says, we are blood sisters. I'm glad she's an ally now rather than an enemy.'

'You say blood sisters. Why is that?'

Lilith gave a small laugh and kissed me.

'Cecilia was Christiano's first sire. I was his third and last.'

I stared at her in surprise.

'You both gave the impression you hardly knew one another.'

Lilith laughed at that.

'We've always kept ourselves fairly distant. We've never been close.'

'Wait. So you have another blood sister out there somewhere?'

Lilith shook her head.

'No. I have a blood brother somewhere. He's called Mark. But I haven't seen him in over 200 years.'

'So, you are hardly close to him either?'

'No and nor is Cecilia.'

'Soon be dawn my darling,' I kissed her.

'Yes, we should sleep now my love.'

Chapter 29

My story now jumps ahead by two years. My father had died and it still hurts to talk about it now, even after so much time has since passed. Suffice to say, cancer claimed his life. He was diagnosed in the May and went downhill very quickly. Mum, Monica and I were all at his bedside when he slipped away.

Also in the two years, Jodie had moved on. She had received more blood from Zang Zing and was now more than capable of looking out for herself. Not that we had anything to fear. The Morisakis were true to their word, thanks to Zang Zing's mighty influence. Lilith and I were free to move around at our will and we even spent the whole of December in Paris as the Morisakis' guests. Zang Zing was back in China for some undisclosed reason so Cecilia was acting as high ruler.

All our past confrontations with her were exactly that, in the past. Now all the bad blood that had gone before was forgotten and my Lily and Cecilia got along just like real sisters. They actually found that they enjoyed one another's company. I got to know and befriend Cecilia's new companion, Garth, a 200 year old vampire from the United States.

We still heard from Jodie on occasion. She was happy and took to residing in Cardiff. She had put James' death behind her but point blankly refused to become involved with another suitor, despite two or three offers from very strong and formidable vampires. She was content doing her own thing.

As for Lilith and I, we had remained living by ourselves in our Camden home. Of course, I still had my own flat, and sometimes we would go there for a change. We hunted and fed when we needed to. We made love most nights and were more than happy.

I take up my story on a hot July morning. We vampires hate the summer months. The days are so long and the nights far too short for our liking. On this particular night I had barely made it back from a hunt before dawn's early light came calling.

'My darling, you must be more careful,' Lilith scolded me.

'I'm sorry Lily. But he was a magnificent feed.'

And indeed he had been! On this particular night I had interrupted a brawl at Jacob's club. His doorman had been stabbed and I had stepped in to save one of his bar staff from being next. I had taken the guy outside and thrown him against the wall. His head had met the brickwork with a resounding crack and before he could die from the injuries I had taken his blood. He had been my first feed for a few days and certainly my first kill for weeks.

'Come my love. Let's get to bed,' Lilith held out her hand to me, as had become her custom.

I smiled and was about to place my hand in hers when the telephone rang.

'Damn early for a call,' Lilith muttered and picked up the receiver.

She said hello and then listened for a few seconds. I saw her eyes narrow and then she was handing me the phone.

'It's your mum.'

I immediately felt a sinking feeling inside. I knew it had to be serious for her to call this early.

'Mum? What's happened?'

'Alex, thank God. You have to come. It's Monica.'

'What? Monica?' was all I could say.

'Yes. Please get here as fast as you can. She's been hit by a car. Oh Alex. I...' My mother started sobbing into the receiver.

'Okay Mum,' I said. 'I'll be with you very soon.'

The truth was I couldn't possibly leave right away. Not with the sun's lethal rays now lighting up the sky. However bad my sister's injuries were, it was just impossible for me to get to her.

I remember cursing God and the world for so much sunlight in July.

'I need to get to Monica but can't,' I fumed to a sympathetic Lilith.

'I know my darling,' she said. 'It's our curse. We have to wait for the night to come.'

I felt so frustrated. I mean, with my father it had been different. He had been an old man and had enjoyed a mostly happy and eventful life. It didn't even enter my head to do something to save him, or even end his suffering. But Monica? Just how bad were her injuries? I had no way of knowing. I tried calling my mother back but got no answer. I had all this power at my disposal but until the sun went down I was as helpless as a new born baby. I could do nothing but go to bed with my beloved and try to sleep a few hours of the deadly daylight.

We awoke to the sound of an aeroplane flying lower than usual and one glance at the clock told me it was now seven in the evening, still daylight of course.

But miraculously it had clouded over while we had slept and Lilith and I took to the air earlier than we had anticipated. After a brief stop at a fast food place for a bite to eat we were soon landing in a field near my mother's house.

I burst in the door calling for her and my mother came out of the kitchen and hugged me.

'Oh Alex,' she said, 'why couldn't you get here sooner?'

Before I could think of an answer my mother brushed past me and went to the coat rack.

'Come on,' she said, 'we'll take my car.'

Twenty minutes later, the three of us were being ushered onto a ward in the intensive care unit.

My mother sat by Monica's bedside, while a doctor came and explained to me what had happened and how bad her injuries were.

'According to the police report the driver lost control of the car and after it had mounted the pavement, it hit your sister head on. Her pelvis was shattered on impact, and her right leg is also broken in two places. She has three broken ribs, a damaged spleen and quite severe internal bleeding. I'm afraid your sister also has a skull fracture and is very fortunate to be alive, Mr King.'

'Thank you Doctor,' I said. 'So how is she doing?'

The Doctor glanced down at his chart on the clipboard.

'I'm afraid it's too early to say. We caught the internal bleeding early and have managed to repair the damage. However, Monica cannot breathe unaided and we are deeply concerned at the severity of the skull fracture.'

I bowed my head and gave a small nod.

'Please be assured Mr King, we are doing all that we can to help your sister.'

'Thank you Doctor,' Lilith said and gave my arm a gentle squeeze.

We were then ushered into the actual ward to rejoin my mother.

For someone who has seen and indeed been the cause of so many deaths, seeing Monica hooked up to this machine and that machine broke my heart. Never in all my time as a human or a vampire did I feel so helpless as I did when looking at her in that condition. Just laying there, having to have a machine do her breathing for her. Having blood pumped into her and God knows what else. Seeing all the bandages and strapping for her injured limbs.

Even with my enhanced vision, it would have been difficult for me to recognise her. Someone who didn't know her very well, might easily not have known the prone figure lying there was her. But for someone who loved her as much as I did, it was very hard to take in. In fact, I had to leave. I mumbled an apology to my mother and ran out of the ward, only just remembering to keep my speed down. I left Lilith behind with her and ran all the way outside and cried in the car park.

I didn't care that people saw me and looked at me. I cried and cried, sitting on a wall.

At last it was getting dark as I made my way back into the hospital. I found my way back to the ICU and took my place by my sister's bedside.

'Are you ok Alex?' Lilith asked, placing her hand upon my arm.

I looked at her and gave her a small nod.

'Yes,' I lied, 'just needed to be by myself for a few moments.'

'Of course.'

My mother came and stood by me, the three of us all as helpless as each other.

We agreed to stay at my mum's house that night, and prayed that the weather would be poor enough the following day so we could visit Monica again early.

But fate was being very cruel that July. Lilith and I awoke to the sun streaming through a gap in the curtains. My beloved gave a little yelp and only just moved her arm out of the way before the light would have burnt her.

'Shit Alex, what do we do?'

I just shook my head and once again cursed everything under the sun I could think of.

'Alex, Lilith. Breakfast is ready. I want to get to the hospital as early as possible,' my mother called up the stairs.

I slumped back onto the bed and gazed up at the ceiling in the spare room. Lilith just looked at me.

'Alex?' she whispered.

'Yes, Lily?'

'You have to tell her.'

'Tell her?' I was confused.

'Yes. Tell her the truth about you, about us.'

It was then that I realised what Lilith was saying.

'You mean tell my mum we're vampires?' I gasped.

Lilith didn't answer, just merely nodded her beautiful head.

'But that's insane,' I sat up again. 'What will she think?'

'I've come to know your mother Alex. I'm pretty sure she'll be rational and accept it.'

I stared at my beloved as if she had suddenly become a crazy person. But of course she hadn't. What Lilith was saying made perfect sense. We were out of options. There could be no excuse for us NOT to go and visit Monica in the hospital. None except for the fact we couldn't step out into a beautiful sunny day like this one.

I finally knew it was time to tell her the truth. Something I wished I could have had the courage to tell my father two years before.

'You're right Lily,' I said, kissing her. 'It is time. Let's get dressed and go and tell her.'

'I think show her is more likely,' Lilith added.

My beloved wore the same green dress she had bought in my hometown. I wore black jeans and a grey sweatshirt as we made our way down stairs to my waiting mother.

'Mum,' I said. 'We can't go to the hospital with you.'

'What? Why not?'

I looked down at the floor and when I looked back into her face I deliberately opened my mouth and showed her my fangs.

'What in the world?' my mother said, dropping the piece of toast she was holding.

'Mum, we really need to talk.'

Chapter 30

My mother looked at me with a mixture of horror and bemusement on her face.
'You are a vampire?' she could hardly say the word.
'Yes Mum.' I said quietly, stirring my coffee.
'And you too Lilith?'
My beloved nodded and showed my mother her flawless teeth.
'I made your son a vampire Mrs King. It was the only way to save his life, believe me.'
At this my mother glanced at me sharply.
'You were dying? And you didn't tell us?'
'I was stabbed,' I explained, 'I was losing too much blood to get to a hospital in time. Lilith saved me.'
'What? By making you into a monster?' my mother almost spat the word.
I shook my head but didn't say anything.
'Mrs King,' Lilith spoke. 'We can apportion blame later on. The fact is we needed to tell you why we can't go and visit Monica on such a sunny day. Yes, your son is a vampire and has been one for two years now. But he remains your son.'
My mother looked at her and then at me.
'You were already a vampire before your father died?'
I nodded sadly.
'And he didn't know? You didn't tell him?'
'Alex couldn't bring himself to do it Mrs King. He really wanted to, but couldn't. If it wasn't for this situation with Monica, we wouldn't be sat here telling you now.'
'This is all some kind of game. A trick. You don't want to see your sister and won't admit it.'
My mother pushed her chair away from the kitchen table and dumped her plate and cup into the sink.
'A trick?' I was stunned to think my own mother would accuse me of not wanting to see Monica.
'Of course it is. I've seen those teeth in party shops. Perhaps you could even have them as permanent fixtures at a dentist.'
Lilith gazed at me then and I knew I would have to do something to convince my mother we were telling the truth.
'Okay Mum,' I said. 'Watch this.'

While my mother watched I pushed up the sleeve of my sweatshirt and bit deep into my wrist.

'Bloody hell!' she swore and immediately went to the cupboard where she kept a first aid box.

'Look Mum,' I instructed her.

She stopped opening the box and looked at my wrist which was already beginning to heal.

I saw my mother's eyes go wide in shock or amazement as the puncture wounds from my fangs closed in front of her eyes.

'If I wasn't a vampire, how else could you explain that?'

'But, but it's impossible. Vampire's don't exist,' my mother had become slightly wobbly on her feet and Lilith helped her to sit back down.

'Oh we exist Mrs King,' Lilith said, 'for thousands of years.'

My mother looked up at her.

'Just how old are you then? You look like you're no older than 30.'

Lilith smiled.

'Actually I'm 31 in human terms. Well, that's to say I was made a vampire at 31. That was over 450 years ago.'

'450 years,' my mother repeated quietly.

'Which is no age for a vampire,' I added.

My mother shook her head.

'This is all so strange,' she said.

'Yes,' I agreed, 'I thought exactly the same when Lilith first came to me. That she was talking nonsense and was some kind of mad woman.'

Lilith gave a small laugh but placed her hand in mine.

'But her tale turned out to be perfectly true, Mum. She has shown me many wonderful things. She has shown me an unwavering love that just grows stronger with each passing day. I owe her my life.'

My mother nodded slowly, taking in my words.

'If that is true then I should thank you,' she said, looking at Lilith.

My beloved gave her a slight nod.

'So you see why we can't visit your daughter? Not until later?'

'I guess not. I've seen films but tell me what's true and what isn't about vampires.'

'You really want to know Mum?' I asked.

'Yes. If you have truly become something other than human then I want to know all about it.'

And so between Lilith and I, we told her what we were capable of. What our strengths were and what could harm us. We deliberately left out the part about having to kill once in awhile. I didn't think my mother would ever accept that part of vampirism. We did of course explain we had to drink blood sometimes, which was true of all the movies and books anyway.

When we had finished my mother looked at me with renewed understanding.

'I can see why you would find it difficult to tell anyone.'

'Yes Mum and you mustn't tell anyone else.'

'As if I would tell my friends: "oh by the way, Alex is a vampire now".'

I frowned at her but she quickly touched my hand.

'It's okay Alex. I'm glad you told me. Does Monica know?'

I shook my head.

'Well, I really should get to the hospital. If there's any change I'll phone you. But please promise me you'll visit as soon as you are able to?'

Lilith and I stood together and both nodded.

While my mother was visiting Monica we slept a bit more and sat around watching television. I have always found it amazing how time seems to fly even when you don't do much.

My mother returned with no news later in the afternoon and Lilith agreed she would sort some dinner out for us.

My mother was as surprised as I had been to find vampires could eat and drink just the same as ordinary people did. And I think she was pleasantly surprised at how well my Lily could cook, for it was a wonderful roast pork meal she had come up with.

While we ate, I explained to Mum about my giving up the job, but that she mustn't worry because money wasn't an issue. I think she was astounded to learn of Lilith's vast fortune but made no comment about the fact.

We had just finished the meal when Lilith suddenly pointed out the window.

'Look! It's raining.'

'Yes it is.' My mother didn't understand the meaning.

'That means it's become cloudy, which means we can leave.'

And so with quick looks up at the sky Lilith and I made our way to my mother's car and she drove us back to the hospital.

Once we were all safely inside we crowded around Monica's bed. It was almost as if we were reliving the same day. Nothing had changed. Not in Monica's condition, for she seemed to be in exactly the same position as she had when I had last seen her.

'Oh honey, why won't you wake up?' my mother sobbed, holding my sister's hand.

I had just placed a comforting hand on my mother's shoulder when suddenly one of the monitors began to beep dramatically. This then led to another monitor to do the same, only in a different tone. Red lights began to flash on and off in rapid succession.

'What's happening?' my mother jumped up in alarm, just as a doctor and two nurses came running into the room.

'She's gone into arrest. We must ask you to leave.' The doctor stated bluntly and made his way to the bed.

'No, Monica,' I shouted, but Lilith was dragging me away.

'Come Alex. Let them do their work,' she said.

The three of us watched through the glass as the medical staff worked to get my sister's heart working again. My mother couldn't watch and instead buried her face into my chest as the charging paddles were placed upon Monica's chest.

'Clear.' I heard the doctor say and then I saw Monica's body jerk under the electricity charge that had entered her body.

Lilith and I both watched as the doctor glanced at a monitor and then put the paddles back into their holding tray.

'Charging,' one of the nurses said.

'Okay. Clear.'

Once the paddles had been replaced upon my sister's chest, another blast of electricity was sent into Monica's prone body, jerking it around like a rag doll.

This time there was a loud beep and the doctor placed the paddles back into their charging holder and stepped back from the bed.

A moment later he came out and joined us.

'That was close,' he said, 'Monica suffered a heart attack. We managed to bring her back but her pulse is extremely weak. She could suffer another attack at any moment.'

My mother began to cry and Lilith led her off to one side while I went back into Monica's room.

'You gave us a fright there sis,' I muttered.

I looked down at her and gently brushed my hand across her cheek.

'What can I do to make you better? Tell me,' I said it out loud but of course wasn't at all sure she could hear me or not.

It was then that the idea came to me. Of course I could help her! Not only help her, but make her stronger than she had ever been!

Once they were satisfied that Monica's heart rate had settled into an even pattern, the nurses left me alone with her.

I had made up my mind. I was going to do it. But before I could bite into my sister's wrist, Lilith came back in.

'Don't do it Alex,' she said softly.

'Do what?' I stood up from where I had been hunched over her.

'You know what. You were about to bite her.'

'Don't be silly,' I lied. 'Where's Mum?' I tried changing the subject, but unsuccessfully.

My Lily shook her head.

'Your Mum is talking with the doctor. Please don't even attempt to sire Monica, Alex. You will regret it.'

This suddenly made me angry.

'Why the fuck not?' I hissed. 'You think I can't make vampires? You think you're the only one who can?'

Lilith looked at me, a sad expression in her eyes and on her lips.

'You've only been a vampire for two years, Alex. Think about it.'

'Yes, I know. So if I sired Monica she would be weak but at least she'd be alive, Lilith.'

My beloved shook her head again and suddenly grabbed my hand in hers. I made an attempt to withdraw it but it really wasn't much of an attempt at all.

'Look at me Alex.'

I didn't at first. Instead my gaze fell onto my sister's unconscious form.

'Look at me Alex,' she said again. 'Please.'

This time I did look into Lilith's beautiful face.

'Ask me and I will,' she said.

Her words confused me.

'What? I don't understand.'

Lilith sighed and gave my hand the slightest of squeezes.

'Ask me to help Monica and I will.'

It was then I realised what Lilith was saying, what she was prepared to do to save my sister's life. Save her life as she had saved mine.

'Think about it Alex,' she said. 'Monica will be as strong as you. As magnificent as you.'

I heard her words but I was again looking at my sister. Again I was reminded at how helpless she looked, how vulnerable.

Before I could give her my answer my mother came back.

'Do it.' Mum said it so quietly that I had to be sure I had heard right. She stepped around Lilith to be at my side.

'What?' I asked, glancing at Lilith, who in turn was already looking at my mother.

'Do it!' Mum said, more loudly this time and with considerable determination.

'Mrs King?' Lilith questioned and my mother turned to her.

'Look, I'm not foolish. The doctors have basically written off any chance of a recovery for my daughter. They said as much just then, outside. You saved my son, now I'm asking you to do the same for Monica. Please?'

Lilith closed her eyes and I knew what was coming.

'I can do that,' Lilith said softly, 'but you do understand that your daughter will no longer be human, yes?'

My mother stared at Lilith for only a second before nodding.

'I understand,' she answered quietly.

'The doctors are correct,' Lilith went on, 'the chances of Monica surviving are very slim. Her injuries are so severe. But I can make her strong again.'

'Yes,' my mother whispered, bowing her head.

'Alex was going to do this himself, Mrs King. That's how much he loves his sister. But it is best that I save her.'

Through her tears, Mum looked up at me.

'Would you really have tried to save her, Alex?' she asked.

'Yes, Mum. I love Monica. It's not her time,' I replied, 'but this is the only guarantee.'

Lilith smiled sadly, nodding in agreement.

My mother straightened up and wiped her eyes with the back of her hand.

'Okay then. What do you want me to do?' she asked.

'Say goodbye to Monica as you know her, for she will wake up rebuilt and more powerful than you could possibly imagine,' Lilith told her.

Mum nodded and slowly bent her head towards my sister. I watched as she gently placed a kiss upon Monica's forehead, careful not to move the bandage at all.

'Come back to us soon,' she whispered and then with one last look, Mum left the room.

Lilith came over to me and gently touched my face.

'Alex, I will need your help.'

'Anything.'

Lilith rolled up the sleeve on her dress.

'When it is time for her to drink my blood, I will need you to hold her mouth open. Okay?'

I nodded but wasn't sure of one thing.

'Will this work? With her being unconscious?'

'Yes,' Lilith answered, 'as long as the blood enters her throat it will find its own way down. Don't worry.'

With one final check that no one was watching, I then watched Lilith bend her head towards my sister's neck and closed her eyes as her teeth bit into it.

I heard her sucking my sister's blood and watched Monica's face grow even more pale by the second.

At last Lilith raised her head up and then nodded for me to open Monica's mouth.

I did so as gently as I could and then Lilith quickly dragged her finger across her wrist, holding it directly above my sister's mouth. We both watched as the powerful blood began to drip into the intended target.

After a couple of minutes had gone by, Lilith drew back and I knew she had given Monica a fair amount, knowing that she would give more once we had got out of the hospital. We were taking a huge risk of being discovered of course, so time was of the essence. I closed my sister's mouth and biting into my own wrist, I wiped the blood onto her neck and closed the bite wounds Lilith had made.

I went around to the other side of the bed and helped Lilith to her feet.

'Now we must be with her when she wakes,' Lilith said.

'How long?' I asked, looking at my still sleeping sister.

'It won't be long, Alex. I promise.'

Chapter 31

Lilith was correct, for it was just a few minutes later when Monica actually woke up. Her eyes remained open for less than a second though, before she squeezed them shut again.

'The light! Too bright!' she almost shouted.

'It's okay, Monica,' Lilith said, 'open your eyes slowly. Your new sight will adjust.'

My sister did as she was told and squinted at me.

'Alex? What's happened? Where am I?'

'You're in the hospital sis,' I said, smiling down at her. 'You got hit by a car.'

Monica opened her eyes wider and shook her head.

'I remember the car. It came at me so fast.'

I nodded and glanced at Lilith who was sitting on the edge of her bed.

'Why is everything so bright? And why can I hear those two nurses talking in the other room?'

'I have something to tell you,' I admitted.

And that was exactly what I did. I told Monica what Lilith had done to her and what she had done to me two years before. The whole story. Including the part where our mother had given Lilith permission to sire her.

I feared Monica would be angry and distraught that her human life was over. But far from it. My sister was excited at the chance to live a new existence and she couldn't wait to get out of there.

'Are my clothes here?' she asked.

'No. They mostly got destroyed with the emergency surgery.'

It was our mother who had spoken and we all turned to see her standing in the door way.

Her eyes immediately went to Monica and I saw a mix of wonder and delight cross her face.

'Sweet Jesus,' she muttered, which came as a surprise to me, seeing as none of us were particularly religious.

'Hi Mum,' Monica grinned at her, and then winced when she accidently tore her lip open with one of her newly grown fangs.

Instinctively, Monica licked at the trickle of blood and I saw the expression on her face change from pleasure at seeing our mother, to a look of confusion.

'My blood! My God! It's…Delicious!' she finally found the word.

Lilith laughed and held her hand briefly, squeezing it gently.

'You think so? Wait until you taste someone else's blood, then you will truly understand what it means to be a vampire,' she said.

Monica glanced at her but Mum spoke next.

'Please don't hate me for letting her do this to you. I couldn't stand it.'

Monica beckoned her over to the bed and they shared a brief but touching embrace.

'No Mum, it's okay. I'm glad you found it within you to do it. Alex told me all about what the doctors had said. That I stood very little chance of recovering. Now I feel so strong and alive.'

'I thought you would hate me,' Mum admitted.

'Not at all. You made the right choice.'

Just then the doctor came back in and almost dropped his chart in astonishment.

'B-b-b-but this is impossible!' he stammered, staring at my sister as if she were a creature from another planet.

Before he could do or say anything else, Lilith grabbed him and gazed into his eyes.

'Listen and hear my voice, doctor,' she spoke slowly and clearly. 'You will destroy all evidence that Monica King was ever here. Her medical files and charts are all to be destroyed and wiped from the computer. Do you understand?'

I saw that Monica's doctor now had a dazed expression on his face, clearly under Lilith's mind control.

'I understand,' he repeated, sounding almost like an android from an American fifties B' movie.

'You will also forget Monica King was here under your care. Do you understand?'

The doctor had just repeated that he understood when a nurse came in.

'What's going on?' she demanded.

Without thinking, I grabbed her and stared deep into her pretty blue eyes.

I quickly but clearly repeated what Lilith had done to the doctor and she was soon under my control.

We watched as the doctor and nurse left the room and I turned to Lilith.

'Is it that simple?' I asked. 'Will they do as we instructed?'

My darling nodded.

'Yes, but we should leave.'

'How did you do that?' my mother was still in awe at having been witness to one of our vampiric powers.

'With ease,' Lilith replied, 'but we need to move. Mrs King, the three of us will leave via that window,' she pointed. 'We will meet back at your house.'

My mother simply nodded and grabbed her handbag from a chair.

Monica kicked off the covers on her bed and was standing beside me in an instant.

'We go out the window? But it's so high!' she looked out.

'Trust me, you'll be fine,' I told her.

Lilith slid the window open with ease and then stepped out into the night.

'Go on!' I urged my sister and after hesitating only for a second, Monica stepped onto the ledge.

'It's only four stories,' Lilith called, 'you can either jump or float to the ground. Tell yourself you won't fall and you won't.'

I glanced at the door to the room and hoped no one would come in.

'Go on, Monica,' I hissed, 'we have to go.'

'But I'm only wearing this stupid gown,'

'It will have to do. You won't feel cold, now go!'

And suddenly she was gone. I flew head first out of the window and saw that Monica was gazing at me in excitement, floating in the air and laughing.

'This is fucking amazing!' she laughed, doing a little mid-air twirl.

'Yes it is,' I grinned at her and then grabbed her hand, dragging her away from the hospital. We quickly caught up with our waiting sire and then the three of us, Monica still laughing in delight, flew away across the now moonlit sky.

Soon we were back at our mother's house, all seated around the dining table.

'Why didn't you tell me Alex? I would have understood,' Monica seemed put out that we had kept our secret from her.

'Surely you must see why we didn't tell you?' Lilith asked.

Monica, who was now dressed in an old top and trousers our mother no longer wore, sat back in her chair and slowly nodded.

'Yes, I suppose. But would you have told me?'

'Yes,' I said, 'I still regret not telling Dad. I always will.'

Lilith touched my arm. It was a simple gesture but I appreciated the comfort it gave me.

'The noise! How do you stand it?' Monica clapped her hands over her ears all of a sudden and pushed her chair back from the table.

'Monica?' Mum asked, clearly concerned.

Lilith glanced at me before standing up and going to my sister, who was now burying her head in amongst the cushions on the couch.

'Listen to me, Monica. Listen!' Lilith was saying.

I watched as she gently pulled my sister's hands away from her ears and I could see Monica was crying.

'Your hearing will adjust. You will automatically tune out things you don't wish to hear. It just takes time.' Lilith told her softly.

I nodded and remembered what it had been like in my first few hours after becoming a vampire.

'But all I can hear is his fucking heartbeat! Boom, boom, boom. It's driving me fucking crazy!'

I glanced at Lilith who shook her head.

'Who's heartbeat?' I asked.

'Mr Brown.'

I didn't know who he was until my mother answered.

'Mr Brown lives next door,' she said, clearly upset at Monica's sudden condition.

'It's all right, Monica,' Lilith stroked her hair. 'You just need to feed. I shall take you soon.'

Suddenly, with a snarl of pure unbridled rage, Monica shoved Lilith out of the way and charged out of the door.

'Alex! Stop her!' Lilith shouted, now lying in a heap on the floor.

I ran after her, calling Monica's name but either she wasn't listening or chose to ignore me.

I was caught off guard, ashamed to admit I was surprised by her speed, even though I should have been ready for it. I guess part of me still thought of her as the sister I had always known and loved.

I caught sight of her as she leapt over the tall hedge that divides our mother's house from her neighbour's.

I heard a crash just as I got to the hedge and knew that Monica had gone straight through Mr Brown's front door.

I landed on a short pathway in Mr Brown's garden and ran inside, only to see Monica already biting into a struggling elderly man's neck.

'Monica! Stop this!' I yelled.

'Hungry!' was all the reply I got.

She was slurping and sucking the poor man's life away.

'No Monica. You have to stop. Please listen to me!' I tried again.

I wasn't sure if I would be able to pull her away from the man but suddenly I didn't have to, for there was an almighty crash as Lilith came crashing through a set of patio doors and grabbed Monica from behind.

Before Monica could do anything, Lilith tore her away from the now unconscious Mr Brown and held her against the living room wall.

'Quick, Alex. Seal her bite marks,' she commanded and I moved to comply.

I checked the man's pulse, and although weak, knew he would survive my sister's assault.

'It…It's okay,' Monica shook her head and gazed at our sire. Blood still trickled down her chin from the corner of her mouth.

'No, it's my fault,' Lilith said quietly, 'I should have taken you out before now and shown you how to feed. I'm sorry.'

I stood up from where I had been crouching down over Mr Brown.

'Is he dead?' Monica asked, as Lilith relaxed her grip on her.

'No, he'll live.' I answered.

'Good, I'm glad. But his blood was amazing. It tasted like nothing I've had before.'

Lilith nodded and stepped away from her, surveying the damage.

'When he wakes up, I'll make him forget he ever saw you and Monica. You two go back next door. I'll make him think this was a break in.'

I nodded and held out my hand, which my sister took.

'I'm sorry Alex. I heard you calling me but something was driving me on.'

'It's okay. I'll explain what happened as best I can.'

Once we were back in our mother's lounge, I explained about the spirit demon that dwells within all vampires.

'Lilith told me that's how we get our enhanced abilities.'

'But the demon doesn't give us immortality for nothing?'

'No, Monica. It makes us lust after blood, although we can control it after a time. The demon also demands we take a life every now and then.'

Mum looked up sharply then. She was still shaken by what had happened next door.

'You have to kill?' she repeated softly.

I looked at her and slowly nodded.

'Unfortunately, yes. If we don't, we slowly go insane and would kill anyway, possibly people we actually care about.'

'I see, so who have you killed, Alex?' Monica asked.

I switched my gaze back to my sister and shrugged.

'Just a couple of evil men. Both Lilith and I have vowed only to take the lives of those who don't deserve to live. In our humble opinion, of course.'

'I knew you would have to drink blood, but I didn't think you would ever be capable of killing someone,' Mum kept her voice low but it was filled with disapproval, which saddened me.

'I'm sorry Mum, but it's who I am now. It's what Monica is too. The spirit demon is like all other demons. Evil. I would love to say we are given these fantastic powers for free but we're not. The price we pay is simple. We do the demon's bidding every once in a while, that the demon can no longer do by itself.'

I didn't know if I was explaining it very well, but one confirming nod from a returning Lilith was all I needed.

'Your son is correct, Mrs King. The price for becoming immortal is a heavy one.'

The conversation had ended there and Mum never spoke of it again. Monica and I were both at her bedside when she died several years later.

I shall always remember her smiling up at me and saying she was glad I had told her my secret. Lilith was there too, and Mum had beckoned her forward.

The last words my mother ever said were these:

'Thank you Lilith, for saving my son and daughter. Despite what you are, the angels all smile down upon you.'

Lilith had thanked her for her kind words and then Mum simply closed her eyes and passed away.

But I am getting ahead of myself, because something was to occur before my mother's death. Something that was to change all our lives, especially my own.

Monica had been a vampire for two weeks and she had taken to it as easily as I had done. With Lilith's insistence, my sister had moved into Jodie's old room and between us, we taught her how to hunt and to use her powers.

Lilith had gone to see Jacob, leaving Monica and me to hunt by ourselves.

We had successfully fed and were making our way back to Camden when suddenly a pain gripped my stomach of the like I had never felt before.

I immediately doubled over and collapsed onto the pavement we were walking along.

It felt as if red hot pokers were being thrust into my stomach and I remember crying out in agony.

'Alex? What is it?' Monica crouched down beside me.

'I don't know,' I managed to reply, 'something's wrong.'
Then all I remember was the pain became too much and I lapsed into unconsciousness.

Chapter 32

I woke up to see Lilith looking down at me, her hand was stroking my hair. She had a worried expression on her face but I saw relief come into her eyes.

The pain in my stomach was still there but now it was a dull ache and much more bearable.

'What happened, Alex?' Lilith asked gently, her stroking continuing.

'I don't know,' I answered truthfully.

Monica must have carried me back home for I was in our bed.

'Where's Monica?' I asked.

'She's asleep. It's almost dawn.'

I tried to put two and two together but failed.

'How long was I unconscious?'

Lilith glanced at a clock we had put on the wall above her dressing table.

'Five days.'

I laughed and went to playfully hit her but my arm lashed out at an uncontrollable speed and sent my beloved flying into the wardrobe.

'Lily!' I cried, 'I'm sorry I didn't...'

But my voice trailed off, even as Lilith got to her feet, shaking her head and staring at me in horror.

'Alex?' she whispered.

'I don't know what's wrong with me. I feel...Strange.'

Slowly, my sire came back to the bed and sat down. There was fear in her eyes now, something I hated seeing.

'I didn't see you move, Alex. As your sire, I should always be able to see you move but you were so...Fast.'

'I don't understand,' I said, 'how long was I really out of it?'

Lilith sighed and placed a hand upon my naked chest.

'I told you,' she said, 'five days.'

'But I...' I didn't know what to say.

Had I really been unconscious for as long as that? I assumed Lilith was telling me the truth as she had no reason to lie.

'Zang Zing should be here soon,' Lilith told me. 'I sent for him, guessing if anyone would know what was wrong with you, it would be him.'

I nodded and looked up at the ceiling.

I then burst out laughing even though the pain in my stomach had got slightly worse again.

'What are you laughing at?' Lilith asked.

'Monica,' I said, 'she's dreaming of a time when we were small.'

When Lilith just stared at me, I wanted to shake her.

'What did I say?' I wanted to know why she was acting in this weird way.

'How can you possibly know what your sister is dreaming about?'

I was about to tell her not to be so silly when my mouth shut and I realised what she meant.

'I don't get it,' I admitted, 'I think of Monica and I can see her lying sound asleep in the next room. Not only that but I can see what she's dreaming about. It's a time when we were playing as kids. Our one and only fight we had growing up. Something so trivial now but seemed important at the time.'

'You shouldn't be able to do that, Alex. What's happening to you?'

'I told you. I don't know. It's almost as if I...'

I didn't get to finish because all of a sudden the pain came flooding back, only at far greater levels.

I remember Lilith holding me down as I writhed in agony on our bed but once again, the darkness swiftly took me away.

The next time I woke up, Zang Zing was seated in a chair beside the bed. I don't think he was aware I had woken, for he simply sat with his fingers steepled together in a pose that told me he was deep in thought.

I closed my eyes again and suddenly I was in the master vampire's head. I clearly saw what he was thinking about. Zang Zing was remembering the confrontation with the Morisakis and their high ruler.

I saw Zang Zing send two council members flying with nothing more than a look. I saw the two vampires crash into a high wall at such velocity that their necks shattered on impact, killing them instantly.

Then the thought pattern changed, and Zang Zing was now sitting out in a large courtyard, high walls surrounding it on all sides.

He was bare-chested and his muscles gleamed in the sunlight. His eyes were closed as he simply sat with his arms outstretched, enjoying the feeling of the sun warming his ancient skin. He was a vampire and this shouldn't be happening but Zang Zing, instead of bursting into flames, was smiling. Gasps of amazement came from other vampires who were watching from the shadows.

'It is as I thought.'

I opened my eyes and saw that the master vampire was now looking intently at me.

I was relieved that the pain was now completely gone and briefly wondered if Zang Zing had done something to end it. But the ancient one shook his head, with a small smile.

'No, Alex. I did nothing to ease your pain. How could I? It was your pain to bear.'

'What? How do you mean?' I asked, confused by his words.

'The pain you have been feeling. It is yours alone because with that pain comes an increase in your power. Do you not feel it?'

In the two years I had known him, Zang Zing's English had got better.

'I feel different, yes.' I admitted.

The master vampire bowed his head slightly and then looked at me again.

'I sense your pain has gone, Alex. Come. It is time you left that bed, for you have lain there too long.'

He held out his hand to me, which I took, and I was pulled out from the quilt. The fact I was naked in front of him didn't seem to bother him and it didn't seem wrong somehow.

'Go and have a shower and we shall talk some more,' Zang Zing explained.

'But wait! How long have I been lying there?'

Zang Zing gazed at me for a few moments before replying.

'Altogether, eleven days.'

I think my mouth fell open but no words came out. I was about to ask where Lilith was when I suddenly saw her seated downstairs in our kitchen, talking to Monica. Both had hands around coffee mugs, almost as if they were seeking the warmth the hot liquid was providing.

'Eleven days?' I managed to say as I grabbed some clothes from my wardrobe.

I saw that the doors on Lilith's side had gone and I was reminded what had happened to them. How I had sent her flying into them with just the merest of touches.

'Don't worry about Lilith,' Zang Zing broke into my thoughts. 'She is fine and doors can be replaced.'

I offered my ancient friend a small smile before trudging off to the bathroom.

Once I had showered I went downstairs and found my three companions sitting in the lounge. I went over to Lilith and was about to kiss and hold her when I saw the fear still evident in her eyes. Zang Zing either saw it or sensed it too for he quickly told her I was alright.

'Alex won't hurt you, my dear,' he said gently.

My beloved nodded and welcomed me into her arms. It truly felt so good to hold her once again. We stayed like that for a minute or so, simply enjoying the embrace. I kissed her neck beneath her hair and breathed in the scent of her, the familiar lavender drifting into my nostrils and sparking memories of all that we had been through together.

I got a flash from her mind as we stood there; Lilith hoping we could be alone soon so we could make love. I smiled to myself and whispered in her ear.

'I want that too.'

We broke the hug and she gazed at me lovingly, all trace of fear and doubt gone from those emerald eyes I adored so much.

'I'm glad you're okay, Alex.' Monica said and I laughed when she too, jumped up and hugged us both. Zang Zing smiled and took a sip from the sherry he was holding.

Monica stood by the fireplace while Lilith and I sat together.

'So what happened to him, Zang Zing?' Lilith asked.

Our ancient friend finished the sherry but still held the glass.

'It is as I thought,' he repeated, 'the pain Alex suffered were the side effects of an extreme increase in his powers.'

'You mean, my brother is suddenly a lot stronger?' Monica asked.

'No, my dear Monica. His strength is just a small aspect. Allow me to demonstrate.'

I didn't know what Zang Zing had planned but I wasn't prepared for what he did next, for the sherry glass he had been holding was suddenly hurtling towards me at an incredible speed. And yet, I didn't only intercept it with ease, I also caught the glass without so much as breaking it. I held it in my right hand, staring at it as if it was something else.

'No vampire on earth would have been able to have prevented that glass from striking them. Do you now see what I was referring to?' Zang Zing asked, looking from Lilith to Monica and then back again.

Lilith spoke first.

'I was aware something had happened but wasn't sure what until I saw Alex holding the glass,' she said.

'And nor should you, Lilith O'Shea. Such is the speed Alex can now move. I may be wrong but I believe he is as powerful as me now.'

'What? But that isn't possible?' Lilith looked astounded.

I shook my head, not quite believing it and Monica simply gasped, her hands flying to her mouth in disbelief.

But Zang Zing simply smiled and waited for us to calm down.

'Your eyes do not deceive you, Lilith. The proof is there. You even told me Alex was seeing into his sister's dreams. He read your mind about you wanting to make love. He accidently hit you without even trying. Need I go on?'

Lilith had actually blushed because Zang Zing must have read her mind too about the wanting to make love but she just nodded and gripped my hand in hers.

'But what does this mean?' Monica wanted to know. 'Will the same thing happen to me?'

The master vampire shook his head and offered her a small smile.

'No, Monica. You are a powerful vampire in your own right. But your brother is unique. His power may well be limitless. Who knows?'

'I'm just glad the pain has gone,' I admitted.

I got up and refilled the glass, handing it back to Zang Zing who studied it carefully.

'Not a single crack. Remarkable,' he muttered before taking a sip.

'Does this mean what I think it means?' Lilith asked.

Zang Zing waited for her to continue.

'Does this mean that if Alex were to sire right now, that vampire would be strong and not terribly weak?'

Zang Zing gave a little shrug.

'I believe that is now the case, yes,' he said.

'Wow, this is unbelievable,' Lilith muttered, still holding my hand.

'Not that I intend to sire anytime soon,' I spoke up.

'You say that now but there is nothing to stop you,' Zang Zing said.

'Perhaps, but I have Lilith's love. That's all my heart desires.'

She lightly hit me on the arm but kissed me anyway.

'Come, young Monica,' Zang Zing drained his glass. 'Let's go hunting, for I can see you need to feed.'

'I do too,' I admitted.

'But love comes first,' our ancient friend smiled, giving me and Lilith a wink that spoke volumes.

Despite my need for blood, my hunger for Lilith's body was definitely top of the agenda. After all, it had been at least twelve nights since we had last made love.

Lilith mounted me and arched her back, controlling the speed and rhythm. I was managing to thrust into her as our bodies worked together, building up the excitement and lust levels that were threatening to reach new heights of our passion.

'Yes Alex! God, yes!' my beloved cried out as the rhythm became such a pace, the room seemed to blur. With each thrust, the room seemed to shimmer in my vision until I felt myself blast my seed deep into her; Lilith's own climax joining mine only seconds later.

The release had been incredible, almost as if it had been our first time.

We lay holding one another, sharing brief but intimate kisses until my Lily rested her head upon my chest while I lay on my back.

'I was so scared, my darling,' she whispered.

'Scared? When I hit you, you mean?'

'Yes but not only that. The fact you were in so much pain and lost in darkness to me for days at a time. I thought I was losing you.'

'I don't really remember much about it,' I admitted, stroking the back of her neck beneath her hair.

'I never want to go through that again,' Lilith raised her face and looked at me.

I smiled and held her face in my hand.

'I can't promise it won't happen again, my Lily.'

She nodded against the palm of my hand and brought her leg up so that it settled in between mine, forcing my legs apart.

'I don't know about you,' she said, kissing me. 'But I'm ready for round two.'

I felt her hand running up and down my cock and it was quickly hard again.

'Me too,' I said.

Chapter 33

I had a request for Zang Zing the very next day and thankfully he agreed to stay in London while I got used to my new powers. Monica offered him her room, saying she would go back to her old place, but the ancient warrior smiled and shook his head.

'You should remain with Lilith and your brother. They have much to teach you. I shall remain at my hotel in Mayfair,' he said.

I shall never forget the thrill of the chase and hunt of my first victim since I came into the power gain.

Lilith took Monica elsewhere while Zang Zing and I flew high and fast until we were miles from London. I found that I could levitate without any effort at all now. I didn't really want to put it to the test but I felt I could probably remain floating in mid-air for hours, perhaps even days at a time. I also found, when I put my mind to it, that I could now fly extremely fast, matching my ancient companion's streak across the night sky like two in control human-shaped comets.

Zang Zing came to an abrupt halt and remained floating in the clouds, but of course I could still see him.

'Very impressive, Alex,' he told me. 'Now let's see how truly strong you are.'

'Okay, but how?' I asked.

Zang Zing smiled and pointed down.

'Far below us is a speeding car. It is doing about ninety miles per hour and putting people at risk. See if you can stop it.'

I remember staring at my friend: surely he was joking? But as if reading my mind, Zang Zing tapped the side of his head.

'It's all in here now, Alex. I am convinced your powers are limitless. If you believe, you will make it happen. Now go!'

With a final glance at him, I turned in the sky easily, arching my back until I was heading back the way we had come. I wasn't aware if Zang Zing was following, for my attention was purely on the speeding car.

I burst out through the cloud cover and clearly saw my target. My friend had been correct. The driver clearly had no regard for other road users or the terrified passenger I could easily see in the back seat. Although dawn wasn't far away, he was a maniac that needed to be stopped.

Just by thinking about it, I increased my flight speed until I had overtaken the powerful BMW.

'If you believe, you will make it happen.'

Zang Zing's words came back to me and I chose that moment to hurtle down like a human missile and crashed into the car's bonnet, fists first.

The impact was huge; far greater and louder than I was anticipating. I was suddenly flying backwards, out of control until I landed in amongst some trees at the side of the road.

Shaking my head, the throbbing in my hands and arms quickly subsided and I slowly got to my feet. Dusting my black jeans and top down, I was amazed to find I was uninjured.

After the collision, the last thing I expected was the silence. But that was what greeted me as I stepped out from the trees and back onto the country road.

The impact had thrown me a good 30 metres from the scene but even from where I now stood, I easily saw the damage I had inflicted upon the speeding car.

The whole engine compartment and front of the car was caved in. In fact, the car was now bent into a V shaped crumpled pile of junk. The middle and back part of the car was at an angle so that it stood upright, the back wheels several feet off the ground. Looking at the front, you would never be able to tell it had been a beautiful BMW only moments before.

The driver's airbag had saved him from serious injury. He was groaning now though, having regained consciousness.

I floated up and looked into the back of the car. To my dismay I saw that his passenger was seriously hurt. Blood was pouring from a nasty head wound and she had already lost a lot of blood. The sticky red liquid had matted the girl's lovely long blonde hair.

I reached down and yanked the back door open, easily ripping it from its hinges. With hardly any effort at all, I threw the car door and watched it soar through the air until it embedded itself into one of the trees. I gazed at it in fascination for a second or two, and for some reason hoped I hadn't hurt the tree too much.

But my attention was quickly drawn back to the dying girl, for she couldn't possibly survive that amount of blood loss. I had to admit the scent of all that blood was intoxicating and it had been several nights and days since I had tasted the magnificent bouquet that blood now offered me.

But I somehow resisted the urge to drink from her and instead ripped off her seat belt and carefully lifted her from the car.

I gently lowered her onto the ground, where she lay completely still. Her eyes were tightly shut and her breathing was shallow at best.

Anger sparked within me then. The waste of a beautiful life, for the girl was lovely. Oh, she didn't have Lilith's classical beauty and vivaciousness. But then, I didn't imagine any woman could ever compare to my Lily ever again. But this unconscious and dying girl was very pretty, despite the blood that was still trickling down her face and into the neckline of her light blue blouse.

'Is someone there? Hey! Help me! I'm stuck!'

The driver was fully conscious now and panicking, but I ignored him and instead turned my attention back to the girl.

'You can save her, Alex.'

I turned and saw Zang Zing standing a few feet away, his hands behind his back in a relaxed posture.

'No,' I said, 'I could never get her to a hospital in time.'

The old Chinese warrior shook his head.

'That's not what I meant,' he said quietly.

'You mean...' my voice trailed off as I realised what my friend was saying.

'It's the only way, Alex. Give her your blood or she will die right here within minutes.'

'But I can't!' I protested, 'what if it doesn't work? What if she becomes weak and helpless?'

Zang Zing shook his head sadly.

'She will be strong, my young friend. I promise you. Do it now before she leaves this earth forever.'

'Who's there? Why won't you help me?'

The driver's voice was pitiful and I snarled at him.

'Shut up! Just shut the fuck up!'

The pathetic man started to cry until I sent a wave of unbridled hatred at him, snapping his neck like a matchstick. The crying stopped immediately so that it was silent once again.

I cleared my mind and actually lapped up the silence. The only other car that was near was on another road. A gentle breeze briefly disturbed a few leaves but all was soon still again.

I glanced at Zang Zing again and to my astonishment saw he was stroking a large stag; its antlers standing proud and magnificent in the moonlight. I felt something touch my hand, and looking down I saw a fawn nuzzling me with its nose, actually giving me the briefest of licks with its semi-smooth tongue. The fawn was one of the most beautiful creatures I had ever seen.

I actually laughed, amazed that these notoriously shy animals were here with two very powerful predators of the night, allowing us to touch and caress them.

But Zang Zing's voice broke the moment.

'Last chance, Alex. Save her, for I cannot.'

I gave the baby deer a final stroke and faced my companion again.

'Why not? You have all the power in the world,' I said.

'Perhaps but I have already sired my three. Make her your first, Alex. Make her magnificent.'

But instead I leaped up and dragged the dead driver from the wreck of his car. I couldn't take it anymore. The sight and smell of all that blood was driving me to distraction and I knew I needed to quench my thirst before doing anything else.

The dead man's head was already twisted at such an angle that access to his neck was easy, so I bit hard and as deep as my fangs would allow, tearing the skin and cartilage with ease.

Even dead, the red liquid rushed with urgency into my mouth and slid down my throat as if it belonged there. As I sucked at the torrent, a vague memory of one of my favourite authors came into my mind.

In her famous vampire chronicles, Anne Rice had made it a golden rule that vampires shouldn't drink from the dead or take the last few drops of blood of their victims. It crossed my mind then that I was ignoring this piece of literature and didn't care.

Sated, I let the driver's body fall to the dirt and crept over to the rapidly deteriorating girl. To my surprise her eyes had opened and she stared up at me with the bluest eyes I've ever seen. Pain was all too apparent and I detested what I had to do to her to save her life. But Zang Zing was right. This girl, who was basically a complete stranger to me, was either going to die in my arms tonight in the middle of nowhere or she was going to be reborn into a creature of power and eternal life.

I bared my fangs and the girl simply shut her eyes, not even having the strength to cry out in fright, but merely accepting the inevitable.

I glanced at Zang Zing one final time, who simply mouthed the words: 'Go on.'

With one final intake of breath, I tore away the collar of the girl's blouse and lowered my mouth towards her neck.

As gently as I could, I bit through the soft skin, nowhere near as savagely as I had done with the driver. The hot flow of her blood began to well up within my mouth and for the first time, I found myself not really enjoying the experience. Maybe it was because I felt sorrow for what I was doing or maybe it was because I was already full from taking virtually all of the driver's blood. I didn't know. But I sucked at her neck for as long as I dared before withdrawing my fangs and mouth.

With her blood still dripping from my open mouth I looked at Zang Zing again.

Both of the deer had long since gone and he now stood impassive, merely watching.

'You know what to do,' he said softly. 'Seal her wound and open your vein. Let your blood into her mouth.'

I did as instructed and bit hard into my own wrist.

Fortunately the girl's mouth had already fallen open and her breathing was now slight and gasping.

'Quickly, Alex!' Zang Zing warned me.

I allowed a few drops of my blood to fall into the waiting mouth but then they stopped. I cursed and realised my self-inflicted bite had already healed. I bit again, harder this time and the flow of blood was more of a stream. I watched fascinated as my life force fell like a mini waterfall into this stranger's mouth and throat.

The girl immediately began to cough and choke.

'Calm and peaceful thoughts, Alex. Remember!' my friend suddenly reminded me.

Panicked, I cleared my mind of all violence and thought of the baby deer nuzzling my hand only minutes before. I thought of the silence of the wood only a few steps away. An image of my darling Lily asleep in my arms came into my mind as well, and the girl immediately relaxed and swallowed my blood, instead of gagging on it.

I thought of Lilith again and saw that she was smiling as Monica sealed her bite marks on some guy in a park, many miles away. Despite the sting of my blood dripping out of me, I smiled too when I saw how pleased both of them were. My sister and my lover, now close friends and both very important to me.

'That's enough, Alex. You can stop now.'

I was broken from my thoughts by Zang Zing's calm but strong voice.

Looking down I realised the girl was now sucking hungrily at my wrist and I had to wrench my arm away from her, especially as I was now feeling weak and tired in a way I hadn't felt in years.

My ancient friend came over and pushed me gently away so that he could look down at the girl.

Although on the brink of sleep I glanced over and saw that the girl was staring up at Zang Zing, her blue eyes shining even more brightly than before. I knew it wasn't my imagination, for there, in that moment I saw the spirit demon in its former form, hiding behind this girl's eyes. A strong and singular horn protruded from out of the right side of its head. Two elongated fangs were clearly visible, sticking out past its closed and ugly mouth. Three bony ridges lined the demon's forehead and for one, just one fleeting moment it smiled at me. It was just a glimpse before the demon dissolved into its spirit form and sank out of view from the girl's eyes.

I blinked, astonished at what I had seen and realised the girl was staring at me now.

'You are safe now,' Zang Zing was telling her. 'You will come to no harm.'

She looked at him, clearly puzzled.

'What is your name?' he asked gently.

'Emilie' she responded, looking from Zang Zing to me and back again.

'Emilie,' my friend repeated. 'What a lovely name!'

'You are English?' the girl asked, her accent was clearly European.

'I am,' I said, feeling better and taking a step nearer, 'and my friend here is Chinese.'

'Chinese? Ah yes, of course.' Emilie nodded and slowly sat up.

Zang Zing stepped away and I held out my hand to her.

I was delighted when Emilie slowly took my offered hand and allowed me to pull her to her feet.

'What has happened?' she asked.

I now recognised that her accent was French.

'I saved your life,' I explained, 'you were involved in that car crash.'

I pointed over to the crushed BMW and when she saw it, Emilie immediately burst into tears and buried her head into my chest.

I instinctively held her and felt her arms hold me too. I was surprised at how strong she appeared until Zang Zing spoke up.

'You gave her almost all of your blood, Alex. That's why she's so strong.'

Emilie broke away from me and reached up and touched her own fangs with her fingers.

'What am I?' she asked, again glancing from me to my ancient friend.

'You are like us,' he told her gently. 'You are a vampire.'

'Vampire? But this is…Impossible!' Emilie stepped away from us, pulling at her teeth in clear agitation.

I was in front of her immediately, and carefully pulled her hand away from her mouth, as she had already sliced into the tips of her fingers.

I gently sucked the blood from her fingers until the cuts were healed and then stepped away again, leaving her to stare at them, speechless.

Emilie then glanced to her left and saw the lifeless body of the driver.

To my surprise she didn't scream or run away. Instead she hurled curses at it in her native language and then proceeded to give him a couple of hard kicks for good measure.

'Who was he?' I asked, after she had calmed down.

'He...How you say? Abduct me?'

I nodded, surprised at this turn of events, for I had assumed she knew him.

'Oui. So he abduct me and I could not escape his car. He drove so fast!'

I watched as Emilie paced back and forth, only pausing to kick the body once more. By now, the lifeless husk was almost unrecognizable for her kicks had shattered bones and squashed flesh to a pulp.

Emilie clearly was as strong as Zang Zing had said she would be, much to my relief.

'Alex,' Zang Zing touched my arm. 'We should go. The sun is fast approaching.'

I glanced up at the sky and saw he was correct, for the familiar orange glow had suddenly appeared on the horizon.

'My name is Alex,' I faced Emilie again. 'You must come with me now. We have to find shelter.'

'I don't feel so good,' the newly sired vampire suddenly fell into my arms.

'Zang Zing! What's wrong with her?' I shouted in alarm, holding the now unconscious Emilie upright.

'Nothing, Alex. The sun is affecting her. Although I think you will be safe from its rays, she will not.'

I looked around and couldn't see any shelter available.

'Where do I go?' I was panicking, not sounding like a super cool vampire at all.

'Half a mile that way. We passed a barn, remember? You will be safe there. Now go, I will follow.'

Without any further delay, I took to the air, Emilie asleep in my arms and headed for the safe refuge that some farmer's barn would provide us.

Within seconds I had landed and wrenched open the battered doors. I got Emilie inside and laid her down on some straw bales.

I glanced up at the roof and was relieved to see that no light was getting in. The walls of the barn allowed light in but only in places far away from the sleeping vampire girl's prone body. Sighing with relief, I knew she was safe and sat down on another bale to look at her.

She was very slim, and with the light blue blouse she also had tight blue jeans.

Of course the blood had long since dried and stopped running from the head injury and I found myself longing to see her without it crusted on her face and matted in her hair.

'She's yours Alex.'

I glanced over at Zang Zing, who had slipped in through the door quietly.

'Mine?' I repeated.

He nodded and went to sit on a straw bale on the other side of her.

'You sired her. She can be the daughter you never had as a human.'

My mouth fell open but no words came out. I stared at him and then at the sleeping girl. Even in her filthy state, I saw that Emilie was no older than twenty, probably younger.

I reached out my hand and gently moved a lock of her blonde hair away from her eye.

'Can it be true?' I whispered. 'Will she accept me as her father?'

Zang Zing shrugged and glanced at me.

'Look into her mind, Alex. See the girl for who she really is. The girl who has become your first sired.'

I gazed at the Chinese warrior for a second or two and knew that I had the power to do as he had instructed.

I closed my eyes and shut out everything else around me, concentrating my thoughts on Emilie and Emilie alone.

Suddenly it was as if I was in her mind, which of course, I was. But this felt more physical than mental. Like I was actually walking around inside her head, best describes it.

Straight away I found out she was a foreign exchange student. She had only been in London a few days when she had met the BMW driver at a club. I saw in her mind, Emilie and the guy dancing, his hands all over her. She was drunk and didn't seem to mind.

The vision shifted until I saw him push her into the car and slam the door.

I knew what happened next so I concentrated harder, pushed though the layers of her mind and saw deeper and more hidden memories.

Emilie lived in Paris with a man she called Uncle. I willed her mind to tell me where her parents were but I failed in this attempt.

In her mind, I saw that her uncle was only too glad to get rid of her abroad for a few months, although I couldn't detect the reason behind this.

My concentration was broken when the girl herself stirred and mumbled a single word.

'Hungry'

My eyes flew open and saw that Zang Zing was already by the barn's door.

'She needs to feed,' he said, 'someone is coming.'

I nodded and realised Emilie was now fully awake and clawing at the bale, her now powerful fingers ripping the straw into shreds.

The door opened and before any deadly sunlight could get in, Zang Zing had grabbed the intruder and thrown him over to me, yanking the door shut in one quick movement.

'Hey! What are you doing in..?'

I didn't allow the farmer to finish his sentence, for I held him with my gaze.

'You will forget we were ever here. You will stand perfectly still while my daughter takes some of your blood. Do you understand?'

I was still amazed at how easy it was for me to accomplish this feat, without really trying or thinking about it now.

The farmer repeated what I had told him and stood meekly still.

'Hungry,' Emilie said again, eyeing the man warily.

'Use your fangs, Emilie,' I said softly. 'Bite into his neck. Take his blood until I say stop.'

She nodded but didn't take her eyes off the farmer. Slowly she got up and approached the perfectly still man. At a guess, I would have said he was in his middle to late sixties.

Zang Zing remained by the door but was watching intently as my first sired completed her approach and then sprang at the farmer like a cat on a mouse, taking me by surprise.

They went down in a heap, Emilie on top of him and before I could stop her, she was tearing at his throat, ripping into it with her fangs. I watched in horrified fascination as blood sprayed everywhere, into Emilie's eyes and face. It was all over the front of her blouse but she didn't seem to mind at all, and instead started sucking at the man's ruined neck.

I sat back and glanced at Zang Zing who shook his head, a small smile on his face.

'I have witnessed so many new born vampires feed for the first time. It never ceases to amaze me,' he chuckled.

I wasn't sure I found it as amusing as him, for Emilie was behaving like a lioness, biting into a gazelle and taking great pleasure in doing so.

'That will do, Emilie.' I said, holding her arm.

To my relief she obeyed instantly and sat back from the unconscious farmer, licking her lips and gazing up at me. A feeling like no other welled up inside me, for I recognized the look for what it was. Adoration.

'I feel strong,' Emilie stated in that wonderful accent of hers, a terrific smile spreading across her lovely face.

'Good, I'm glad. Now seal the man's wound with your own blood.'

Emilie frowned and for a moment I wondered if she would do as I told her. But I needn't have worried for she sliced a finger-nail across her wrist to draw blood and smeared it over the farmer's torn neck. I watched with satisfaction as the wound magically healed.

Emilie watched too and I saw her eyes go wide in amazement. She glanced up at me again.

'You gave me this?' she said. 'You gave me these powers?'

I nodded, unsure what she was going to do or say next. I certainly didn't expect her to fling herself at me and hold me tight in a crushing embrace.

'Merci, merci' she kept saying over and over in my ear.

'Bravo!' Zang Zing applauded from over by the door and I knew that Emilie was without doubt the daughter I had always wanted as a human.

Chapter 34

As always seems to be the case, the sun beat down for most of that day, meaning we were stranded in the barn. In order not to arouse suspicion, Zang Zing woke the farmer up and after capturing his gaze, sent him home.

We moved around in the barn so that Emilie wouldn't have any chance of getting a burn, as the earth continued its orbit. We also used the time to explain who we were and what exactly we did. Naturally, Emilie was full of questions, even though her English wasn't perfect.

'What is this spirit demon inside me?'

Zang Zing patiently explained that demons once ruled the world before man came along.

'Fallen angels?' Emilie asked.

'Some, yes,' my Chinese friend answered, 'but certainly not all. One of the most powerful of these demons was Morisakis. It is been said Morisakis is the father of all vampire kind, and that it is his spirit and no other that dwells in all vampires.'

'But how did it start?' Emilie wanted to know.

Zang Zing shrugged in that easy-going way of his.

'According to the scriptures, Morisakis tried fathering a child with a female demon called a succubus, but after numerous attempts, when no child was forthcoming, Morisakis killed the succubus in a fit of rage.'

'But wait,' I said, 'I thought succubi were immortal just as vampires?'

Zang Zing smiled and bowed his head in acknowledgment.

'You are quite right, of course. The succubus did what Morisakis would eventually do, and that was to return in spirit form and to take over a female human from time to time. By now, mankind had begun to spread throughout the ancient world and it was to a human woman that Morisakis now turned. The first woman he tried to seduce died from her injuries. The second was driven insane and killed herself. The third was a success and became pregnant with Morisakis' child.'

I was amazed, especially as Lilith hadn't told me any of this.

'A demon child was conceived?' Emilie said in awe.

'No,' Zang Zing shook his head. 'Only half demon. The woman was human, of course. She died giving birth but the child survived.'

The ancient warrior paused in his narrative as a low flying plane passed overhead.

'What happened next?' Emilie asked.

'Before he even had a chance to hold his own child, Morisakis was said to have been killed by an avenging incubus, the male equivalent to the succubus.'

'How did he die?' it was my turn to ask a question.

'The same way most vampires have died since. His head was cut off. Not satisfied with that, the incubus burnt his remains.'

'But Morisakis returned from the grave?' Emilie questioned.

'Not exactly, but his spirit did return and entered the body of his own child, creating the first ever vampire. This is all according to the vampire scriptures that were written many centuries ago. Whether or not that is how our species started, we only have ancient texts to go by.'

'Do you believe it to be true, Zang Zing?' I asked.

'It does not matter,' he said. 'What's past is past. I care only for the present and the future.'

We all fell silent, digesting his words until Emilie spoke again.

'What became of the child?'

Zang Zing gazed at her and answered.

'He resembled a human boy but of course now had his father's demonic spirit within him. He was originally called Calios but later took his father's name.'

'Morisakis,' I said the name softly and my friend nodded.

Soon after that conversation Emilie settled down and slept some of the daylight hours away. I expected to find myself getting weak too but after just two hours sleep I was wide awake again.

Sitting up on my bale, I looked over and saw that my newly acquired daughter was sound asleep. Zang Zing was staring at me intently, a pleasant smile on his serene face.

'Have you realised it yet?' he asked.

I gave him a questioning look, not having a clue as to what he was referring to.

'Think back to the car crash,' he told me. 'What happened?'

I gave the matter some thought and shrugged.

'I stopped the car, killed the driver and saved Emilie.'

'Yes, but how did you kill the driver?'

I laughed and for a moment thought that Zang Zing might be losing his memory, for he had clearly seen my actions.

'I broke his neck and drank most of his blood,' I replied.

'Yes, this is true,' Zang Zing nodded, 'but how exactly did you break the man's neck?'

'That's easy, of course. I grabbed his head and twisted it sharply to one side.'

Zang Zing didn't reply but instead stared at me with the same intense expression.

'What?' I said, becoming uncomfortable under his scrutiny. 'Did I do something wrong?'

The oldest vampire on earth laughed then and shook his head.

'I saw what happened, Alex. I saw everything.'

I waited for him to continue.

'You killed the man by snapping his neck, yes. But you did it without using your hands.'

'What? Of course I did. That's crazy. How else could...?'

I stopped talking and stared at my friend.

'Yes?' he prompted me.

'I didn't use my hands,' I whispered. 'I remember being so angry that I lost control briefly. And then he was dead.'

Zang Zing stood up abruptly and faced me.

'Why can't you admit what you did?' he suddenly asked.

'I have,' I protested. 'I broke his neck, end of story.'

'No it isn't! You broke his neck with the power of your mind, Alex. Don't you see?'

I was about to deny such an absurdity when I stopped before any words came out.

'Yes, Alex. That is right. You clearly demonstrated the power of the mind strike. As far as I'm aware, I'm the only vampire who can use such a weapon. Until I witnessed you use it today.'

I stood up and walked a couple of paces away from him. When I turned back, he was once again sitting on his straw bale.

'I killed him with my mind,' I said quietly.

Zang Zing simply nodded, glancing across at the sleeping Emilie, before returning his gaze to me.

'You have accomplished many things on this day. You have lots to tell Lilith when you return.'

'Lilith!' I gasped. 'She will wonder what has happened to us.'

'You forgot your mobile phone again?' Zang Zing laughed, which made me laugh too.

'Yes,' I admitted. 'Even though I was in I.T, I didn't use it very often. Old habits and all that.'

My powerful friend shrugged and nodded at Emilie.

'You have created a wonderful creature. Keep her safe, Alex. Teach her our ways.'
I smiled and looked adoringly at my sleeping child.
'What do you think Lilith will think of her?' I asked.
Zang Zing stared at me for a second before answering.
'I think she will adore her as much as you.'

Before I returned to Camden with Emilie, we both needed to feed. I took us through Hyde Park shortly after dark and as luck would have it, we didn't have to go far before we came across a man mugging another man, much smaller than himself. This was just on the other side of the park.
'There's your target Emilie,' I whispered. 'You know what to do.'
She nodded at me and took off at a run to intercept the mugger.
I watched with fatherly pride as Emilie leapt into the air and landed a kick in the middle of the big man's back. He went down with a cry and Emilie landed a few feet away, doing a lovely forward role as if a born gymnast.
'You bitch,' the man growled and it was then I saw he held a baseball bat.
'Be careful, Emilie,' I called out.
The man looked over to where I was watching and went down again when Emilie ran and landed an open handed punch to his jaw. The man was flat on his back, the bat rolling uselessly out of his reach.
He tried to sit up but my daughter jumped on him. Although much smaller than him, her vampiric strength was more than a match for the brute.
I watched as Emilie straddled the man's chest and sank her teeth into his neck, not caring his turtle neck sweater was in the way.
I listened and smiled with satisfaction as Emilie began to suck the man's blood. He tried desperately to shove her off and away but Emilie slammed his shoulder back to the earth and I clearly heard the dislocation from where I stood. He howled with new pain but was soon silent as he lapsed into unconsciousness.
I walked over to where they were and gently laid my hand upon Emilie's shoulder.
'That will do,' I told her quietly.
Once again, Emilie did me proud by stopping when I asked and without me even prompting her, she sealed the man's wound too.
'Did I do well, Father?' she asked.
I remember staring open-mouthed at her for several seconds and Emilie asked if she had done something wrong.
I laughed and shook my head.

No, you did great,' I said, 'the fact you called me Father, surprised me, that's all.'

Emilie lowered her gaze and lapsed into silence. It was my turn to worry.

'Emilie?' I asked.

She looked up at me again but quickly averted her gaze.

'I'm sorry. I should not have called you that,' she said.

I laughed again and gently held her by the shoulders, raising her chin in one hand so that she had to look at me.

'You misunderstand me. I was thrilled you called me your Father.'

'But you are!' she blurted out, her accent becoming thick with passion. 'My Mother died when I was young and my Father gave me to my uncle, saying he didn't want me. My uncle is not a loving man and is glad I am away from his home.'

'Will he miss you?' I wanted to know but suspected I already knew the answer.

Emilie gave a short, bitter sounding laugh.

'No. How you say? He is…Arsehole?'

I laughed and hugged her tightly.

'Emilie,' I said, 'I would be honoured if you called me Father. I already look upon you as my daughter.'

No more words were needed. I was rewarded with a beautiful smile that emanated from her at my words. This was more than enough, and soon we were on our way home.

Back in the barn, I had explained about my living with another vampire and Lilith welcomed her with open arms.

'You sired her, Alex?' she stared at Emilie in wonder.

'Yes. It was either that or allow her to die. It was my fault she was hurt in the crash anyway.'

'Crash? What crash?' Monica asked.

I sighed and knew I had to explain what had happened.

After I had finished, we all sat down in the lounge. Although I was the only male in the house, Zang Zing having returned to his hotel, it didn't bother me in the slightest.

'I'm not sure where you can stay,' Lilith admitted, and I hadn't given it much thought either.

Emilie was about to say something but Monica beat her to it.

'That's okay,' she said. 'We're only small. She can share with me tonight and I'll go back to my place tomorrow.'

'No, you don't have to do that,' Emilie's accent was strong again as she protested.

'It's okay,' my sister smiled at her. 'I'll be fine.'

I knew I would miss my sister, but I also knew I needed Emilie in the house with us.

'This is crazy!' Lilith said. 'We aren't short of money. Why don't you stay in the same hotel as Zang Zing for a while? It's a lot closer than your town and besides, you still have lots to learn.'

Monica glanced at me and I nodded, knowing it was a good idea.

'Alright, I'll check in tomorrow.'

Soon I was in bed with my Lily, having bid goodnight to Monica and Emilie.

'I still find it incredible that you're as powerful as you are, Alex.'

'I know,' I said softly, nuzzling Lilith's neck and biting gently into it.

'And now you've sired your first, my darling. I sense her power too.'

"You do?" I asked, teasingly. I began to suck lightly at the blood that was beginning to trickle from the wound I had made.

Lilith arched her back and I felt her arms and hands grip my head, pushing me into her neck.

'Of course. Oh I do love you, Alex. I loved you the moment I first saw you.' She whispered, stroking my hair as I continued to lick at her blood, and suddenly a vision came to me. It was of Lilith as a slightly younger woman than she appeared now. At a guess I would have said she was around Emilie's age. In the vision I watched as Lilith received a hard slap on the face from a large man with a great bushy beard.

I bit into my beloved's neck again because the wound had healed. I wanted the vision to continue and to my relief it did.

The large man struck her again, this time sending her crashing into a kitchen table, plates and cutlery went flying off of it.

I continued to drink my Lily's blood and now in the vision I saw Lilith as she was now, a powerful vampire. Not as old as she was now of course, but still powerful thanks to Christiano. I saw the same large man, his beard still full but more grey. He stared at Lilith with fear etched on his grizzled face. Then I saw Lilith slash her nails across the man's features, drawing blood down his right cheek. I then saw her bite the large man's face, crushing his nose in her teeth. Blood streamed down his face and Lilith began to lick at it like a cat with cream.

Again, I reopened the wound on her neck and this time in the vision that came, I saw Lilith drive her elbow into the same man's chest, shattering his rib cage. Then with pure rage and hatred, I saw her dig her nails into the man's still moving chest and rip it open. Blood and bone flew in all directions and the large man screamed in agony as Lilith ripped out two of his ribs and threw them at the kitchen wall. Just as the vision began to fade for the final time I saw my beloved pulling out the man's quivering heart, which she then sank her teeth into.

I pulled away from her neck which had healed again and looked into her eyes.
'That was my husband,' she said, almost in a whisper.
'I saw how he beat you,' I said.
Lilith nodded and grasped my hand in hers.
'I never loved another man again until I met Severin.'
'You loved him? That bastard who beat you?' I asked, incredulous.
'Yes Alex. I married him, although truthfully it was more my father's idea. Joining of families you know?'
'An arranged marriage?'
'Not quite. More of a convenience I guess.'
I nodded and knew that in days gone by marriages like that were common place.
'Will you marry me Alex?'
The question completely took me by surprise.
'What?' I just stared at her.
'Will you marry me?'
Up to this point, I hadn't even thought of marriage. We were living together, yes, but I assumed vampires didn't get married.
'You're serious?' I asked.
'Of course. I love you. You love me. We've got an eternity to live so why don't we do it as a married couple?'
I looked into that wonderful face. The face I knew I could never grow tired of looking into. The face I know every line of, every little crease, every little frown that appears and every single smile that has registered.
'Yes Lilith,' I smiled. 'I will marry you.'
My beloved smiled too and we kissed a long and lasting kiss.

After we had made love shortly before dawn, we lay naked in one another's arms, Lilith's head resting upon my chest.
'Were you ever going to ask me Alex?' she said quietly.

'To marry you?' I stroked her hair.

'Yes.'

'I might have done. I wasn't sure vampires got married.'

Lilith gave a small laugh and tickled my stomach.

'Vampires who don't have a fear of God can enter a church just like anyone else.'

I looked up at the ceiling and thought about that.

'Is that where we will get married? In a church?'

Lilith raised her head and looked at me.

'We can get married wherever you want, my darling.'

I smiled and then groaned when Lilith sank her teeth into my stomach.

'When?' I asked, through gritted teeth because it was quite painful for Lilith to suck my blood from there.

She stopped sucking and again looked up at me, blood dripping from her fangs onto my chest.

'We can start making arrangements whenever you want.'

I nodded and grimaced as she bit into me again and took more blood.

'Who will we invite?'

Lilith this time sat up and licked her lips clean.

'Anyone we like.'

'Then let's start making plans tomorrow.' I said.

'It is tomorrow,' Lilith replied, glancing towards the black curtains of our bedroom window. Light was just beginning to enter around the edges.

'Yes,' I agreed. 'We really should sleep.'

'And yet...'

Lilith left the comment hanging in the air as she slowly and deliberately slid down my body.

Chapter 35

All the while I had been human, I had always wanted a wife and family. I just hadn't met the right woman. Now of course, as a vampire, those particular dreams were coming true. The most amazingly exquisite creature I had ever known had asked me to marry her and a lovely young girl now looked upon me as the father she had never had. In the space of just two amazing days, my life had changed forever.

Sure, biologically Emilie wasn't mine, but it simply didn't matter. More than once during those first few days, she came up to me and thanked me for saving her life. The fact that I had been the one responsible for the crash in the first place simply didn't concern her in the slightest.

'But Father,' she said, 'he probably would have killed me anyway.'

We would never know if this was true of course, but Emilie was moving on with her life and quickly settled into our little Camden home.

She was the first to admit her English wasn't brilliant, but after staying with us for a couple of weeks, it came more easily to her. I would often stand outside the study door and listen to Emilie read aloud, going over the same line three or four times until she was happy with her pronunciation.

Three weeks after I had sired her, Zang Zing had gone back to Paris, satisfied I was in control of my new found abilities.

He had been gone less than half a day when Cecilia and a man I had never met before arrived on our doorstep.

The man had very short fair hair and piercing blue eyes, not too dissimilar to Emilie's. The new-comer towered above Cecilia, and she isn't exactly short.

'Ah, Alex. I want you to meet Mark. He is our blood brother.'

Surprised by the announcement, I offered my hand anyway and Mark shook it eagerly, a wide smile on his face, although not enough to reveal his fangs.

As expected from a creation of Christiano's, Mark's grip was strong and was it my imagination or did his eyes narrow when I felt his grip tighten? I felt a slight pressure on my hand and fingers as his handshake lasted just too long, but if it was meant to hurt me, then he must have been disappointed.

'Cecilia has told me a great deal about you, Alex,' Mark finally broke his grip and then his eyes lit up as I felt the presence of my beloved behind me.

'Lilith!' he beamed, 'so good to see you again.'

I was ignored for the moment as Mark brushed past me, his arms out for an embrace. He was met with a stern expression and crossed arms.

'Hello Mark.'

That was the cool response he received from my future wife.

He tried to hide it but I saw Mark's face fall and his smile definitely dropped a few notches.

Before he could say anything, Cecilia interjected:

'Mark has been staying with us in Paris but insisted on coming here.'

'Did he now?' Lilith stared briefly at her blood brother before turning her attention back to Cecilia.

'Haven't you forgiven me yet?' Mark blurted out. 'It happened so long ago, Lilith.'

My Lily gazed at him for a few seconds before choosing her next words carefully, or so it seemed to me. As to what he was referring, I didn't have a clue.

'I do not want to discuss that here and now, in front of my fiancé.'

If Mark was disappointed before, his expression was now one of complete dejection.

'Your fiancé?' he stammered.

'Yes, Alex and I intend to get married. And soon,' she added, smiling at me and grabbing my hand.

'Well, congratulations,' Cecilia said. 'You make a lovely couple.'

'Thank you,' I smiled at her.

'Yes, congratulations,' Mark muttered and looked down at his shoes.

Lilith led the way down the hallway, still holding my hand.

'By the way, Cecilia. I want you to meet somebody,' I said.

'Really? And who might that be?'

I grinned and pointed at a seated Emilie, reading a book about the English language.

'Emilie, my first sired.'

Cecilia's mouth dropped open and for once she looked anything but regal. Of course, she quickly recovered and went over to my now standing daughter.

'Hello,' Emilie smiled at her.

The two female vampires were of equal height so that their eyes met with ease.

'You created her?' Mark's voice was filled with wonder as he too approached Emilie.

'Yes. It was either that or allow her to die,' I replied.

'Remarkable!' Cecilia was saying, 'I sense her power, Alex. For a fledgling, this is most unusual.'

'I agree,' Mark added, staring first at Emilie and then at me.

'Zang Zing said Alex could make a powerful vampire, despite the fact he's only been one himself for two years.' Lilith said, standing beside me.

'Most impressive,' Mark said and sat down on one of our sofas.

Cecilia continued to look at Emilie, and if my daughter was uncomfortable under such scrutiny, she didn't show it.

'So then Mark,' Lilith handed him a cup of coffee. 'Where have you been these past few years?'

'He can fill you in on that later,' Cecilia broke in, 'but tell me Alex, how did you meet this charming creation of yours?'

Her impatience surprised me a little but I quickly related the story, all the while becoming more aware of the fact Mark's interest in Emilie had become more heightened.

From where I was now sitting with Lilith, I saw he kept looking over at her. Emilie, for her part, avoided his gaze and instead glanced at me or at Cecilia.

'But what made you save her?' Cecilia wanted to know. 'I mean, it would have been easier for you to have let her bleed to death.'

'Zang Zing encouraged me to save her, and I'm glad I did,' I said, smiling at Emilie who grinned at me.

'And you are training her yourself? Or is Lilith schooling her in our ways?'

'Father is teaching me,' Emilie spoke up, 'but Mother helps me too.'

Obviously her French accent was still there but her words were clear and I felt Lilith's hand tighten in mine for just a moment.

'You called me Mother?' she whispered, staring at Emilie who shrugged.

'Of course. That is what you are, yes?'

Lilith looked at me and then back at Emilie, who was now worried she had said something wrong.

But my future wife smiled and went over to give Emilie a big hug.

'If you call me your mother, then that's what I shall be.'

I must admit I was relieved to hear Lilith's kind words. Yes, she had accepted Emilie into our home but it was another matter entirely too suddenly be called Mother.

'Well, isn't this nice? One big happy family.'

To my astonishment, Mark threw his cup of coffee at the fireplace and stormed out.

'Mark?' Cecilia called out and went after him, leaving the three of us staring at one another.

'Typical!' Lilith spat and went over and picked up the shattered pieces of cup.

'Why did he do that?' Emilie asked.

'God only knows,' Lilith answered, 'he's a law unto himself. Always has been, always will be.'

In this passionate outburst, Lilith's Irish accent became pronounced.

I went out to the kitchen and picked up a dishcloth.

As soon as Lilith had picked up all the broken cup pieces, I wiped up the spilt coffee.

'What did he mean earlier?' I asked. 'About being forgiven?'

Lilith ran a hand through her hair and looked at me.

'A long time ago, Mark made a pass at me. Said we should be together. It wasn't long after Severin's death, and I wasn't at all interested.'

'So what did you do?' I prompted.

'I told him in no uncertain terms to forget any idea about there being an 'us'. That he was nothing but a brother to me, and a distant one at that.'

'And I take it he didn't react well?'

Lilith looked up at me and slowly shook her head.

'He attacked me, Alex. Mark tried to rape me and would have probably succeeded if Christiano hadn't appeared.'

I stared at her in shock, not realising what Mark was capable of. I was beginning to understand his fascination with Emilie too.

'You see, Mark has always been stronger than me. I couldn't resist his strength that day or even now. He had ripped my dress open and had me pinned beneath him on the floor when Christiano threw him off me and swore he would destroy Mark if he saw him again. Until today, I hadn't set eyes on him since.'

'Now he's back.' Emilie said quietly.

'But surely Cecilia knows what he did?' I could see that the assault still shook my beloved, so I held her.

'Perhaps she thinks he's changed,' she spat. 'Or perhaps she's more forgiving than I am. Either way, she wasn't the one he tried to rape.'

'No,' I agreed. 'I can see that.'

Just then, Cecilia returned, looking more upset than I had ever seen her, and with no sign of Mark.

'I'm sorry for his temper,' she said.

'You should never have bought him here!' Lilith actually lashed out in her anger and the slap landed hard on her blood sister's cheek. The sound of it echoed around our lounge and I saw Emilie stare in amazement, having never seen Lilith angry before.

Cecilia rubbed her sore cheek and nodded at my sire.

'You are right, I'm sorry. I thought he had changed. He's been so... Well, charming I suppose, as our guest in Paris.'

'Leopard and spots,' Lilith glared at her.

'Leopard and spots? I do not understand,' Emilie said.

'I'll explain later,' I told her.

'So where is he now?' Lilith asked.

'I could not find him. Since Zang Zing gave him some of his blood, Mark's powers have grown. Only to be expected of course.'

At this remark, I glanced at Lilith before asking the next question.

'Why would Zang Zing give Mark blood?'

Cecilia sighed and sat down beside Emilie.

'When he came to us, Mark was in a very weakened state. Told us he had been attacked by another vampire. He had a large knife sticking out of his back and had lost a lot of blood.'

'Pity it didn't kill him,' Lilith said with venom, of the like I had never heard.

'Oh it very nearly did. The attack occurred only a couple of streets away from our chateau. He was lucky.'

'Why was he in Paris?' Lilith, despite herself, was curious.

'Mark claims he was just passing through. He says he has travelled almost non-stop for the past century.'

'Well, I don't want him in London,' Lilith said, defiantly.

'Or anywhere near this house,' I added, glancing at Emilie.

'I can't prevent him from going where he desires,' Cecilia protested.

'No, but Zang Zing can. And I can too,' I said, determined that Mark wouldn't come near my family again.

'But I don't know where he's gone.'

I thought about that and decided to try something. I excused myself and walked out into our little garden.

I let the sounds of the city slide away and closed my eyes.

I thought of Mark. I saw him crouching high on a roof-top, his fingers gripping the parapet so tightly that the concrete had great gouges in it.

Suddenly I knew he was aware of me and this made him smile malevolently.

As if he was standing next to me, I heard him speak:

'You have Lilith's love when it should have been rightfully mine decades ago. I will be coming for her, Alex. And if I can't have her, then I'll come for your daughter instead.'

I focussed my thoughts harder and told him he would have to come through me.

'You won't stop me, Alex King. No one will.'

Again I focussed my strength of will and told him that Christiano had stopped him all those years ago.

This only served to make Mark laugh out loud.

'Yes and he paid the price for choosing her over me. I killed him while he slept. Drove an iron spike through his head and drank all the blood that spurted out. You can tell Lilith and Cecilia their sire is no more.'

I shook my head, losing concentration. I was aware that Lilith was now standing behind me, just as Mark stood up and threw me one last comment.

'Soon, Alex. Soon.'

And with that, I lost all sense of him. Desperately I tried to track him but my efforts came up with nothing but a blank empty void. I was in no doubt that Mark was now blocking me somehow.

I slowly opened my eyes and turned to face the woman I loved.

'My Lily,' I said softly, 'I have bad news to tell you.'

Chapter 36

When I told her the news, Lilith stared at me in shocked silence. Then slowly, her hands balled into fists at her side and she spoke in a harsh whisper.

'I don't care how you do it Alex. I want him dead. Do you understand? I want him dead.'

I touched her arm briefly and smiled grimly.

'I will try my darling. But Mark is a powerful opponent.'

Lilith shook her head and gazed into my eyes as she placed her hands upon my shoulders.

'I've seen what you can do, Alex. I know you can destroy him.'

Cecilia and Emilie came then and I broke the news to Christiano's oldest and first sired.

She reacted differently, readily accepting the fact Christiano was gone.

'I'm not surprised,' Cecilia sighed. 'I will avenge his death, of course. It is what Christiano would have wanted and expected of me.'

'Can you defeat him?' Lilith asked the question that had entered my mind.

Cecilia gave a small shrug and smoothed a crease out of the dark red dress she was wearing and gave her answer:

'If I die trying, so be it.'

And with that, Lilith's blood sister took to the air leaving the three of us to a brooding silence.

Days came and went, with no sight or sound of Mark. I tried again to locate him with my sensory power but to no avail. Cecilia looked for him briefly, but was called back to Paris for Morisakis business.

Lilith made a call to them and spoke directly to Zang Zing, but even the master vampire himself couldn't detect Christiano's killer.

In the meantime, I continued to show Emilie our ways and she was becoming a natural hunter. I was pleased that she was using all her senses to track her would be victims; and she was especially good at using stealth, hardly making a sound when she crept up on her unsuspecting target, even on a surface such as crunchy gravel.

Cecilia had made an interesting suggestion just before she'd returned to Paris:

'I don't wish to intrude on the girl's upbringing but I can show her the ways of Bushido, if you wish.'

I remembered Cecilia's use of the sword and knew it would be a huge advantage in combat for Emilie if she was trained in the art of it.

'What do you think, Em?' I asked her.

'I would like that very much,' she admitted. 'But how would I do this, Father?'

'You could come and stay with me.' Cecilia told her.

I had to admit I was a bit reluctant to let her go so soon, but Emilie had jumped at the chance of returning to her homeland.

'I can stay at the chateau?' she asked, excitedly.

'Of course. You would be our guest, and don't worry, Alex. She will be perfectly safe.'

'Father?' Emilie questioned with such hope in her eyes that I sighed.

'It is your decision. We shall support it, whatever you decide.'

'Thank you. I should like to go very much.'

I smiled despite the sinking feeling I now had deep inside.

'Then you shall go,' I told her.

Lilith bought her a first class night flight and we promised to visit her soon.

So there we were; just the two of us again. Of course, we still saw Monica sometimes but she no longer required our help or instruction. In fact, my sister had gone back to her job at the museum, although how she avoided daylight I did not know. The main thing was, she was happy doing her own thing. Same old Monica, I suppose.

One evening we were curled up on in front of the fire in our dressing gowns and had just shared a long and passionate kiss when a breaking news item flashed up on the muted tv screen.

'Wait,' I stopped Lilith from untying my gown and pointed.

The camera closed in on a house's back garden and a street address flashed up that wasn't too far from our own.

I hit the remote button and the sound came back on.

'...The victims are all thought to be women, aged between sixteen to forty years of age. Police say they are of mixed race and although refusing to speculate on the cause of death, however it is believed each victim was drained entirely of their blood. As to the identity of the four women, it is not known at this time.'

I wanted to know more but the news item ended and the regular programme resumed.

'What is it, Alex?'

I looked at the woman I was to marry and told her what was on my mind: 'I can't really explain it but I just know that Mark is responsible.'

Lilith was silent for a few seconds.

'Are you sure?' she finally asked.

'Yes and I wouldn't mind betting the women were raped as well.'

Something in Lilith's eyes darkened at the R word but it was gone in a second.

'So Mark has been here in London, all this time?' she said quietly.

'I don't know. I just have this feeling it's his doing.'

'Oh I believe you. If anyone knows what he's capable of, it's me.'

'Yes, so what can we do?' I asked.

Lilith shrugged and brushed a few stray hairs out of her eyes.

'About the murders? There's nothing we can do, Alex.'

'We could go to the police,' I blurted out.

'And tell them what? That some psychotic vampire is on a killing spree? No Alex. We can't expose ourselves,' she said firmly.

'Perhaps we could warn people. I don't know.'

I was finding the situation very frustrating. Not only was such a monster loose on the streets, there didn't seem anything we could do to stop him.

'Maybe you'll find him,' Lilith suggested, but even as she said it, she didn't look convinced it would happen.

'Perhaps I'm wrong,' I said. 'Perhaps this isn't anything to do with a vampire.'

Lilith gently touched my face and looked me in the eyes.

'Tell me Alex. Did you trust your instincts as a human?'

Even the simplest of touches I found to be erotic, but putting those thoughts aside, I thought about my answer.

'Not really.'

Lilith nodded and held my chin in her hand.

'Then listen to me, my love. Always trust your instincts as a vampire.'

I smiled and bent my head towards hers, and soon all thoughts of the television were lost to our passion. Our kisses deepened and our robes quickly opened.

As I moved in between her thighs, Lilith switched off the tv and let the remote fall to the floor.

Chapter 37

We waited in vain for further news developments but none were forthcoming, despite the fact we searched the internet and Lilith had various contacts in the city. In fact, when the murdered women story faded from the headlines, Lilith and I began to plan our wedding.

'Who shall we invite?' I asked one day while we were enjoying bacon and eggs for breakfast.

'It won't be many,' Lilith said. 'Your Mother, Emilie and Monica. Jacob, Zang Zing and Ceclia. Anyone else?'

I had to admit I couldn't come up with another name and to me, the list seemed pitifully small.

'Hey, don't look so glum! A small ceremony will be lovely.'

I grinned at my sire and knew she was right.

'That's settled then,' she said. 'Now we have to choose when.'

'And where,' I added but was surprised when Lilith shook her head.

'No Alex. I have already spoken to Zang Zing about this and according to him there is only one vampire priest in existence who can marry us. Luckily, he is here in London.'

I followed Lilith into her small office and there by the computer, was a phone number written down on a notepad.

'How about the last Saturday in August? It is still two months away, allowing us plenty of time for other arrangements.'

'Sounds good to me,' I agreed but something was troubling me, and I knew what it was.

'How can there be such a thing as a vampire priest, Lilith?'

My beloved paused in picking up the phone and gazed at me. Then she actually gave a small laugh and shook her head.

'I don't actually know his story. I can only assume he no longer holds regular congregations. I can ask him if you wish, Alex?'

I shrugged and smiled back.

'It just strikes me as odd, that's all. That a vampire can still be a priest.'

I watched as Lilith tapped in the numbers on the phone.

Since my power increase, my hearing was now even more superior than ever, and I easily heard what the priest was saying.

'You do realise Lilith O'Shea, that yours shall be the first vampire wedding ceremony I have performed in over a hundred years?'

'All the more reason to go ahead then, Father.'

The priest gave a small chuckle.
'I would be delighted then. You know where to find me?'
Lilith told him yes and the date was fixed.
'One more thing, Father. We were wondering how you have remained a priest all these years?'
Again there came that small chuckle.
'Oh I no longer serve God as I once did. But I firmly believe the Lord loves all his creatures and forgives us of our sins, my child. Despite our origins, I still regard vampirism as a gift. I thank God for the gift of immortality, not Lucifer. This is why I will perform your ceremony, Lilith O'Shea.'
Everything I knew about religion, which wasn't much, was being turned upside down. I was lead to believe that if you took another life, then it was always regarded as an evil act. We kill as vampires, which makes us evil in my book. Yet, here was this priest fully believing otherwise. It baffled me but if he was the only one who could perform our marriage, then I was willing to believe anything.

During the next few days, nothing much happened. There were no more murder victims and as far as we knew, the police were still hunting the killer. Perhaps one telling clue as to the killer's identity was the fact they briefly held a man who vaguely resembled Mark for questioning. Apparently, an observant member of the public had been out walking their dog when they had spotted a fair haired man in the house's vicinity.
But the police released the man without charge a day later, leaving Lilith to observe:
'It would seem Mark has been careless. No self-respecting vampire is ever seen near his victim's bodies.'
'Perhaps he did it on purpose?' I suggested.
My lover thought about it and I saw her eyes narrow.
'To what end?'
'Maybe Mark wanted to send out a warning that he was still in the area.'
'You could be right.' Lilith agreed.

The next night I was tracking my next target, as I needed to feed. Zang Zing had been correct when he had said that despite my power increase, my bloodlust would actually diminish.
But I had left it for as long as I dared and the lust was growing within at such a rate that I might kill anyone or thing just to satisfy it.

My would-be victim was a bad man. Lilith had it on good authority that Jack Morgan was a professional killer: a hired gun that killed without mercy as long as his fee was met.

But now it was Morgan's turn to be hunted.

I followed the course of the man's dark Mercedes via the rooftops, easily keeping pace. Even from a distance I could tell the car was new and top of the range.

The night air was hot and humid but I felt no discomfort as I tracked the car to a quiet business park. From my lofty perch, I saw the Mercedes pull up smoothly next to the only other car there, a sports car of some sort. Crouched on the rooftop opposite, three stories up, I watched as Morgan dialled a number on his mobile. After a brief pause, he spoke into it:

'I'm in position. Have my money ready, Mr Johnston.'

That was the extent of the conversation, for he rang off and sat back in his seat.

I thought briefly of my beloved and saw in my mind that she was relaxing in a bubble bath. I smiled at the image and then re-focussed on my target. Morgan was talking again but this time to someone in the car with him:

'Quit your whining. You know this is what I do. And anyway, you don't complain when I buy you nice stuff.'

'Oh, whatever, dad,' a female voice replied, although I couldn't see who it belonged to. I assumed she was sitting in the back as Morgan now turned angrily in his seat.

'Don't give me the attitude, Bethany. Why I agreed to look after you I'll never know. I should've got shot of you years ago.'

'Well, I wish you had! And don't call me Bethany. It's Beth!' the girl shouted back.

Morgan muttered something about her bitchy mother and then slid out of the car.

He was dressed in an expensive looking dark suit and with a final glare at the back of the car; he made his way towards the nearest building. I watched with interest, as he now held a revolver in his gloved right hand, and with his left, was screwing a silencer onto the barrel.

Morgan quickly checked the weapon and silently slipped inside the building.

It was some kind of warehouse, not too dissimilar to the one where I had made my first ever kill. But instead of using the main shuttered door, Morgan had used a smaller side entrance.

I didn't move but instead focussed my attention on the car. I was quietly surprised when a girl of Emilie's age suddenly got out and walked away from it, towards the warehouse opposite. She had short spiky red hair, and was wearing a black denim skirt with purple leggings beneath. Her black t-shirt had a band logo emblazoned across her chest, although I didn't know who the band was.

The girl disappeared in the shadows around the side of the warehouse, although whether she was hiding or leaving her dad, I didn't know.

Even with the silencer on the gun, I still heard three shots echo from within the building and took that as my cue to act.

I dropped silently down the three stories and landed smoothly, walking immediately without pause across the tarmac towards the now silent warehouse.

However, I wasn't quiet as I entered. In fact I slammed the side door open so hard it splintered and fell off its hinges, sounding like a cannon shot as it landed on the hard concrete floor of the warehouse.

Without a word, Morgan fired at me, but by now my speed was more than a match for the bullet.

I calmly stepped to one side as the slug of hot metal zipped past and embedded itself in the brick wall behind me.

He immediately fired again and I had to give him credit for trying, at least. This time I ducked, all the while keeping my eyes on the target. With my new invisible strike power, I crushed his right hand so that Morgan automatically dropped the gun, a shout of pain and surprise quickly followed the reflex action.

He stood holding his now-useless hand with his other, staring at me in bewilderment.

'W-what are you?' he stammered.

'The last thing you will ever see,' I hissed, baring my fangs.

I knew that if I let Jack Morgan live, he would kill again, so after drinking almost all of his blood I let him slump to the floor. Concentrating all of my mind's incredible power, I snapped and crushed almost every bone in his body until all that remained of Morgan was a crumpled heap of a body still encased within an expensive but now completely ruined suit.

I saw a forklift truck parked nearby and with my supernatural physical strength, I picked up the truck and placed it on top of the body, making it look as if he'd been crushed by it.

I then remembered that Morgan had shot someone here, so on further investigation I found a dead man sitting in his chair in a small back office.

I didn't know who the man was but obviously someone had wanted him dead. Probably the Mr Johnston Morgan had placed a call to a bit earlier.

The three shots I had heard had all found their target; two to the man's chest and one in the middle of his forehead. No doubt a professional kill, but one Jack Morgan wouldn't be getting paid for.

I left the small office and walked back out past the crushed body of Jack Morgan and on out into the night. A nice and gentle breeze had lifted and I enjoyed the night air as I stood outside the warehouse.

I was about to take to the air and return home when a girl's voice called out.

'Is he dead, mister?'

I turned and saw the same red-haired girl from earlier, sitting on a pallet of old oil drums.

I now saw that around her neck was a collection of necklaces, featuring crucifixes, skulls and little dragons. I also saw that she had thick black eyeliner and dark lipstick, clearly identifying herself as a Goth.

'Well, did you kill him?' she asked again, tapping her booted feet against one of the drums.

'Yes, he is dead,' I confirmed.

I wasn't too sure what I was going to do about this situation. Obviously the girl was a witness to her father's murder, so I would have to prevent her from telling anyone. At the same time, I knew I couldn't just kill her. I may not have the same morals as most people, but I do have some. I had made up my mind to capture her gaze and command her to forget when the girl suddenly laughed.

'Good! I'm glad the bastard scum is dead. I hate you! I hate you, you fucker!'

I watched in silent amazement as the girl hurled abuse into the otherwise quiet warehouse.

Then she took me by surprise by jumping off the pallet and running up to me, throwing her arms around me and giving me just about the biggest hug I had ever received; certainly from a human.

'Thank you! Thank you!' she was saying into my chest.

I held her briefly and then gently pushed her away.

'Who are you?' I wanted to know.

'I'm Beth. That bastard in there was my useless father. I'm glad he's dead, so thank you.'

I held up my hand and stopped her from hugging me again.

'Well, if you are truly happy I killed him, then good. I'm glad. If not, then I'm sorry.'

The girl then looked at me as if for the first time and I saw that her eyes were almost as green as my beloved's.

'What's it like, mister?'

'I'm sorry?' her question confused me.

'Being a vampire, silly!'

I stared at her in surprise, my mouth falling open revealing my fangs.

'You know what I am?' I was incredulous that this teenaged girl was so utterly unafraid of me.

'Of course. I'm into vampires and stuff. I always had a suspicion you were real.'

She gripped the front of her t-shirt and I glanced down at the band depicted upon it.

'The Dead Awaken? I don't know that band,' I admitted.

Beth gave a small groan and let her t-shirt drop again.

'Gothic rock at its finest!' she almost sung the words out and then she broke into a song about zombies being slaughtered or something.

I was finding the whole scene quite surreal and to be honest all thoughts of capturing her gaze had left me.

Here I was, a tremendously powerful vampire fresh from his kill, listening to a young girl sing about zombies and death, when really I should have been back in the arms of my fiancé.

Beth suddenly stopped singing and prancing about in her boots and faced me once again.

'So what is it like?' this time she stood with her hands on her hips, obviously her way of demanding an answer.

'It's pretty cool, actually,' I smiled.

'I knew it! Oh wow! This is fricking amazing!'

'Look, I really must get home,' I told her.

'Do you live near?' she asked, going over to the pallet of drums and sitting down again.

'Not far. Just across the city. You?'

'Half an hour's drive.'

I blinked a couple of times and said what was on my mind.

'I can't believe your father took you on one of his hits.'

'Why not? He always used to brag about being this hired killer. I hated him.'

'Wasn't he afraid you would turn him into the police?'

For the first time since the song, Beth averted her eyes and looked at the tarmac instead.

'Beth?' I prompted softly.

When she looked up again, tears had come to her beautiful green eyes.

'I couldn't tell on my dad because I killed someone once.'

This time tears came flooding out and she dissolved into mournful cries that melted my heart. I went over to her and held her close, allowing her to shed her tears into my chest until finally, they were reduced to little sobs a minute or so later.

'Who did you kill, Beth?' I asked gently, still holding her by the arms but far enough apart so that she could look up at me.

'It was a girl at school,' she said quietly. 'She bullied me with her friends for two years until finally, one day after school I finally snapped. She was alone behind the gym smoking and she made a move to trip me as I passed. She laughed as I stumbled but remained on my feet. I then shoved her as hard as I could and to my amazement, she fell back and smacked her head on the wall. I panicked when I saw the blood and ran home. I told my Dad what had happened and he just laughed and said it was about time I stood up for myself.'

Beth fell silent and I quietly finished the story for her.

'And the girl died from her injury?'

Beth slowly looked up at me again and slowly nodded.

'I know it was an accident but I'm still guilty. Three years later she still haunts my dreams. You're only the second person who knows.'

I nodded and stood up, releasing her.

'Your secret is safe with me, Beth,' I smiled at her.

Suddenly, the girl took me by surprise once again.

'Can I come home with you, mister? Please? I only had my useless Dad taking care of me. I don't have anyone else.'

'I can't do that Beth. I'm sorry if killing your father has left you all alone in the world, but…'

'I don't have to be alone,' Beth interrupted, 'Take me with you. Make me a vampire and I'll be yours forever then.'

Beth made a move to hug me again but I held her at arms-length and shook my head.

'No Beth, it cannot be. I am very much in love with my fiancé.'

This stunned her into silence but not for long.

'You're getting married? Is she a vampire too?'

I laughed at how excited Beth had become again, pleased she had taken my rejection so well.

'Yes. Lilith made me and I love her more than anything.'

'Cool or what!' Beth's face lit up even more. 'Take me with you. I don't care if you're getting married. I just want to be like you.'

'No, Beth. I can't. It...'

'Why not? Are you the only two vampires out there or something?'

Beth's fierce words took me aback and I knew I had to tell her the truth.

'No, there are more of us. I actually have a daughter of similar age to you.'

I thought of Emilie then and saw that she was fast asleep in the Morisakis chateau far away.

'Yes! That's it!' Beth said excitedly. 'Make me like you. I can be your second daughter. Please!'

I had to admit her desire and passion for becoming a vampire was having an effect on me.

Would it be terribly wrong of me to give her what she wanted? To bestow upon her the gift of immortality and make her part of the family? I admit I was feeling the absence of Emilie a great deal, and perhaps I was secretly looking to fill the void she had left. But was it really fair of me to give that position to a girl I barely knew? Beth broke into my thoughts with another question.

'What is she like? Your daughter? I mean, she can't be your biological child if she's my age. Not unless you conceived her when you were about eight!'

I laughed and shook my head.

'No. Her name is Emilie. She is actually French.'

I told Beth the tale of what had happened and why Emilie had been over in this country. The more I explained, the more excited Beth got.

'You see? Perhaps it was destiny that we should meet like this. You kill my father and take his place. Some divine plan or other: makes sense to me.'

I stepped away from her and thought about all she had said. When I turned back to face her, I looked at her but didn't capture her gaze.

'Do you really want to become a vampire, Beth?' I asked softly.

'Yes, I do. Please!'

'Let me make this absolutely clear to you okay? Once the transformation begins, there is no stopping it. I cannot change you back. Do you understand?'

Beth held my gaze for a second or two before nodding once.

'I understand.' She answered quietly, but with a determination I admired.

I took a deep breath and gave in.

'Very well. Lie back on the pallet and hold out your arm.'

I watched as Beth did as she was told without question or hesitation.

'I'm going to bite into your wrist as gently as I can. I will take most of your blood and you will become very weak. I shall then give you some of my blood and the transformation will occur.'

'Will I fall asleep and wake up reborn like the movies?' Beth looked up at me as I approached the pallet.

'Perhaps,' I said, 'or maybe you won't fall asleep at all. There is no given set of rules when it comes to making vampires; only that I cannot make more than three.'

At this piece of news, Beth sat up and stared at me.

'What? You mean after you turn me, you can only do it one more time?'

'Yes, that's exactly what I mean.'

'But why? That doesn't seem fair.'

'It is our way. It is how it has been for centuries. We cannot allow our population to grow unimpeded. Think of the consequences.'

Beth did so.

'Obviously, the more vampires around, the greater risk of discovery. Also, the more danger to the human race.'

I nodded, pleased she had understood.

'But I still want to be like you. Be a part of your family, even though you haven't told me your name.'

I laughed and knew that this was absolutely right; that I would be proud and honoured to call Beth my daughter. I only hoped Lilith would understand when I took her home, but I was sure she would.

'Forgive me,' I said. 'My name is Alex.'

Beth smiled and gave me her hand.

'I will call you Dad.'

Chapter 38

When I returned home with Beth, Lilith was a bit surprised to say the least. After the briefest of hellos, my beloved slowly circled the new vampire, saying nothing. Her silence was both confusing and dramatic.

My new daughter glanced uneasily at me, her emerald eyes shining more brightly thanks to the power of the vampiric blood.

Finally, Lilith stepped back and looked at me.

'You have made her well, Alex, but you do realise you can only sire one more?'

'Of course,' I answered. 'I don't regret giving Beth my blood. Not one drop of it.'

Beth grinned at me and then spoke to Lilith.

'I know you weren't expecting me and I'm sorry if my being here upsets you.'

For the first time, my fiancé smiled and took hold of Beth's hand, gently shaking it.

'Not at all,' she said. 'You are most welcome.'

Naturally I was relieved to hear those words and soon Beth was relaying her story to us; about how no one had suspected her of the girl's death but as a result, her studies and grades suffered, and she left school without any qualifications.

She was now eighteen, and had recently started her first job, waiting tables in a back street café, but hadn't really liked it.

'Men would come in and think they had the right to touch me up. Worse thing was, my boss encouraged it! Said his customers were loyal and besides, it probably meant I would get bigger tips out of them.'

It disgusted me to think that kind of thing was going on but Lilith quickly voiced the sad truth.

'It's the way of the world, I'm afraid. It's been going on throughout the ages; even now pretty women in all walks of life are often regarded as sex objects.'

Beth gave her a surprised look.

'You think I'm pretty?' she asked, clearly amazed at the notion.

We both nodded and Beth laughed, clapping her hands as she did.

'Oh wow! I've never been called pretty before. Grungy and weird, yes, but never pretty.'

We went and sat in the lounge and soon we had coffees on the go. Beth went on to tell us how her father would often leave her on her own for hours at a time, sometimes for days.

'He gave me cash to buy food and stuff but that was about it.'

'What about your mother?' Lilith asked.

Beth shook her head and took a sip of coffee.

'She left us years ago when I was small. Dad never gave a reason. I went to bed one night and by morning she was gone.'

'Did they fight a lot?' I wanted to know.

'No, that's the weird thing. I always thought they were happy.'

'How old were you when she left?'

This time it had been Lilith's turn to ask the question.

'Six, I think. Six or seven.'

'And how did your mother respond to the fact your father was a hit-man?'

'I don't think she knew. But to be honest, it was a long time ago so I might not be remembering it right.'

I found her tale to be strange and suspected that perhaps her mother had discovered her husband's secret and run away. Either that or he had murdered her. Both were possibilities and one glance at Lilith told me she was thinking the exact same thing. Neither of us voiced our suspicions aloud though.

'What about friends? Boyfriends?' Lilith asked. She was clearly glad to change the subject, and I think Beth was too.

'Neh,' Beth shrugged. 'I've always been a bit of a loner. Thanks to my Dad, I've got used to my own space and doing my own thing.'

I had to ask the question which immediately sprang to mind.

'If that's the case, what made you want to come with me?'

Beth was suddenly quiet and was now looking down at her boots.

'I don't know,' she mumbled. 'I guess I thought it would be different. Even cool, you know?'

She looked up then and gave us a wonderful smile.

Lilith and I exchanged glances and both smiled back at her.

'We shall do our best,' Lilith told her. 'But for now, you need to feed.'

As with Emilie, Lilith allowed me to teach Beth our ways; to show her what it was really like being a vampire.

Of course, after I had given Beth a lot of my blood, I needed to feed as well and quickly found two old drunken homeless guys in Regents Park.

It was three in the morning and no one else was around.

I grabbed my chosen target and quickly drained him, sealed the bite mark on his neck and let him live. He was asleep on one of the park benches while Beth silently went after her target.

The old tramp had been so far gone with drink that he hadn't even noticed me grab his companion. Now he staggered up the pathway, muttering to himself about how the government had let him down or something.

I had already warned Beth that her first feed was the most difficult and sure enough, things didn't go well.

I was about to warn my daughter that the tramp had wandered beneath a security camera but before I got the words out, she pounced. Much as Emilie had done in the barn, Beth's ravenous hunger overtook my instructions and her teeth were already ripping into the back of the man's neck. I cursed and ran up to them but then remembered the camera. Shaking my head at the great sucking sounds that were now emanating from my daughter, I jumped up and grabbed the camera, twisting it off its metal spine with ease. Landing back on the gravel path, I crushed it with one stomp of my foot. Of course I had to be sure the film itself was destroyed so I ripped the camera open and stuffed the disk into my pocket.

All this had happened within seconds but seconds the tramp didn't have, for Beth was now sitting on him, her eyes closed and licking her lips.

'Beth?' I asked softly.

She opened her eyes and I could see them shining with an intensity they had never shown before.

'He has nothing left to give,' she said.

I gestured for her to move and checked for a pulse I knew I would not find.

'Did I do it wrong, Dad?' Beth was clearly bemused by my actions.

'Yes and no,' I replied, standing up. 'You took all his blood, which you shouldn't have done. But it's my fault, I should have stopped you.'

Beth then saw the smashed security camera and gasped.

'I didn't see that!' she was suddenly alarmed, and begun to pace up and down.

'It's alright. I took care of it. But these damn things are popping up more and more and we have to be careful.'

'I'm sorry, Dad.' Beth muttered and hugged me.

I patted her on the back but knew we had to get away from the area.

'Seal the man's wound like I showed you and place him next to his sleeping friend.'

I inspected Beth's handy-work and had to admit she had done an excellent job, especially considering the amount of damage her fangs had inflicted.

She quickly picked up the dead man with ease and carried him over to the bench where his companion was still fast asleep.

We then left, quickly putting a good distance between ourselves and the park.

Soon we found ourselves walking along a quiet street and Beth asked the question I knew was coming.

'Why was it wrong? Taking that guy's blood, I mean. Isn't that what vampires do?'

I sighed and quickly explained all about the spirit demon. I then went on and told her of the vampire laws we had to obey. At this point, Beth was clearly disappointed.

'I thought vampires could do whatever they wanted.'

I shook my head.

'No, Beth. If we killed whoever we liked, humans would soon discover us and hunt us down. We have to be discreet, it's the only way.'

After teaching her a bit more about using her now enhanced senses, we made our way home.

I showed her Emilie's old room and was about to say goodnight when she called out to me.

'Yes?' I answered, pausing in the doorway.

'I'm sorry I killed the tramp. I promise to do better next time.'

I nodded and told her that tomorrow we would fly and use mind control.

'Cool. Night, Dad.'

I smiled and closed the door.

Chapter 39

The following day I kept to my word and soon Beth and I were soaring high above London, zooming in and out of the thickening cloud cover. I had to admit I had got so used to the sensation of defying gravity that it took me a bit by surprise when my new daughter shrieked out with pure delight, opening out her arms and spinning in mid-air. But up so high in the clouds, I knew no one could possibly see us and laughed along with her.

After spinning around once more, Beth stopped and faced me, hovering just a couple of feet away.

'What will Emilie think of me?' she asked.

I pondered the question and was alarmed I hadn't even thought about it.

'I'm sure she will love you, Beth. Why do you ask?'

'Because she's your first sired. I don't want her angry at me for taking her room.'

'I'm sure she won't be like that.'

'Why is she away?'

I quickly explained that Emilie was staying with Cecilia and receiving extra training from her.

'I see. And will I get to meet this Cecilia woman too? She sounds like a bad ass.'

I laughed and there was a time I would have agreed with that description of Lilith's blood sister.

'Of course you will meet her.'

As it turned out, Beth got to meet both her and Zang Zing much sooner than I anticipated, for just two days later, the pair of them came to visit us in our Camden home.

After the introductions were made, Cecilia stood by the fireplace but Zang Zing began to pace around the living room. I had never seen the ancient vampire look so agitated before.

'We bring grave news, Alex,' he turned to face me.

I immediately knew something was wrong but one quick thought-search for Emilie confirmed it wasn't anything to do with her, as I could see her reading in what I assumed was the Morisakis library.

As if reading my thoughts, Zang Zing placed a hand on my arm.

'Emilie is fine.'

'More than fine,' Cecilia added. 'She has a remarkable capacity for learning, Alex. It is a joy teaching her.'

I smiled but it was brief, for Zang Zing then spoke again.

'Have you noticed a sharp rise in vampire activity in London?'

I glanced at Lilith and we both shook our heads.

'None that we have noticed, Zang Zing,' Lilith answered.

The mighty vampire frowned and shook his head.

'What is it? What's wrong?' I asked.

'Something is very wrong. I can sense it. Someone is siring vampires at an impossible rate.'

I was about to ask who but Cecilia answered for me.

'We believe Mark is building himself an army. To what end, we aren't sure but of course it won't be for anything good.'

'What?' Lilith sounded startled and for good reason.

Zang Zing held up a hand and we all looked at him.

'Mark let his guard slip. It was only for an instance but it was long enough for me to see that he was still in London,' he explained.

I tried to sense Lilith's twisted blood brother but I got nowhere.

'If Mark is indeed siring more vampires, then you are in danger. I'm sure you don't need to be reminded that any vampire he might make would be very strong; and more than likely, vicious too.'

'What do you suggest?' Lilith asked, now holding my hand as if seeking comfort. I only hoped I was giving it to her.

'We suggest you come with us to Paris. Allow the might of the Morisakis to protect you,' Cecilia replied.

'But this is our home,' Lilith protested. 'Surely he wouldn't dare attack us here?'

I turned her to face me and gently caressed her face.

'I think we should go,' I said. 'We all know what he is capable of.'

'Alex is correct,' Zang Zing spoke again. 'I am hoping I can confront him while here and make him see reason.'

'But you don't have much hope of that,' Cecilia added.

The ancient Chinese vampire sadly shook his head

'I fear not.'

And so it was with great reluctance that the three of us began to pack some things for our unplanned stay in Paris. Naturally, Beth didn't have much in the way of possessions as we hadn't had a chance to go to her old house. But Lilith and I just looked at one another in our bedroom, while Zang Zing and Cecilia waited downstairs.

'This isn't right, Alex. This is our home. We shouldn't be afraid in our own home.'

Lilith was close to tears and so I held her, resting my head against her hair.

'It will be okay, my darling,' I whispered. 'I promise you. Besides, we're getting married soon and I won't let anything stop you from becoming my wife.'

In between her sobs, my beloved laughed and playfully smacked my shoulder before giving me one of the longest kisses I could remember.

Soon we were ready to go. We were all outside with various packed cases in the back garden but Lilith suddenly remembered something.

'Wait! I forgot my keys.'

I nodded and watched her dash back in.

That's when the attack came.

Three vampires landed just a few feet away and rushed me. I had just enough time to shout out Lilith's name before my arms were grabbed by two of them and the third one grabbed me around the neck.

Suddenly there were vampires everywhere. I struggled in their grip and saw five more converge on Zang Zing. Cecilia tried to go to his aid but she herself was set upon by three more. I snarled in fury as I saw Beth get hit by yet another vampire, her head rolling with the blow as she went down, clearly unconscious.

I seethed in anger and frustration but was unable to break free. I tried to see what was happening to Zang Zing but he was buried beneath a pile of vampire bodies, all shouting and raining down blows. These vampires were unlike any I had seen before. They were feral and nasty. The kind of vampires writers loved to bring to the silver screen in Hollywood to bring as much death and gore to the watching public as possible.

I desperately tried to wrench my arm free as the vampire who had hit Beth ran into the house.

A powerful hand was placed on my mouth just before I could scream Lilith's name again.

One of our attackers suddenly flew past, landing face first with a crunch into our garden wall. I turned slightly and saw that Cecilia had thrown him off but then two more came from over the wall and took his place, pinning her to the damp grass.

I felt the hand on my mouth pull away and I immediately called out to my beloved.

'Shut up!' the one behind me yanked my head back by the hair just as there came a crash of breaking glass. I struggled to see the vampire who had gone into our house was now lying unconscious on the lawn, having been thrown through the kitchen window.

I saw Lilith then. She was standing in the open doorway, pure and unbridled rage on her lovely features. She took a step forwards and her eyes widened when she saw the utter chaos in her own garden, but before she could do or say anything, a vampire came from around the side of the house and shot her in the chest. The noise was deafening, for it was a shotgun he had used; the blast taking my beloved off her feet and crashing into the garden wall. Her body disappeared from view behind the shrubs and bushes that were planted there.

'Lily!' I cried out, but there was no response. I glared at the new-comer with the shotgun and realised it was Mark himself, dressed entirely in black, an evil grin etched across his face.

'There is no use struggling, Alex,' he smiled. 'I made them very strong. Don't you agree?'

'Why are you doing this?' I hissed. I tried sending an invisible strike of power at my adversary but Mark blocked it somehow.

'There's no use trying your mind tricks on me, Alex King. I have some of Zang Zing's blood in my veins, remember?'

I shook my head, trying desperately to think how I could get out of this situation; to get us all out of this situation.

I then saw that Beth was coming around but Mark saw it too and with a swift kick to her head, knocked her out again.

'I see she has her mother's eyes,' Mark indicated my daughter. 'I shall enjoy playing with her later.'

His threat made me struggle again and the captive on my right made the mistake of stepping into my view. I immediately sent out a wave of furious power at him and watched with some satisfaction as his head blew clean off his shoulders and sailed high over the wall.

I couldn't celebrate for long though because I suddenly felt a great pressure on my chest, building in intensity. It felt as if my heart was being slowly squeezed and I realised that was exactly what it was, for Mark was staring at me, his eyes narrowed in concentration.

I gasped with the pain and just when I couldn't bear it any longer, everything became dark and I slumped in my captive's arms.

The world, or rather my living room, slowly came back into focus as I found myself bound to one of our armchairs by heavy steel chains.

Something didn't feel right and I saw Mark standing by the fireplace watching me.

'I took the liberty of taking some of your blood. Quite a bit of it actually. I would say a nice vintage but then again, you're still very young for a vampire.'

That was why I felt so weak. I focussed my mind and tried to break the chains but it was no use. In my weakened state, my powers weren't strong enough to break them. I needed blood and fast.

'Nothing to say?' he taunted me. He still had the shotgun held against one shoulder and now prodded me in the chest with it.

'Why didn't you kill me?' I snarled through gritted teeth.

Mark smiled and indicated Beth, who was unconscious in the other chair; her face badly swollen and bruised from where she had been hit.

'I kept you alive so you could witness me killing her.'

'Bastard!' I struggled against the chains but they refused to move.

Mark just laughed and gently ran his hand down Beth's face.

'I'm intrigued, Alex. Why is it you haven't asked about your beloved Lilith?'

I gasped in shock and immediately thought about my beloved. I could see in my mind that she was where I had last seen her. Lying face down, unmoving in the flowerbed. I immediately began to cry for I knew she should have recovered by now.

'Pity really. I would have thought she would have survived the gunshot. It just goes to show our beloved master didn't make her as strong as he should have.'

'No, no, no.' I was shaking my head, refusing to believe she was gone and that I would never get to hold her again.

'Yes,' Mark continued speaking, oblivious of my heartbreak. 'If she had survived I would have made her suffer. Oh yes. I've waited years to make that bitch suffer. I would have raped her and killed you in front of her, making her watch every painful bit of it.'

Suddenly he stepped forward and struck me across the face, my head rolling to one side with the force of the blow, which hurt a great deal.

I then thought of Zang Zing and saw that he was lying on the grass, a vampire guarding his body. Was he dead too? I couldn't tell but I certainly couldn't detect any movement.

Mark stepped away from me and went back over to Beth.

'I admit I have a lust for women, especially those with green eyes. I don't know why, just the way I am I suppose.'

I tried again to break the chains but my arms weren't strong enough. Instead I sent a wave of power at Mark but he laughed acidly.

'Your power merely tickles me now. See? I didn't even bother to block your pathetic effort.'

I knew he was right and then looked on in horror as Mark ripped open Beth's black shirt, the buttons flying off in all directions. He cupped her right breast and began fondling it.

'Yes, I can see why you made her. Such a sweet girl, Alex. You've done well.'

'Leave her alone!' I snapped but he paid no attention and instead began groping her other breast, the fabric of her bra moving more fiercely this time.

'Please. I'll do whatever you want, just please don't hurt her.'

I'm not ashamed to admit that tears were coming thick and fast now. I was becoming more and more lost to my misery and grief; grief that Lilith was lost and that Beth was in serious danger and that we all might not survive this night.

Mark stopped touching her and faced me again.

He then laughed and struck me again. Somehow I remained awake and Mark then surprised me by calling out.

'Bjorn, get in here! You too, Don.'

I wasn't sure what was going on but two heavyset vampires came into the room.

'Did you check on Cecilia?' he asked.

Bjorn, a big guy with long blonde hair nodded.

'I did, sir. I stabbed her myself with a fence post. She's dead, sir.'

Mark actually clapped his hands with glee and glanced over at me.

'Oh dear. It really doesn't look very good for this little gathering, does it? The mighty Cecilia slain by one of my puppets.'

If he was insulted by the comment, Bjorn didn't show it. In fact he smiled and simply nodded in agreement.

I thought of my Lily again and to my astonishment, actually saw that she was awake, lying on her back, staring up at the stars; her green eyes shedding tears for I knew she was still in a great deal of pain. But she was alive!

I somehow managed to keep the joy to myself and knew that we still had a chance. It wasn't much of one but if Lilith could recover, I was filled with renewed hope. I only hoped Mark was so busy gloating about his victory he wouldn't sense her survival.

'So what exactly can you do for me, Alex?' Mark suddenly turned on me again and gripped my face with his right hand.

I knew that I had to buy Lilith time and to do that I needed to keep Mark talking.

'You're building an army right? I can make powerful vampires for you.'

He narrowed his eyes and for some reason my mind switched to Cecilia. Sure enough, I saw she was lying on her back, a large wooden fence post sticking out of her chest. But Bjorn had been wrong for she too was still alive! Her eyes were blinking and I now physically saw her grip the post with her hand and began to slowly withdraw it, inch after painful inch.

'And what makes you think I would have need for vampires you create?'

I focussed my mind back on Lilith and now saw she was crawling across the ground towards the guard standing over Zang Zing.

'Come on Mark,' I said. 'I know how it works. It takes a lot out of you to sire vampires. You need recovery time before you can do it again.'

Mark's eyes narrowed again and glanced over at the now-waking Beth.

'What you say is true,' he muttered and took a few steps away, clearly thinking about my proposal.

I thought of Cecilia and saw that she had now removed the post entirely and was slowly sitting up, the wound in her chest already beginning to heal, thanks to her age and power.

Suddenly my focus was drawn back to Mark as he grabbed hold of my daughter and yanked her upright until she was standing in front of him.

'What are you doing?' I gasped, not liking the sudden turn of events.

Beth was clearly terrified for she was looking at me, panic in her eyes.

'Let's see how good you make them, Alex,' Mark snarled and suddenly sank his teeth into Beth's neck.

'No!' I cried out in shock and saw my daughter instantly begin to slump in her attacker's arms. But just a few seconds later, Mark released her and pushed Beth back into the chair. She was weakened but still awake.

'Yes!' he grinned at me, blood dripping from his fangs. 'She is a strong one. I can use her and others like her. Alright Alex, you have got yourself a deal. With your help I can build an army that can storm the Morisakis and take over. We will rule the vampire population and keep adding to it.'

I let him carry on with his delusional speech, all the while thinking about Lilith. She had now grabbed the vampire guarding Zang Zing and was about to bite him when Cecilia shook her head and pointed at the fallen master. Lilith paused and then shoved the guard at Cecilia who quickly began feasting upon the unfortunate vampire.

'Tell me Alex. Why would you make me this offer? Especially after I killed your beloved?'

Mark's question brought me back to the living room and I knew I had to make my lie the best one I had ever told.

'Truthfully?' I asked.

Mark nodded, gently stroking the shotgun again.

I thought of Lilith before answering and saw she was kneeling down beside Zang Zing's body.

'I loved Lilith,' I said. 'I really did. But the thought of marrying her? No fucking way! The very thought of it made my skin crawl. I was only going through with it to shut her up. She was good for sex but nothing much else.'

Beth gasped and knew she believed what I was saying but Mark slowly shook his head.

'Nice try for the Oscar, Alex. But not convincing enough.'

Mark slowly raised the shotgun and I had the vision of Severin's death again; ironically, the same death that was about to befall me, but a shout outside stopped Mark from shooting.

'Now what?' he spat, and stormed off, taking the vampire called Don with him.

Bjorn was clearly unsure what to do so I tried talking with him.

'You can't be happy at being called a puppet.'

The blonde vampire hissed and grabbed me by the throat.

'It is of no concern of yours!'

'No,' I smiled. 'But she is.'

I had provided all the distraction required, for Beth was suddenly upon him, ripping at the back of his neck with her fangs. Mark obviously hadn't taken enough of her blood to weaken her too much.

Bjorn cursed and tried to fend her off but lost his balance and fell against me. Without hesitation I bit deep into his exposed arm and drank hungrily, feeling my strength and power returning at an exceptional rate.

Beth withdrew and allowed me to finish him as we heard more shouting outside.

I heard Mark's voice cry out:

'No! What have you done?'

I didn't need my mind strike power to break the chains, for my vampiric physical strength was back to its best. I easily raised both my arms and the chains creaked and broke, falling to my feet as I shot up out of the chair and bolted outside, Beth right behind me.

The sight that greeted us will forever remain in my memory.

My first glance was of Cecilia, standing with two lifeless vampires at her feet, including Don, her furious glare directed towards her blood brother.

Next, I saw that Zang Zing was truly dead, his lifeless eyes staring up at the stars and moon but seeing nothing. But the smile on his face was one of serenity and I knew his end had been a peaceful one.

Finally my searching eyes found my beloved Lilith. She was floating in mid-air, power literally crackling around her. She looked absolutely beautiful, despite the gaping hole in the middle of her dress. She also looked terrifying as her hateful gaze bore into the man who had once tried to violate and murder her.

Mark still held the shotgun but was seemingly unable to use it.

And then the woman I loved with both of my souls spoke:

'Zang Zing sacrificed himself, Marcus. He gave me his blood. Every. Last. Drop.'

My Lily said those last few words slowly and deliberately. A wave of absolute power was sent with each one. With the word Every, I saw Mark's right arm shatter so that he was forced to let go of the gun.

When she spoke the word Last, another wave of power shattered both of his legs so that Mark toppled over. And yet, he still didn't cry out. It was as if some invisible force was preventing him from moving at all.

Then finally, with the word Drop, Lilith sent a blast of invisible energy that ripped through Mark's chest, sending shards of rib cage and flesh flying outwards in all directions.

Blood immediately fountained out onto our lawn but Mark was somehow still alive. He gazed up at us, blood pooling beneath his battered body and dripping out of his mouth.

'May I have the honour of finishing this?'

It was Cecilia who had spoken. I saw that her eyes were locked onto her younger sister, still floating within the circle of radiating energy.

Lilith simply nodded and glanced at me, smiling for the first time.

I smiled back, still amazed by the sheer amount of power that she now possessed.

She slowly lowered herself to the ground and I immediately went to her.

'I thought I had lost you,' I hugged her so hard and we both laughed as static snapped between us.

'Never, Alex. You will never lose me,' she kissed me then and for all intents and purposes it might as well have been the first ever kiss between us, for sparks literally flew into my mouth and I gasped, staggering back a couple of steps, but Lilith held me.

'Forgive me. I'm not used to this kind of power yet,' she said softly.

I nodded and we both looked over as Cecilia hefted the shotgun and aimed it at her blood brother's head.

'Well, beloved brother, your time is at an end.'

Mark at last gasped and coughed up more blood before whispering to her.

'Go to hell.'

He smiled and Cecilia shook her head.

'Goodbye.'

And with that simple word, Cecilia pulled the trigger and blew his head to smithereens.

We all stood and waited for the echo of the blast to fade away before speaking.

Cecilia sighed and dropped the gun, glancing over at us.

'It is done,' she said simply and then marched off into the house.

'Dad?' Beth walked over and I hugged her, relieved that she was safe.

'It's okay now Beth. It's all over,' I told her.

I looked at my fiancé as she stared at Mark's headless body.

'And look at you,' I said, 'so much power.'

Lilith tore her gaze away and smiled at me.

'Let's try that kiss again,' she grinned and came at me.

This time there was just the merest of tingles when our lips met, but it was something I could easily get used to.

Epilogue

After two shotgun blasts, it came as no surprise when the police banged on the door. As if expecting them, Cecilia answered and spoke quickly before the officer did.

'They weren't gun-blasts at all, officer. The sounds heard were from a car backfiring. That is all.'

The officer was about to argue but Cecilia simply repeated what she had said and it was evident to me she had caught the policeman's gaze.

'A car backfiring?' he repeated, sounding every bit as if he was being controlled.

'That's right. No cause for alarm here,' Cecilia gave him a dazzling smile and slowly closed the front door.

'I don't understand why Zang Zing died.'

Those were the first words I spoke once we had all seated ourselves in our lounge and knew the police had driven away.

Cecilia and I had carried in the ancient vampire's body and placed it gently upon the floor.

Beth in particular looked shaken by the evening's events but then again, I think we all were.

'He wanted to die,' Cecilia said.

'Wanted to?' Lilith repeated.

She had gone up and changed out of the ruined dress and was now dressed in simple white cotton trousers and dark blue t-shirt. Being taller than my Lily, the trousers didn't fit properly, but otherwise she looked fine.

Cecilia sighed and looked at her.

'He told me just last week that he felt his time was coming to an end. He welcomed it, after being on the planet for so long.'

'You mean he knew this was coming?' I asked.

'Well, not this attack exactly but Zang Zing did say that given the opportunity he would pass on all his power to someone else, so that they could carry on protecting vampire kind.'

I nodded but was still trying to see the logic behind his reasoning.

'But, why me?' Lilith asked. 'You were there in the garden with us. Why didn't you take his blood?'

Cecilia shook her head and stood up, straightening her t-shirt as she did.

'And what would you have thought if I had taken it? You would have said it was my intention all along. So no, blood sister, I allowed you to take the master's blood. End of story.'

I stared at her, shocked she would even think that of Lilith, but from one glance at my beloved, I knew there was some truth in her accusation.

Lilith stood and faced her sister in blood, both created by the same vampire but so very different. The two gorgeous creatures of the night stared at one another before Lilith slowly extended her hand and Cecilia gently took it.

'It is true,' Lilith began. 'There is a lot of bad history between us. I felt you could have done more for me in my early years, and especially when our own blood brother attacked me. But he's dead now and we should move on. What's past is past.'

Cecilia nodded and said: 'Agreed.'

They shook hands and then embraced.

I was a bit surprised, having thought all the bad feeling had already gone, but clearly Lilith had kept it hidden from me. I'm not sure how I felt about that but when she turned and smiled at me, all other thoughts disappeared.

'You really thought I was dead, Alex?' she asked, her voice no more than a whisper.

'Yes,' I hung my head, ashamed to admit it. 'Mark believed it too.'

Lilith laughed and then actually vanished right before our very eyes! I stared at the spot where she had been standing and then felt her warm breath on the back of my neck, and her arms sliding around my chest.

I looked down and saw her materialise, holding me against her.

'It's a good thing that his puppet was too lazy to check properly,' she whispered in my ear.

I laughed, astonished she had become invisible until I remembered Zang Zing had performed the same feat on more than one occasion.

'You really have all the old guy's powers?' asked a familiar and very youthful voice.

We glanced over at Beth and both laughed at her choice of words.

'Yes, it would seem so,' said Lilith, smiling at her.

We then watched as my Lily went over to Zang Zing's body and placed a simple kiss on his forehead.

'Thank you, my lord. May your final journey be a peaceful one.'

She stood up and glanced around at the house.

'I think it's time for a change,' she declared.

I didn't know what she meant. As far as I was aware the house had suffered only a small amount of damage.

'You want to redecorate?' I asked.

Lily looked at me and smiling, shook her head.

'No, Alex. I believe it is time we moved on from here. I will miss the house, of course. I have many happy memories but it is time to make new ones.'

I smiled and went to her, taking her hand in mine.

'I shall go wherever you want to.' I told her.

'Well, I was thinking about Paris.'

My eyes widened at this statement but Cecilia spoke first.

'You will become the council's high ruler?' she asked.

But Lilith shook her head.

'No, Cecilia. I'm keeping out of vampire politics. That's your field of expertise. You should become the new high ruler.'

We looked at the vampire who had dealt the final death blow to the evil Mark and she smiled grimly.

'It will be an honour,' she said, solemnly.

Lilith nodded and glanced over at Beth.

'What do you say Beth? Do you want to come to Paris with us? Meet your blood sister?'

My daughter didn't hesitate and ran over to us, hugging us both, laughing all the while.

A commanding voice disturbed our family reunion.

'I hate to bring the subject up but we have several corpses to dispose of.'

We knew Cecilia was right of course and broke our little family hug.

'I have a friend at the morgue,' Lilith said. 'I can contact him in the morning.'

Cecilia nodded and then glanced over at our friend's body.

'We should have a proper ceremony for him,' she said, sombrely.

'Agreed, but where?' Lilith asked.

Cecilia had the answer ready.

'He loved the garden at the chateau. He shall be buried there.'

It seemed fitting that the vampire who had ruled the high council should be buried within their grounds and my Lily said she would arrange transportation.

'I will leave you now,' Cecilia said. 'I should make preparations in Paris. Tell the high council their leader has been lost.'

Lilith nodded and the two sisters embraced one final time before Cecilia left.

'Well, I think that's quite enough excitement for one day.'

I agreed with my fiancé's opinion and Beth quickly said goodnight.

I went over to the shattered kitchen window and examined it.

'We should board this up,' I told her but Lilith shook her head.

'No, leave it, Alex. It will be fine. If a thief wants to break into a house belonging to three vampires, then good luck to him.'

I laughed and we held one another, kissing for what might have been the billionth time.

Zang Zing was buried in his beloved garden beneath the moon and stars. The Morisakis high council were all in attendance, as were Lilith and I. Beth struck up an instant friendship with her new sister, and I was amazed at how far Emilie had come, under Cecilia's tuition. Not only were her fighting skills formidable but her English was now almost without flaw. My two daughters stood side by side at the ceremony while we said goodbye to our ancient and very wise friend.

We finished repairing our house at Camden and it quickly sold, much to our surprise. I still had my old apartment and so we moved back in while we tied up the paperwork for our new property.

Cecilia had told us about a glorious chateau which was located on the outskirts of the French capital. With five bedrooms and two bathrooms, it dwarfed our old Camden home. The front and back gardens were large in size and on the east side, a large orchard ran the length of the entire property and carried on past to the wooded area to the south.

We both fell in love with the place the first time we viewed it and the peace and solitude it offered was yet another selling point.

On the eve of our relocation to Paris, Lilith and I were married in a little chapel hidden away in Soho.

Cecilia brought Emilie over with her and the whole occasion was a reunion of sorts. My Mother came along with my sister and if she was at all perturbed by the presence of so many vampires, she didn't show it.

Jacob gave Lilith away and my best man wasn't a man, because my sister, Monica, stood at my side while we took our vows.

Emilie and Beth were bridesmaids and both looked very pretty. As for Lilith, my bride looked incredible wearing a white wedding gown that was straight out of the Victorian era.

'I am and shall always be yours,' I told her after I had lifted the veil.

'I know, Alex. You have made my eternal life complete again. Thank you.'

Then we kissed to whoops and cheers from our gathered friends and family.

That night, Beth went with Emilie to Paris while Lilith and I returned to my old apartment for perhaps the last time.

I unlocked the front door and, before she could protest, I grabbed a laughing Lilith and carried her over the threshold, straight into my bedroom.

I kissed her hungrily before remembering to go back and shut the front door. When I returned to her, Lilith was stretched out across the bed, naked and holding out her arms to me.

'Make love to me, my husband,' she said in a seductive and yet soft voice.

I froze for a few seconds, just staring down at this bewitching creature before moving past the bed and stood at the window, looking out into the night.

Rain was beginning to fall and my thoughts went back just a few short years; when the very same woman I had just married came to me in the dead of night with her fantastic tale of death and passion. I recalled it had been raining on that night too.

'Alex? What's wrong?'

I turned away from the window and smiled down at her.

'Nothing,' I said. 'Nothing's wrong, not in the slightest.'

We made love. For the thousandth time? The millionth? It didn't matter. All that did matter was Lilith and I were together and that for the moment, everything was as it should be; that everything was alright with the world.

And so my tale of how I became a vampire comes to a close. I have enjoyed sharing aspects of my life with you. I sit here now in the garden of our wonderful new home, a glass of fine red wine in my hand.

My beloved Lilith is with me, pointing out various things that could have perhaps been improved. Of course, I'm fully aware that my descriptive powers are rather lacking at times but really, I have more than enough other powers not to let it concern me. After all, as the Buddhists would say, only God is perfect.

'So where do we go from here, my darling?' I ask my wife.

Lilith smiles at me and we share a long and lingering kiss, the familiar scent of lavender filling my nostrils once again.

'Oh I think we have many more adventures to come, Alex.'

I look at the woman who has given me so much, changed the world I lived in. Thanks to her extraordinary gift, I know I will never age and become ill. I can continue to defy the laws of physics at will and know that she will always be at my side.

I can sum up my story with one simple sentence.....

Lilith and I were meant to be.

And then we kiss, not caring that the wine is spilt, landing like splashes of blood at our feet. Imagine that.

Alex and Lilith will return in book two of The King Family Vampires:

EPONINE

Printed in Great Britain
by Amazon.co.uk, Ltd.,
Marston Gate.